The Right Man

By the same author

A Good Enough Dad

THE RIGHT MAN

Nigel Planer

[signature]

HUTCHINSON
LONDON

1 3 5 7 9 10 8 6 4 2

This edition first published in 1998 by Hutchinson

Random House (UK) Limited
20 Vauxhall Bridge Road, London SW1V 2SA

Random House Australia (Pty) Limited
20 Alfred Street, Milsons Point, Sydney,
New South Wales 2061, Australia

Random House New Zealand Limited
18 Poland Road, Glenfield, Auckland 10, New Zealand

Random House South Africa (Pty) Limited
Endulini, 5A Jubilee Road, Parktown 2193, South Africa

A CiP record for this book is available from the British Library

Papers used by Random House UK Limited are natural,
recyclable products made from wood grown in sustainable forests.
The manufacturing processes conform to the environmental
regulations of the country of origin.

ISBN 0 09 177733 X

Typeset by Deltatype Ltd, Birkenhead, Merseyside
Printed and bound in Great Britain by
Redwood Books Trowbridge, Wiltshire

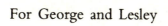

For George and Lesley

ONE

OH DEAR, I'M not yet forty, and I seem to have gone straight from my adolescence into my mid-life crisis without a pause for the prime of my life. There's never been a bit where I felt, if not exactly in control, then at least at ease. The last two thousand years of much-publicised male supremacy are meant, surely, to have rubbed off on me somewhere along the way. Surely I should be basking even. But it hasn't felt like that at all. Blimey dimey no. Even now, I am aware how difficult it is for me to admit that there are problems. I am meant to solve problems, not bleed them on to a page.

People always say, 'You must have known. Some part of you, inside, must have known.' I contest this. Why must I have known? I did not know. Maybe all the signs were there but I did not go looking for them, maybe I even ignored them. I hate being undermined by those who talk of 'knowing somewhere inside yourself', as if it was Muggins's fault not to have been more introspective, more self-doubting, more bloody Freudian. Accidents happen. You walk in front of a bus – maybe your mind is on other things – you don't know somewhere-deep-inside that it's going to accelerate and break your pelvis. Sometimes it just isn't possible to tell whether to feel extraordinarily buoyant, or the other thing. Especially in this business. I didn't think about it. That I accept. I just didn't think. Actresses are notoriously promiscuous. Of all people, I should have known that, of course. Liz was not happy, I knew that, and I had redoubled my efforts to make her life more fulfilling. I'd tried to spend more time at home. To switch off work. But our special mornings set aside for romance had been a disaster – difficult when you've both been up sharing the feeds – and of course

I

even with all the phones turned down, you can still hear the answerphone click. But Liz had gone off me sexually well before Grace was born. She no longer bothered to go through the motions, and flinched like a scalded mongoose if I touched her. And when I tried to put my arm around her she would say, 'I'm not your puppy, you know.' The underwear I bought her after the birth went down like a serrated steak knife. I was doing my best to change but these days it seemed I couldn't do anything right.

I just put it down to what she told me to put it down to: that she was worried about getting pregnant, that she was pregnant, that she was breast-feeding, that it had been too late at night, that it had been too early, that it had been too quick for her, that it had been too slow. When we did make love, she used to bark instructions at me, up a bit, down a bit, harder, softer, don't stop, stop. She chinned me once with her knee, when trying to find a suitable position in a small hotel bed. She'd laughed then and I'd had to go to the doctor with a split lip. After a couple of years of it, I have to admit, I had turned into a bit of a Freddie Fumble and could have won a gold at the Olympics if they had a premature ejaculation event. But I still don't see how I could have actually known.

'Hello. You don't know me. My name's Sara Henderson. I'm Bob's wife.' The voice had a husky waver to it, with the faintest hint of a European accent. Sara was pronounced with a long 'aa'. As soon as I was sure I'd made the connection, I transferred from the 'announce' speaker to line 3, my personal one, cutting out all the warring sounds from the busy office, and Joan, who had taken the call for me, returned her attention to others.

Bob Henderson, Bob Henderson. The slight pause that followed allowed me to run through the two hundred or so names in the immediate-recall part of my brain. Nothing. Either Bob Henderson was not directly connected to me, my clients or any public broadcasting or independent production companies, or my memory was indeed beginning to hit overload. Premature dementia how do you do.

'Oh, Mrs Henderson. Yes,' I said with a smile in my voice. This is where I live, in the one-on-one world between mouth and earpiece. This is where my waking hours are spent. 'What's this in connection with?' I didn't want to let her know that I hadn't a wit-not-wot who she or her husband were, in case I should have known. It worried me that nowadays, Naomi – the Ketts half of Mullin and Ketts – was right; I was beginning to lose my edge.

I pushed up 'Henderson R.' on my Psion.

'I would like to talk to you, Mr Mullin. I'm sorry to ring you at work like this.'

'That's all righty. It's what I'm here for.'

The only thing to come up was Henderson and Giggs, a company of solicitors who had represented the Elephant film studios in that breach of copyright case with Carlton TV two years ago. Nothing really to do with me, I don't even know why I had them there.

'It's about Bob and Elizabeth.'

Elizabeth Heyton. One of my lesser actress clients was a few names down the list on my Psion. She'd done a fair amount of voice-work, some of it must have been for Elephant; my mind was making wild connections. Had Elizabeth Heyton been uncharacteristically inebriated in a dubbing session and wrecked the joint?

'Could we perhaps meet for a cup of coffee or something? I can't go into all this on the phone. I'm round the corner from your office at the moment actually. I'm sorry,' the Saara woman purred.

In the main office, Naomi and Tilda, our trainee, had the champagne out early – celebrating some minor revenge they'd wreaked on the BBC. I declined to join them for a plastic beakerful, put on my coat and went out into the raging cacophony of the Soho day. Like an unbearable unstructured concrete jazz piece with an intrusive brass section. I'm very sensitive to noise.

It was surprisingly warm, with a breeze. The outside world disappears when at work in Meard Street, suddenly to hit you in the face on descending into Soho. London was gearing up early for the tourist influx. Up in the control tower of Mullin and Ketts one might as well be on the moon or in an arctic shelter for all one is aware of the seasons, or the natural world. When it's cold, we all say it's cold and turn up the heating. When it's hot, we curse and open the windows. It's not a frightfully modern building and so doesn't possess air-conditioning, which is just as well as far as I'm concerned; the constant sound of humming gets on my nerves.

I suppose I love Soho, but more from a sort of protracted osmosis than any actual passion. I've been squeezing a living out of it for more than a decade now. Tucked up behind Shaftesbury Avenue, its narrow buildings – some of them like ours at Meard Street dating back to the eighteenth century – heaped on top of each other in a jumble of opposites. Old Soho ironmongers and delicatessens are the off-beats to a rhythm of changing restaurant fronts. The gay and street-bar scene co-exists with traditional prostitution and strip-joint businesses. Below grimy plastic signs saying 'Model' open doors lead to uneven narrow staircases. Outside skin-flick houses, bored and over-made-up women say 'Live girls, sir' to the street in general. It would be no place to bring up a child.

Patisserie Valerie was crowded as usual and I had to squeeze in between two pony-tailed 'indie' execs to get one seat and hold another. In here the sharp edges of the hubbub were dampened by the cakes and bread on the shelves which lined the walls. I scanned all the faces of women on their own for a possible Sara Henderson. No one reacted particularly. I ordered a coffee.

An expensive- and theatrical-looking woman found the door and after peering through the window, came in and stood anxiously by the crowded counter, looking for someone inside. For me. She was wearing unnecessary dark glasses and had on a considerable amount of jewellery. I waited a couple of seconds, taking her in, before lifting my hand to draw her attention. She turned her gaze rather dramatically in my direction and started shaking her head. Puzzled, I stood up and squeezed back past the pony-tails.

'Mr Mullin? We can't talk here, it's far too public,' she said and plucked at my sleeve. She had too much lipstick on and little deposits of it had clustered at the corners of her mouth. There was an enveloping scent as well.

'Well, I . . . Let's go somewhere else then,' I said. And without thinking, held the door for her. She seemed to expect it.

If this woman hadn't been, or at some point aspired to be, an actress, I would have eaten my Filofax.

'Where will you take me?' she whispered, like a slave girl in a Spartacus movie, as if it was a foregone conclusion that I wanted to ravish her.

We were heading towards the Groucho and the Soho House but somehow I didn't fancy taking this unknown Bette Davis figure among the biz-folk. Who knows how embarrassing she might turn out to be?

I turned into the first sandwich bar we came across and sat her down in the back, away from the window, on a little black wire chair.

'Is she very beautiful, your Elizabeth? Tell me. Do you love her a lot?'

'Listen. Mrs Henderson. You're going to have to go previous a bit with this. I really don't actually know who you are, or what I'm doing here.'

'I am Sara.' Again, with the long Russian-sounding 'aa'.

'Well, I'm Guy. How do you do?'

'You have a child, Guy?'

'Yes, we have a child, Grace, but . . .'

'This is very difficult for me,' she said and went quiet as my coffee and her mineral water arrived.

We sat in our own pool of silence for a few seconds in the middle of the shouting sprawl, during which she looked at me all the time, and then she picked up her tiny black designer handbag and, with unsteady hands, picked out a tissue and a photograph.

She dabbed at her nose with the tissue. Her nails were perfect and painted. She passed me the photograph, putting the tissue back in her bag, which she left open on her lap.

The photograph was of three rather ugly boys in white shirts with matching tartan ties, aged probably between eight and eleven. It wasn't a relaxed home pic but a formal studio job, with the boys lined up in size order, on a bench. Their faces professionally angled in three-quarter profile, their hair neatly parted. I nodded and handed it back to her. It went into the bag with a snap.

'I don't like to do this,' she said, 'but these are my boys.'

Momentarily, I considered taking out the photo of Grace, standing with no knickers in a bucket in the garden, which lives in my wallet. But it seemed inappropriate.

'He has a family from before as well,' she said. 'He has done this before.'

She had taken out a ten-pound note and put it on the table under her glass. She rose.

'Forgive me,' she said. I stood and sat again. At the door of the sandwich bar she gave me a long, intense look, the meaning of which was obscure and then turned away swiftly and left. Perfect timing had we been in a black-and-white 1930s movie; somewhat camp for Soho in 1998.

I sat finishing my coffee. I took out the photo of Grace in the bucket and put the tenner in my wallet. I paid with change from my pocket and walked back towards Mullin and Ketts.

Without really thinking, I walked past our door and all the way up Frith Street to Soho Square. I walked around Soho Square. I walked into Soho Square and sat on a bench, just across from three cider drinkers. One of them started to approach me so I left Soho Square and walked north.

The entertainment business fizzles out somewhere beyond Great Titchfield Street, although I did have to smile hello at a video editor I know, and at Johnnie Starkey, an elderly agent, who must have been on his way back to Golden Square after a Greek lunch.

I kept walking.

Things like this don't happen to me. Its meaning was surely clear and yet so clichéd as to be unbelievable. I ran it past myself several times to see if I could get the joke. Had Sara Henderson been hired by someone? Was she a sort of 'affair-o-gram'? It was half past four and the sound of the traffic was getting to me. Back in the office, the girls were already a tad pissed. As I hurriedly got my things together to leave, a not-joining-in-ness from Naomi told me that the females had probably been talking about me while I had been out walking.

I have discussed infidelity often with Naomi – in theory, of course – and once or twice with Joan and Tilda. You get to do that kind of thing if you work in an all-female environment. They don't like those close to them to hold differing opinions, I've discovered, there has to be a sort of common ground. They want everyone to feel the same way about things, and about men in particular. One year they even managed somehow to

6

synchronize their periods. That was tough on me, as you can imagine. One thing agreed by all the women in the office was that the secret to a good relationship is finding the right man. The moment he shows signs of being typically like other men, non-attentive or unable to commit, or just plain wrong, then the consensus was he should be dropped or avoided and the search must continue.

The irony of this wisdom as far as Naomi Ketts was concerned was that she was an absolutely hopeless judge of character, falling again and again for charismatic men with power, money and, inevitably, wives and children. She would announce these disasters regularly at work and in wine bars, well, to anyone willing to listen actually. The last one was with quite a big-shot BBC producer, whose name I withhold, who got dropped in the franchise reshuffle and moved to Nottingham with his wife and kids. We always knew when old Ketts had found one. She would become indignant, self-pitying and shirty for a few months. Angry with her lot in life. A tough and brassy woman at work, but in her lonely flat in Highgate a hopeless co-dependent looking for big daddy. When I asked her if the man's wife knew, she said, 'She must have known, everybody knew.' It was true that everybody did most likely know. Naomi is never the most discreet of women when it comes to sexual matters. But in this case I suspected 'everybody' included everybody except the man's wife. I felt sorry for them all, and for Naomi's shrink, who must have had even more of an earful of it than all of us at Mullin and Ketts. I wondered if I was the only person in the whole of glorious show-business who didn't know about Bob Henderson and my Liz.

The female orgasm, that's the rub. That's the blinking bafflement. With men, the word orgasm refers to a specific moment in time: the moment of ejaculation − or, as the Australians would have it, 'slime', as in 'Have you slimed yet?' However, with women it seems to be more of a generic term, and is something on which surprisingly few of the women of my acquaintance seem to agree. In my years of working in an all-female environment, I have heard the female orgasm defined in so many different ways as to warrant a sub-section in the dictionary, like the Innuit and their supposed hundred and fifty words for snow. Some women say they have never had an orgasm, some only when masturbating, some are exclusively clitoral, some come all over, others from nipple stimulation, one maintaining that only breast-feeding was truly orgasmic. Some go multiple, others once a year. Some can only achieve fulfilment within intimacy, others only with illicit lovers, casual sex or strangers. If the ads are to be believed, high-calorie ice-cream has something to do with it, as do motorcycles, chocolate, caring conversation and model boys covered in car grease. Tania in the office flies in the face of current accepted wisdom, claiming she can come only from repeated vaginal penetration with her boyfriend in the missionary position. Highly unfashionable. Despite this multiplicity of opinion, 'You never made me come' is still one of the worst put-downs available to a woman when trying to humiliate an irritating mate. There is also the faking option – unavailable to men – although my Liz would not have bothered with that one. I sometimes wish she had; it might at least have shown willing.

Once I timed her. I know that's unromantic, but twenty-four minutes! Eighteen minutes of stimulation with no sign of life from her, then a few brief minutes of arousal – still with her eyes closed – followed by her orgasm: twenty seconds of groaning and a slight tremble followed by silence. Maybe I should have tried harder, been sexier, but my arm was tired. I was worried I might develop Repetitive Strain Injury. I ran out of dirty talk after four minutes, which may make me sound like a wimp, but four minutes is one minute longer than a pop record and eight times longer than the average commercial.

Ever onwards. In the half-hour I'd been out dealing with Mrs Henderson and her theatrics there were nine call-back messages for me, three scripts to skim and the problem of the undelivered manuscript of Neil James's first novel to deal with. Neil was turning into a problem client in general. A blunder kid. Too much mopping up to do, not enough creative play.

Naomi Ketts and I worked ridiculously hard to get this agency off the ground and keep it flapping about in the sparkly blue. It's taken us ten years of near obsessive dedication. We've been through a lot together and now have developed a working relationship which is completely symbiotic. Often, we don't even need to speak, we know what the other is thinking before it has been thought. But unlike me, she still gets a thrill out of the whole shebang. She still flies off the handle, shouts at the girls, gets rip-roaringly drunk to celebrate a deal clinched. Still goes to see all the new shows. Studies the business press like a circling vulture. Still vibrates to the electric charge of it all. She still needs that entertainment-biz petrol.

I can't really call it a mid-life crisis – I'm too young for that, I hope – but in the last couple of years I've definitely gone through some sort of sci-fi dooweeoo time shuffle. Much of what goes on at work just seems, well, adolescent to me now, and it's definitely to do with Grace. April the fifth 1994, 2.30 a.m., 8lb 3oz. When they bunged her, covered in white stuff, her fanny all blue, into my arms at Queen Charlotte's that night, I had a profound feeling of something. Not that everything else became meaningless, not that. But priorities suddenly seemed to shift into a different focus. A new sense of proportion prevailed.

What I've been trying to do since Grace was born is to narrow down my field of hands-on operation to just seven clients, my 'heavy seven'. Maybe a couple more: Jenny Thompson perhaps, Simon Eggleston – Barbara Stenner of course – but basically, keep my personal client list small enough to be able to take a more active role in child-rearing. Ideally, I would like to work only three days a week, maybe doing the rest from home. Obviously I could never stop seeking out new talent – that would be unsafe – but I am very happy nowadays to delegate work on my forty or so other clients, to Naomi or Tilda in the office. Both of whom are more than competent.

To succeed, to get anywhere as an agent, you have to burn with it. You have to wake in the morning with last night's prime-time TV ratings figures beckoning you into consciousness. You have to put down the office phone, look at your watch and realize that it's half past eight at night already and that you haven't eaten for the last seven hours. You have to be able to keep a cast list of names, faces and phone numbers at the forefront of your mind for fourteen hours on the trot. For it to be fun, which it can be, requires that you engage your third gear after breakfast, if you believe in breakfast, and keep it engaged until bedtime. Coast along in fourth or pause to admire the view and some other nippier vehicle will overtake you, probably picking up your passengers on the way. I suppose it's the same in any field of entrepreneurial work, which covers almost everything these days since the privatizations of the late eighties. It seems as if, traditionally, mothers and midwives knew what they were doing keeping men away from childbirth. It's not so much that men weren't interested in babies but that the women couldn't afford to risk having their husbands lose the plot, going all philosophical and sentimental on them, taking their hands off the steering wheel of commerce when, as new mothers, they were most in need of security and support, and money of course.

Not that I've gone completely soft or anything. Wood and Walters no. But no one ever said on their death bed, 'I wish I'd spent more time at the office', did they? Well, maybe my father, and that speaks for itself. To get where I am required a finely tuned killer instinct and I don't know whether I will be able to stay here without it. Nowadays, for instance, when I put down the phone and look at my watch, I'm aware of another timetable, running alongside my own: 12.30 p.m. nursery pick-up – and, as of this September, 3.30 p.m. big school pick-up – 6.00 p.m. bathtime, 6.30 story and bed. The women in the office are pretty good on the whole about me turning up later than I used to, and I leave early now on three afternoons a week, whenever possible. Tilda's got an eight-year-old, so she's the most sympathetic, but she has a live-in granny, so it's easier for her. Naomi got a bit stroppy at the beginning but that was fair enough, I suppose; I was turning up zombified from lack of sleep and she had to take the load, especially through Grace's ear infection stage. She did badmouth Liz a fair bit I know, but not to my face, to the others.

The trouble is, my concentration's gone somewhere without a paddle. These days I seem to have a sort of twenty-four-hour undertow of concern that something bad might happen to Grace. It's my fault she was born after all, I got her her first break as 'twere, she didn't ask for it. She didn't write in with hopeful ten-by-eights asking to be taken on. Well, mine and Liz's fault, obviously. When she stopped waking through the night I just couldn't get myself back into uninterrupted sleeping patterns, so I started having these recurrent nightmares about her. Funny how the system plays tricks on one. They'd always involve some danger she was in which I would have to get her out of by putting myself in it instead. A kind of Abraham and Isaac in reverse. For instance, we'd be walking along the cliffs in Cornwall or somewhere windy, the path would be steep and rerouted due to some of the cliff having fallen away. There would even be a danger sign and a rickety clanking fence. Grace was at the edge, not being naughty, just there, almost as if I had put her there. The limestone began to crumble and tufts of gorse pulled away from the path. A loud sea below competing with the roar of the wind in our faces. The ground beneath her feet didn't crumble fast but slowly enough to present me with the main dilemma of the dream, almost as if it were written on the wooden sign. I would have to throw myself over the cliff in order to spare Grace. The cliff only needed to claim one of us. Would I throw myself to the shingle below? I would. Indeed it was almost as if I had brought us to this dangerous point for that very purpose. Some kind of primordial deal with the devil.

And that's another thing, since the little bleeder was born I seem to have been in touch with something elemental, something primeval. Some force which isn't about happy couples putting up wallpaper together like in the ads, or about couples at all, something which is altogether unknowable, which is a matter of life and death. My death, Grace's life. As if now she's here I no longer really matter. As if there were some tide which has blown me to the edge of relevance like an amateur wind-surfer on the horizon whose disappearance is a mere holiday statistic. From now on my job is to be benign because what else is left? A player no more, a carer from here on in. My career a mere shelter providing domicile, my grandiose dreams redundant, my nightmares flabby fiction. Suicide would now be merely an insult to those who needed me. Everything must bend like the wind-blown branches of an ancient oak to the whims of Grace's survival.

I took Neil James's bloody unfinished manuscript out of its used brown envelope and scanned through the first few pages, trying to see a point. *The Right Man* by Neil James. Not another novel by a TV comedian. That had been my first, but of course unexpressed reaction. A funny thing seems to happen as soon as somebody gets successful in a certain field in this business. They immediately set about seeing how grandly they can fail in other fields. Pop stars want to be actors or charity workers, actors want to be pop stars or politicians, writers want to be stand-up comics, and TV comedians, as we all know, have to write rip-roaring, roller-coasting novels. I wonder what real novelists want.

Of course this mass envy-pre-emption exercise can be very useful for someone in my position. It can take me into new areas, where there is new talent to be found. I hate putting it like this, but I have always been very talent-led. Talent will lead you to other talent, and Neil had done that for me several times before, unbeknowns to him, of course.

Despite certain initial doubts, more to do with a somewhat saturated market area than with my faith in Neil's as yet untried ability as a novelist, I went along with it. The publishers were keen, and seemed to have inspired Neil with confidence after their initial meeting with him – at some rained-off charity cricket match for Children in Need, I believe it was. Now the poor bod needed rescuing. Sandra Subtlety would be required.

'Hello, Neil m'dear. Listen, I've spoken to Marc Linsey and he agrees we should have a meeting . . .'

'Oh no, not another meeting . . . What's the point of another meeting?' Neil was getting bolshy too. Unattractive, that.

'I know, meetings are a complete backside ache, but look, m'dear, I think if we can get him to come up here to us this time . . .'

'I hate coming in to the West End, man.'

'God, so do I. So does your editor, for God's sake. That's the point. How about if we have lunch?'

Being the artiste, Neil was less fond of meetings than the rest of us. To me, meetings should be an art form in themselves: where to have them, how long to let them go on, how much to say or not say are things which have to be considered and practised if one is to get a meeting right.

The best meeting is one whose outcome has already been decided before the arranged time, either by the possession of fresh information, to be ponged in at the appropriate moment, or by separate and prior conversations with most of the parties concerned. A well-designed meeting should be like a neat and totally rehearsed one-act play, with everyone playing their role – room for a certain amount of improvisation, yes, but preferably only from the party who has been kept in the dark until the last moment; usually the one who will have actually to write a cheque or OK a budget at the meeting's conclusion. You have to know more than your adversary does. It's all very Zen. A deal is struck when all parties can come away from a meeting feeling that their needs are being met. It's no good going into a meeting with the intention of making someone squirm – you will not get the best out of them that way. Aggression should be used sparingly, and even then only when dealing with those who are impressed by it, Americans say.

'Can't we make it the end of the day? I lose a day's writing if I come up to the West End for lunch, and I'd have to get a new inner tube.' Neil was very hot on environmental issues, and political and gender issues. Well, any issues really.

'I'll see what I can do. How's tomorrow looking?'

'You should know, Guy, you're my agent, man.' I hate being called man.

'OK. I'll call you straight back.'

The end of the day for Neil means five o'clock, just around Grace time for me. Time to go and relieve Liz of the adorable little devil before her brain turns completely to jelly. In any case, I know there's no way I'm going to get Marc Linsey to come up to the West End at the end of the day – he lives beyond Wimbledon, family man – and it's important not to go and meet him on his home territory, at his leathery board room in Kensington. Firstly, he'll be overconfident there and may call in the contract. And secondly, Neil always gets wound up by those large designer buildings. He's liable to smoke, or criticize the furniture or something. He can be charming and funny with a couple of glasses of Chardonnay inside him and I've got to keep it on a carefree wavelength. Got to let Marc think all is going well. Nothing heavy, keep it light and wacky. It's got to be with food. We are over a year past the delivery date after all.

'Hi, Marc, me old mucker? It's Guy! How the devil are you? How are Beccy and Sidney?' These days the business has changed; one has to take an interest in the whole person. Tough 'lunch is for wimps' talk is last week's teabag, and a little extra family chat is cost-effective.

'Guy! I was wondering when you'd call. I'm fine. Seem to be encrusted with children these days. Just got back from Florida, of all places. Disneyed the little buggers . . . I've done my bit for this year.' The public-school drawl of the publishing world.

There followed a minute or two of nice caring stuff about Marc's wife and kids, Beccy and Sidney, whose names were punched up on my Psion in front of me, although I didn't need to look at them. I have a hard disk of a memory for names and phone numbers when I need them. Unfortunately, it is only available to me when necessary for work; it lets me down socially, much to Liz's annoyance – I need a larger power chip. I arranged a lunch for the next day at the Soho House and called Neil back to tell him. Grudgingly, he agreed to come.

There is a sort of code to the truth and lies in agenting. You can always lie *for* your client but must never lie *to* your client. Would that things were so clear in personal relationships. Now, technically speaking, I had just lied to Neil. I told him the only time Marc could make was tomorrow lunch, when of course I hadn't actually asked for any alternatives. However, I justified it to myself with the thought that I knew the weakness of Neil's negotiating position. He was a year late with the manuscript. It wasn't the manuscript that he had been asked to provide, it was a dark and depressing dirge, instead of a light and frothy romp. It was about 60,000 words short, but most importantly, he had already had the signing fee. I really didn't want him to have to pay that back.

A lunch in the West End might just save his streaky bacon. So in this sense, although I was not telling him the entire truth about the meeting time, I was undoubtedly acting in his best interests. Lying both to and for my client, if you like – in any case saving him from himself – and I liked Neil, even if he did need saving from himself rather more than other folk I could mention. I found him when he was doing his own sort of performance-art/mime thing, and after a fair amount of input from me he'd become a more than adequate comic turn. When I say I 'civilized' him, I mean it purely in the television sense of the word, in that I feel I had enabled him to make whatever he had to offer acceptable to a greater number of people. There had been client satisfaction in that. He seemed to have foundered on

14

the rocks recently though. Gone all political. Too much navel-gazing. All this self-awareness lark, v. bad for business. He had the required oodles of talent but had started questioning everything, analysing his own motives. Risky as hell in light entertainment. Blind talent or complete lack of talent are easier to deal with. Certainly easier to exploit. I hate that word 'exploit' and I use it here strictly in its business sense: the exploitation of talent for the benefit of all concerned. 'Nurture' sounds too New Age, but that's what it is. I suppose, as a good agent, I should invent a new term, more fitting with the caring nineties, because it's true that five years ago the word 'exploit' would have sounded perfectly alright. 'Expand', maybe, or 'mine', or 'broadcast', even. Yes, that's good. Thankfully, most of the eighties terminology is now dying out. We no longer talk about 'getting into bed together' with a TV company over a project, or 'getting a director pregnant' with the idea of casting a certain actor, but vestiges of eighties-ism still remain. I must remember to expunge them from my vocabulary when they come up.

It was a shame about Neil. He was a funny man. Not Stephen Fry by any means, nor even Hugh Laurie. But he'd had a certain amount of exposure – another horrible eighties word. I should start making a list. His trouble was that he didn't quite fit into an easily identifiable image category. He hadn't been to Oxford or Cambridge and hence lacked their sublime diffidence and fogeyness. But neither was he from Liverpool or Belfast or some chip-on-shoulderworthy place. He was middle-class, educated and – probably the worst attribute for a really stonking career – he had a social conscience. And then he'd got this idea to write a novel. In theory I'd been all for it: raise the profile – another horrible expression for the list – possibly leading to a more broad-based career. And there's another one. He'd stopped doing stand-up gigs altogether and concentrated on writing. I hadn't been able to achieve one of those massive TV-star's-first-book advances for him, but he'd been happy with that, saying that he didn't like the idea of that kind of pressure, but also that he didn't want it to seem that he was only being published because of his television 'visibility'. That's another obnoxious term and I'm sure he wouldn't actually have used it. Being Neil, he would probably have said something along the lines of 'I'd rather be judged on the merit of the work.' Absolutely right sentiment but a very difficult one to explain to the marketing department of someone like Hodder Headline or Random House.

In the meantime, I wouldn't have to worry about what to do about Neil until tomorrow lunchtime. I put his rather thin manuscript into next day's script pile and wrote the lunch down in my mini-Filofax. On the whole, I still prefer pens and pencils and paper to the Psion, and wherever possible, I use my notebook or little green diary, certainly when meeting clients. It looks more personal than anything digital and people relax more when they see that you are human. Of course, everything's logged on an Apple at the office by Joan anyway, so we're covered.

At the conclusion of this bit of business the thought of Saara Henderson and her three little tartan boys came blowing back into my mind like the aching sough of wind in high trees.

'It's your favourite person on line three,' Joan sniggered at me.

'Oh, not fucking Marcus Mortimer again,' I said, putting the unhappy Hendersons on my back burner where they couldn't grind at the machinery of the day.

'Uh uh. Female.' Tilda, who'd been going though radio schedules with me in my office, raised her eyebrows suggestively and left the room, grinning to herself, and through the glass I saw our accountant Tania's eyelids drop swiftly back down to the computer screen on her desk. She shared the joke with all the women in office. It must be Susan Planter, Jeremy's wife. Jeremy Planter. Yes, he's one of mine actually. Even Naomi thought there was something between me and Susan, and in a way, I suppose there was. Something. Not sexual, as my female colleagues would have it, but an understanding, a sympathy. I didn't fancy her at all but I did like her, do like her, and she likes me, I know. We can talk. She's interesting and, blessed relief, nothing to do with the business, unless, of course, you count being married to Jeremy Planter, who was fast becoming Mullin and Ketts' top-earning client.

Terrible bloody name, Jeremy Planter, terrible couple of names actually. As if Planter wasn't bad enough, to prefix it with a Jeremy should have been show-biz suicide. Originally we advised him to change it but that was ten years ago and we were wrong. Jeremy has had a Dr Faustus of a career for the last year or so. After years of playing second or even third fiddle on other people's shows, there suddenly seemed to be nothing he couldn't do. Mind you, he wouldn't attempt anything that he didn't know he could excel in. He was a dream client in that he knew his limitations. The total opposite of Neil: no two-year sorties into the world of novel-writing for Jeremy. Nor months in Hollywood trying to swim amongst the sharks without armbands like Doug Handom, my little Brit-pack movie star – cover of *Esquire* last month, by the way – which of course has been the sinking of many promising careers. Not everyone has Doug's ability to deal with loneliness and American sincerity; Doug Handom's the exception. No, Jeremy had a totally practical attitude to his talent, if you can call it that. He was quick-thinking and, despite the generally awkward appearance – the terrible physique and the speech impediment – hugely attractive. There are those who say he is difficult to work with, and he can be, I've seen it, but he is, to fan the embers of a cliché, a perfectionist, and has no qualms about making someone's life a misery until they get it right. It's going to be his reputation on the line at the end of the day after all and, since the cliché is well and truly alight now, I might as well add, he doesn't suffer fools gladly. I'm very proud of what we've done for Jeremy. He's virtually become a bloody brand name, for Christ's sake. In fact the other day I even heard someone on *Loose Ends*, John Hegley I think it was, describe a certain way of pausing before a punchline as 'Planter-esque'. You can't get much better than that. Funny to think that the famous Planter timing actually comes from a stammering cure programme which Jeremy was put through by his mother in his early teens. But he's amazing like that. He can turn even his worst flaws into advantages. The millions of people who watch his game-show regularly have actually begun to love him, I believe. They have taken him, or what they think is him, into them by a sort of drip-feed. Maybe they can sense how much he needs their approval, their adoration. And he really does need it, more than food, or sleep, or even sex. I could go all analytical, as Sunday journalists have tried recently, and make connections between his humble origins in a two-bedroom flat by the railway at Mortlake, the fact that he was an only child abandoned by his father, da di da di da and so on, but what would be the point? He was probably making all that stuff up anyway, and who cares? Jeremy Planter is a phenomenon. It must have been a nightmare for Susan being married to the bastard all this time.

I pushed line 3 and flicked the adjoining office door closed with my foot. A pointless gesture, because any one of the women in the office could have listened in on line 3 had they wanted, but it was all part of playing along with the game.

'Susan. Sue. Hello, m'dear.'

There was an un-Susan-like pause before she spoke.

'Guy, I'm really sorry to call you like this.'

'Pas de problemo, Susan. I like to speak to a real person at least once a month. How're Dave and Polly?'

'They're fine. He loves the tennis racquet.' I'm godfather to Dave, the Planters' eldest. There are some agents who prefer to keep all their client relationships on a purely business level, knowing nothing about their clients' personal lives or inner thoughts. They don't really take any interest in what makes an artist tick, so long as he or she is still ticking. I am not that kind. I couldn't operate like that. I like to know everything that is going on. It's more satisfying this way, more fun, and also, I believe, better business in the long run. Artists trade off their emotional life – they're a one-product line – and it's as well to know what's going on in it so that you can get a feel not only for what they say they want but for what other possibilities there might be. What they may want in, say, a year's time, so that you can use the old intuition.

'Have you spoken much to Jeremy recently?'

'Well, we haven't had one of our curries for a while, but I was at the recording Friday before last, so . . . Why?'

'The halfwit has gone off with one of the bimbos, Chrissie or Bella or Samantha or something, something tacky like that, some piece of furniture. Do you know her? He says he's in love with her. Well, he sort of nodded sheepishly when I challenged him about it. He means it, Guy, he hasn't been back here for eight days, except once when I was at work, to pick up his camera equipment, the little bastard.'

'Oh, Lordy Lord.'

'He didn't mention any of this to you?'

A 'definitely not' noise from me.

'No, well he wouldn't, would he? Cowardly little shitbag. I'm sorry to do this to you, Guy, but I'm really distraught back here. The kids are going bonkers. Did you know anything about all of this? Anything at all?'

'Christ, no. Oh, this is awful.' After years on the phone I can have a very convincing tone when required.

I knew that Jeremy had done a fair amount of shagging in the past. He was easily flattered by the attentions of women – well, by any attention, come to think of it – and I suppose in the last couple of years he had been increasingly exposed to temptation.

'I think there's a photograph of them together, of him coming out of her house or something yukky like that, Guy.'

A tabloid headline using the famous Planter delivery shuttled across my mind and flickered there awhile. 'J-Jack the L-Lad J-Jeremy W-Wants to P-Plant One On 'Er.' I must admit that, for the teensiest moment, I did consider whether this affair would be a good thing or a bad thing for Jeremy, career-wise.

'Oh, no. That's the last thing we need,' I said, and then, 'How is it your end sewer-rat-wise?'

'Oh, you know, pretty hopeless really. We had the *Sunday Mirror* going through the dustbins last night – I thought it was an urban fox. Luckily they didn't wake the kids. And last week I had this woman with a bicycle pump and a CND sticker on her duffle-bag, claiming she came from some women's group and would I like to talk to her, she knew how I felt, et cetera. Turned out she was from the *Sun*. I saw her off the premises. I mean, he's only a game-show host, for Christ's sake. A cheap, shitty little scummy fucking arsehole of a game-show host.'

I murmured an affirmation. I reminded her to ring round any relatives and friends and warn them not to be taken in by phone calls from anyone who was 'an old friend of Jeremy's' but who'd 'lost his number'.

'They're not really doorstepping us or anything. Yet. But me and the kids had one of those guys with the snoopy lenses bugging us in the supermarket.'

I crushed the bit of me that was disappointed that my client

19

wasn't considered worth twenty-four-hour surveillance by the gutter press and tried to deal with what was actually happening to my friend.

'Listen, Susan, I didn't know about this, I promise you. I knew about that stupid . . . What was her name?'

'Selina Barkworth.' One of Jeremy's flings. The one I knew that Susan knew about.

'Yeah. I knew about that but that was ages ago. But this . . . He's kept it very quiet, which isn't like him, is it?'

'No, that's why I'm worried, Guy. I'm . . .'

Oh, lawks. I really can't stand hearing someone cry down the phone. Especially Susan, who isn't the crying type − I mean, who doesn't, I mean, she's usually so strong. Being a man, even one who spends all day in an office full of women, I can't just let emotional or sad things happen. I have to try and make them better, I can't help it. I can't just sit there and empathize.

'He's a fucking stupid shitty bastard,' I said, and then in slightly less than perfect Planter, 'He's a f-fart, he's a w-wanker, he's p-p-pathetic, what does he think he's doing? He's an arsehole,' I added, and then, rather inappropriately, 'He's a c-c-cunt.'

Luckily, I don't think she was listening to me at all, anyway. My direct line was bleeping and I pushed it on to hold. Only eight people have the number of my direct line, so I knew it must be one of my heavy seven, or Liz.

She snorted a half-laugh. The direct line stopped bleeping. Whoever it was had given up, or Joan had taken it.

For a moment, I was aware of a twingette of jealousy. I'm sure guys like Jeremy actually have a nicer time than Mugs Mullin here on the end of the phone. Sara Henderson's husky voice came snapping up to me from the depths: 'He's done this before.' For guys like Jeremy, and Bob Henderson, whoever he was, there would always be new bimbos at the end of the rainbow.

'You feeling a bit better now?' I said, and added, 'And listen, call me any time, OK? I mean it, any time.'

'Thanks, Guy. I'm sorry. I feel terrible. I didn't even ask how you were.'

'Oh, I'm fine, fine,' I said. 'Well, reasonable really. My father died last week, so . . . but apart from that I'm fine.'

'Your dad died? Oh, Guy, I'm sorry, I didn't know. And here's me blubbing down your phone.'

'No, it's OK. We knew he was going to. I've got to sort out all the gubbins, though, that's the only pain.'

'I'm sorry, Guy. Have you had the funeral?'

'Last Wednesday, no, tell a lie, Thursday.'

'And how's your mum?'

'Unchanged.'

I don't know why, but Susan was the only person with whom I could talk about the inconveniences and realities of life without fear of intrusion. None of the women in the office knew I even had a father, for instance. And with Liz, it was always best to keep problems down to a minimum. I didn't want to load her down. Liz was stressed enough as it was, stuck indoors all day with our progeny. I don't think she or I had realized what an enormous task having a child would be, and how career-compromising. But Susan, on the other hand, seemed to have an extraordinary ability to soak things up without throwing any of them back at you. Confidences and disclosures were safe with her and I hope she felt safe with me. We got off the phone and I immediately got Joan to put in an inconsequential and routine call to Harry, the producer of *Planter's Revenge*, which was the name of Jeremy's latest vehicle. Harry was in a meeting and would call me back. I accepted that nonchalantly. No point in sounding any alarm bells yet. I kicked the door back open and waved across at Naomi that I needed a chat when she was off the phone. I called Joan in for the rest of the afternoon's bumf.

'Simon Eggleston called, something about his tour dates not fitting in with *The Bill*. I've told him they'll have changed again by September anyway but he's fretting. It's John Egan's birthday on Tuesday. I've got you a card, here, and Jeremy Planter called you but said it's OK because he was biking something round to you and you would know what it was all about.'

I pride myself on being able to have my face register absolutely nothing of what I am thinking if it's a question of avoiding unnecessary upsets. Even Joan, who's known me three years after all, would have no idea that the package from Planter would have any significance other than routine. I OKed John Egan's card – we never sign things in this business, we 'OK' them – sixty-five, bloody hell, he was getting on, and left Joan to sort out Simon Eggleston and his National Theatre/television dates clash.

I went into the main office where Tania, our accountant, was putting on her jacket.

'I'm just taking Cleopatra for a walk, OK?' she said in her squeaky little girl's voice.

At the word 'walk', the large tail of a very ancient Alsatian dog started banging against the metal underside of her desk. Cleopatra got up stiffly and tottered to where her lead was kept on the door. I don't know what Tania saw in her dog. Five operations and arthritis in three knees. Anyone else would have surely given up on her years ago but Tania had a morbid attachment and seemed to love her more for her pitiability. I'm not being unfair here: Cleopatra had been six years old and fairly smelly when Tania first got her out of Battersea Dogs' Home, so there must have been something in Tania that preferred an ill dog to a fit one. Tania is a completely kind-natured girl, or I should say woman because she is over thirty after all, even if she does still have the high, scratchy voice of a nine-year-old. She cares about things and seems to live her life in a constant torment over animals. Articles about battery farming, vivisection, the ivory trade, zoo conditions and veal transportation have, at various times, been pinned by her on to the cork board. And on her computer, a wealth of wildlife stickers. Anyone accidentally kicking the lampshade collar around Cleopatra's neck, when she had doggy eczema last year, would get the kind of look from Tania that could make you feel guilty for weeks. She was the best part-time book-keeper ever, though, and probably the only person in the office who really knew the inner workings of Mullin and Ketts.

Naomi Ketts was wearing the big pink jacket. I've often thought that a darker colour would suit her complexion better, and something without the shoulder pads and wide pockets might make her seem less daunting, but I would never suggest it, despite a decade of proximity. We don't have that kind of relationship. Anyway, her sartorial aggression is probably deliberate; she likes to have people on the defensive. Through the partition window in Naomi's office where I was slouching on a filing cabinet, I saw Joan signing for a Jiffy envelope.

'Oh, typical bloody man. Fucking typical male behaviour. It's pathetic. You're all the same,' said Naomi. 'Little bit of cash in the pocket, little bit of success, couple of TV shows and whoopsie doopsie I think I'll trade in the bint for a more nubile model.'

'Yeah, I agree. It is rather standard bloke stuff,' I said, 'but we've never been under any illusions about our Mr Planter's moral standing, now have we?'

I raised my eyebrows at Joan and she came in and gave me the envelope, closing Naomi's door again. It was addressed to me and marked 'Personal'.

Not wishing to tell tales out of school, and Naomi Ketts does have some remarkable qualities, but an awareness of the effect she has on people is not one of them. Even at her age and stature, she seems determined still to see herself as a hard-done-by little girl. Once I saw her petting in a corner with a cameraman, saying with a child's lisp, 'Pleathe look after me, won't you, becauth I get tho lonely and losht.' A bizarre sight, particularly taking her height into account. To justify her hopeless love life, she would say: 'What other kind of men could someone like me get?' Yes, Naomi had had a lot of trouble finding the right man. I had tried persuading her that 'Hello, are you the man who's going to have visiting rights to my children?' is not the most enticing of pick-up lines, but then she did have a point that most men would find a woman her size, with an aggressive sense of humour to match, somewhat threatening.

'What do you expect from the male of the species? Different bloody planet! Well, he's a dickhead, that's all I can say,' she said.

'Yes, we've known that for years, but a very talented and popular one – well, popular anyway,' I said, tearing open the package. 'Don't worry, though, I'm on the case. I just wanted you to know in case we have a "life-change" situation on our hands.'

'Well, he's your client. You know how to handle him. I don't want to have anything to do with the little shit. God! Men!' And she threw her little gravel-bag toad against the picture of Steve McQueen on her wall.

'Fair enough,' I replied. 'I'll let you know if it gets to RFA dimensions.'

RFA is Mullin and Ketts jargon for Red Fucking Alert. In this interchange I was using it to imply the danger of losing a valuable client. You see, when a man or woman, but usually a man – as Naomi put it so succinctly – ditches one partner suddenly for a younger model, it signifies a possible desire for 'life-change'. This might be perfectly harmless, but more often than not, the publisher, editor or producer is the next to be dropped, and then, inevitably, the agent. This Bella/Chrissie/Samantha could be working on our Jeremy even now, suggesting new vistas to him. The new sex had obviously made him feel confident enough to abandon his wife and kids. In the après-sex, she might be urging him to new professional heights, inspiring him to bigger, better shows, tougher deals, a new agent.

You don't have to be a Zen master to work this one out. What possible good to a Bella/Chrissie/Samantha, with her sprightly nipples and tight box, would the old representation be? Previous alliances from his old pre-bimbo life. She would know pretty soon, if not already, of Jeremy's long-standing relationship with Mullin and Ketts and of my friendship with Susan; of my being Dave's godfather, even. None of this would make her feel secure in her new role as Queen Planter. If this were sixteenth-century Italy, we could all soon expect poison in our soup.

Inside the package was a note from Jeremy and his front-door key Sellotaped to the back of an autographed Walker-print of himself. The note asked me to go round to his place to pick up certain things for him and bring them to the office. He would explain all when I next saw him. No pleases, no thank-yous. So it was beginning already.

Asking your personal representation to do little favours for you is definitely on the cards and is normal: checking your travel arrangements, booking tickets for you, ringing people to apologise for you. Going round to water the plants while you are away is stretching it a bit, even for an artist with whom one has a very personal relationship. This is something that could be left to a cleaning person or neighbour. So Planter's graceless request was a sign that he had relegated me, and therefore Mullin and Ketts, to the role of skivvying for him. I wondered if he had already been lunched by one of the big agencies, like ICM or

Peters Fraser and Dunlop. I wondered how long the ugly process might take. I pocketed his front-door key and threw away the note. It was half past three. I had been hoping to see round a couple of flats for my mother this afternoon, but that would have to wait until some other time. Mum had agreed with me that it would be best for her to move after Dad's death. I rang the estate agent's to let them know, and I wrote a memo for Tania, to call up all monies unpaid to Jeremy Planter and chase them. I went to the Planter file and took out his last seven contracts, photocopied them, putting the photocopies in my bag, and with lighthearted apologies said my 'hasta lasagnes' and left the office.

The evening was a total bastard. I was twenty minutes late getting back from the West End, so Liz and I passed each other at the front door. She was going to the gym, or to see her best friend Heather, or both. For the first time, I wondered whether all this was true. She was in a frazzled state; Grace had obviously been winding her up all day. She doesn't go to day nursery on Wednesday, the original idea being that I'd be able to get back early on Wednesdays, but that turned out not to be possible on a regular basis. Liz left without a word to me. It must be tough for women who have to stay in all day with the baby, brain turning to gelatine.

Grace tried her not-eating-anything gambit again, but I soon put paid to that by ignoring her and taking exaggerated enjoyment out of eating my own egg – the old Tom and Jerry trick, works every time. No doubt Grace would get wise to it sooner or later, but for the meantime it meant we'd get through another night without 'I'm hungry' at a quarter past ten. I was able to watch two of the nine videos I had to look at over the weekend after Grace had her bath. Although I get Tilda to do most of my viewing nowadays, there are always some which I have to watch. Not watch them properly, of course, like I used to, but fast-search to the scenes which my clients are in. It's no good having a client on telly and having to explain to them the following week that you didn't even see their work. But there are ways of lightening the load: just taking a couple of notes about salient points and mentioning them with emphasis can give a client the feeling that you have been avidly following every nuance of their perf. Theatre is more wearing on the vertebrae, of course, you have to be seen to have actually been there, and leaving in the interval is risky – the scenery may fall down in the second half and you wouldn't know. 'I thought you paced your performance brilliantly in the second act, m'dear' would soon be sussed if your client had had a fainting fit in the final scene, or been too pissed to finish the show. Not that we have any real piss-artists at Mullin and Ketts, I can't be doing with them.

Once Grace was asleep I cracked open a bottle of something and got out the week's script pile. Again, a skim-through would suffice. Size and type of part, then check to the end to see which characters die, and if there are any major plot reveals one should know about. Drinking alone is not something I used to do, but in the evenings, with Liz out and Grace asleep, it was becoming, dare I say it, a bit of a routine. Liz wouldn't be back until two or three in the morning now, so I'd turn in at twelve and leave the hall light on for her. I contemplated ringing her friend Heather to see if she had really gone there, but couldn't bring myself to do it.

I've discovered with Liz that equality between the sexes is a difficult thing to achieve, let alone maintain. There are 168 hours in a week. That's how many there are in total. Not a particularly magical number, but the actual one. If we say that eight hours every day are spent sleeping, that leaves 112 waking hours. Then take away three hours a day for preparing, eating and clearing away food, and you have got ninety-one hours a week left each. It's already looking stressful and tight. Other deductions common to us all were harder to make. Like home administration and repairs, tidying up, working to get the money in, and ablutions, of course. I found myself making allowances for her when it came to ablutions. Women are allowed to spend longer on washing. Evidently they have less naturally oily skin and so need to put on creams and things, and, of course, they are judged on their appearances so much more than men – whether we like it or not – so I gave her an extra hour a day on that in my theoretical calculations. This made it necessary, after the ninety-one hour mark, to divide us into two, according to our gender, and that's really where the arguments started, I suppose.

It soon became apparent that although an hour is an hour and it lasts the same time for everyone, some hours have different values from others – rather like a currency – and it was virtually impossible to work out a fair exchange rate. For instance, Liz hates cooking and sewing, so an hour doing either would, for her, go very slowly. I, on the other hand, enjoy cooking very much and am good at it, whilst I find sewing very difficult and frustrating. I'm crap at it. Here, Liz has an unfair advantage over me, in that her mother taught her to sew from the age of four. So that although she doesn't like to do it, she could complete all of our sewing in a quarter of the time it would take me.

Trying to establish a fair sharing-out of the tasks became even harder when I took actual work into account. Work is impossible to evaluate. There is work you do because you have to and there is work you do because you want to, and unfortunately it is usually the former which brings in the money at the end of the week. But then, the six months or so that Liz would spend waiting for another acting job, whilst not earning us any immediate cash, might one day bring in a fortune if she got lucky.

It became complicated, but I'd persevered, even writing down columns of figures. Whichever way I juggled them, however, I ended up, in my column, with more than the available 168 hours – an impossibility – whilst Liz usually had about six hours a week to spare.

It was no wonder I got headaches so often, and it would have been fair enough, I thought, for me to develop some psychosomatic stress-related illness. However, it was always Liz who got these. From the flakiness around her hair line to her overwhelmingly tired and floppy stints. These attempts of mine at a Maoist kind of equality were, I think, what used to drive her out of the room, slamming the door so that the door handle fell off again, and into the bedroom. She wouldn't talk to me then for some days. I would sit there thinking of screwing the counter-sunk lugs back on the door handle, for what must have been the twentieth time, but decided it might be better to replace the handle altogether with something perhaps less aesthetically pleasing, but which would at least survive her tantrums.

I suspect it was my reasonableness over matters like this that must have driven her to Bob Henderson in the first place. By reasonableness, I don't mean understanding. I wouldn't claim ever to have understood her. Nor do I mean that I was easy-going or even-tempered. Far from it. I suppose I mean more the inescapability of my logic, or at least my inability to escape from it.

The trouble was, if we had done things her way, obeying only our feelings, bills would not be paid. Not just because there would be no money but because she habitually left all that kind of thing to me. Accounts, administration, insurance were activities she looked down on. And she looked down too on my pedantic tenacity with them. No doubt there are other more flamboyant men who can deal with these everyday tasks with a flourish and to whom Liz would be more suited, but I am dogged about these things and this scrapes the blackboard of her nerves.

I bet Liz's lover-boy, Bob Henderson, doesn't care about things like equality between the sexes. I bet her Bob is casual and confident in his power. I bet, being a proper man, he would not tell her of impending bankruptcies, would not trouble her little head with the everyday bureaucracies of their lives. I bet he is on-line to his bank. I bet he is connected by modem to his accountant and I bet a piece of paper only ever crosses his desk once. Smiling girls with clean hair talk to him on those mini-microphone headset telephones about how his shares are doing. And when his washing machine breaks down, the service company not only answer the phone, they actually specify a time when they can turn up, so that his au pair can know when to be in. But of course, he would have one of those German washing machines that never break down, made by a company who got big using slave labour from the concentration camps during the Second World War. But that thought would not trouble him, would not occur to him. Men like Bob have in-built opposite magnetism to suffering. Suffering's southern pole is repelled by his unrelenting northness. Robert Henderson. Old Hendo. Our Bob. A man blessed because the day he was born, God had run out of consciences.

Grace was playing on a pebbly beach. I'd taken her there. The sound of receding surf sucking at the shingle was irritating, nauseating. She was laughing and enjoying jumping over the little incoming waves as they sauntered in, mockingly. At each new ankle-deep incursion she was further from the shore, and looked back to me for reassurance, which I gave her. Go on, my daughter! Grow! Learn! Swim! Then came a moment when she was frightened. The water was up to her waist now and the noise of it dragging on the stones beneath our feet was overwhelming. I had brought us here, I had encouraged this expedition into the treacherous tide. As usual, at the last minute, I put myself between her and the vengeance of the pulling water, waded in up to my chest, letting the sea claim me instead, leaving her on the land. Luckily I was saved from the moment of watery lungs by waking up.

Liz was snoring like a lorry. Three a.m. She farted and rolled on to her side. After ensuring that she was still asleep, I farted in sympathy. The thing now was to fight the temptation to creep out of bed into Grace's room to check if she was alright. It was only a dream, my problem. My rational resolve didn't last long. After a minute or so of monitoring Liz's breathing, I slipped out from under the duvet and went silently to stand in Grace's doorway for a few moments. I couldn't hear anything so I went in a few feet, then a few feet more until I was right over the safety bar of her bed. Very quietly, and from what seemed a long way off, I heard the gentle lapping of her breath. I went back into the bedroom where Liz had rolled again, cocooning herself in the duvet. I lay on my side of the bed with no cover for a few minutes, until, realizing I was cold, I quietly reached for my T-shirt on the chair and slipped it on.

Later in the night, I must have managed to reclaim some of the duvet, because I woke in the morning with a corner of it over my shoulders. I got up and dressed quietly, making Liz a cup of tea. I had to go to work. As I prepared to leave, Grace woke and started bawling at me. She wouldn't let me go. I ended up bunging her in with her mum – much to Liz's annoyance – plucking her off me like an unwanted burr.

TWO

IN HINDSIGHT – SOMETHING we don't usually have time for in this business – it was probably a mistake to let Neil James meet Marc Linsey at all. Neil had changed more than I had appreciated since *Every Other Weekend* had gone off air. *EOW* was a situation comedy about two divorced fathers and their children, quite big a couple of years ago, completely forgotten now. Neil was somewhat type-cast as the soppy one, remember? No, I'm not surprised, it wasn't earth-shattering stuff, but it was a good little earner and an easy gig for Neil which looked like going on for at least a couple more seasons. But then came the franchise débâcle and all the ministers of television had a cabinet reshuffle. *Every Other Weekend* was dropped as being too 'blokey' and Neil was left with a rather small commission from the publishers and 100,000 words to write. It was my fault really. I just don't get the time to stay on top of clients as much as I should any more, since Grace. Not even my heavy seven. If I'd known what kind of a state he was in I think I'd have somehow engineered to keep them apart.

Not shaving can look pretty good on actors, and execs can turn up to high-powered do's with a few days' growth these days. Even heads of departments at major broadcasting houses sport a just-got-out-of-bed look. It's a way of showing that you are one of those people who still care about content of programmes, that you have definitely not turned into an accountant. But there's not shaving, and there's Not Shaving, the latter having something to do with not washing either. As he shambled into the downstairs dining room at the Soho House, half an hour late, Neil might as well have had 'I have let myself go to pieces' emblazoned on his T-shirt. Maybe he felt that now he was a bona fide commissioned novelist it meant that he didn't have to change his underpants or say hello to people properly any more. As he lurched towards the beautifully linened table where Marc and I were chatting about babies, a young waiter with a music journalist's haircut asked him if they were making any more of *Every Other Weekend*. Neil brushed past him without even an acknowledgement. Not good to do that to Josephine Public, not good at all. Bad for Betty Business. I clocked Marc sneaking a side glance at his watch, so I cut the pre-chat chat and suggested we order. Neil looked at the menu as if it were a breakdown of ex-Tory MPs' private earnings and sneered at me for ordering Gravadlax and a rocket salad. While we waited for the wine, he finished all the breadsticks and lit a Marlboro. And before I make it sound as if he was cutting an artistic or even romantic figure, let me add that he had also put on at least two stone. Oh, Lord.

I decided to accept a glass of wine although I had no intention of taking more than the merest sip of it. Marc, being in publishing, was happy to drink at lunchtime, and Neil joined him. After a few words of positive encouragement about the original quality of Neil's writing, his unique turn of phrase and Marc's continuing interest in the basic idea, Marc came gently on to the matters in hand. He wanted to establish an understanding over certain aspects of the so-called story, questioned Neil's proposed title, *The Right Man*, and then – as I was dreading – asked quite firmly about possible delivery dates. This seemed to make Neil's pulse rate increase. The Soho House had run out of their own brand of mineral water so I was gulping down the fizzy, which I never like.

To tell the truth, I had been surprised that Marc Linsey had accepted the initial, and I thought rather flimsy outline, but I had, possibly wrongly, kept my misgivings to myself. The 'right man' of Neil's story was a stalker, a prowler who sneaks around the same woman's house for years so that he knows every creaking floorboard, what time of the month it is for her, what she is wearing that day, which garments need mending. But he never makes himself known, this man, and he never does anything nasty other than the snooping. So despite the lack of gratuitous or even comical violence this thing was hardly going to be a zappy comedy. Marc pointed out gently that this idea did not afford Neil the opportunity of writing any dialogue, or indeed any action. Neil looked exasperated and assured us that it was based on a real case he'd heard of, although there's no reason why that should have made it good fiction, let alone funny. I've been in many script meetings where the producers complain that a scene doesn't work, to be told by the writers, 'But it actually happened.' Nobody cares whether it actually happened or not. Actually happening is not an excuse for putting it on telly, or in a script or, in this case, a book. So with Neil's outline, rip-roaring and roller-coasting were not descriptions which sprang immediately to mind. However, we'd got this far into the water, so we had to swim or choke.

Neil was talking rather a lot now roused, and Marc sat quietly listening, with that little curly smile people have when they are the ones who can pull the plug on you. Evidently, Neil's 'right man' was also going to be like the elves in the night – you know, the ones who help the shoemaker to meet his deadlines by nocturnally doing all his mending. He was going to secretly fix this woman's fridge for her, or darn her clothes, or help get her children off drugs, I don't know. Neil's point being, if I understood it correctly, which is unlikely, that no matter how much a man may think he is trying to help a woman, in the end he is only interested in power over her. Possibly a valid one, but it didn't inspire one to think of Neil's name embossed in silver on paperbacks in airport bookshops. Marc Linsey's attention was evaporating.

Neil was in need of some good-luck elves himself, but none had been forthcoming. His first deadline had come and gone without really a murmur from this affable and lunch-providing editor. People are always late, we said. Ben Elton is probably late, we said. Probably even Martin Amis is late. When, last September, Neil had delivered a few thousand words only, of unpublishable masturbatory fantasies without a gag in sight, slight alarm bells began to sound. I intercepted, and that draft, if you can call it that, had never appeared on Marc Linsey's desk. Thankfully, Neil had accepted my position.

I had tried, but not over-hard, to distract him by finding him work elsewhere, but he seemed to have become obsessed with the thing. He'd stopped ringing in for work. Always a bad sign. I tried to move the conversation on to the hopefully less contentious subject of the proposed title.

'You don't understand,' said Neil between gulps of Chardonnay. 'It's got nothing to do with looking for Mr Right or singles bars or anything like that.' Oh. Pity, I thought. 'It's a psychological term and it's sometimes used in the profiling of serial killers. A right man is someone who has to be right whatever happens. Like Peter Sutcliffe thinking he was a saint saving all those women he banged over the head with a hammer.' The wine was making him garrulous, or maybe he'd had a couple of drinks already before coming into town. Either way, the lunch was definitely not going the way I would have liked.

'Maybe you should just call it *Right Man*?' I offered, with my helpful raised-eyebrow look. 'Too many books have a "the" in the title. Too many first books by TV comedians. *The Liar, The Gun Seller, The Gobbler, The Tosser* . . .' I ran out.

'So this guy is a serial killer, right? I mean, he's a serial killer, is he? That's right?' said Marc, looking marginally more interested.

'No, he's not,' said Neil, becoming a tad aggressive now. 'No, no, no, no, no. It's like a complex, you know? A right-man complex. It's about a man who can't see that he is damaged, so he thinks the world must be. It's sometimes called the Roman Emperor Syndrome.'

'That's quite a good title,' said Marc.

'Or just *Roman Emperor Syndrome*,' I said, trying to make sense of my own logic. 'I mean, it's not *The Crime and the Punishment*, is it? It's not *The Pride and the Prejudice*.'

Neil was not touching his pasta, but had poured himself another glass. The conversation had veered a long way from where I wanted it to go.

'So where does fixing this woman's fridge fit in?' asked Marc with barbed innocence.

'I'm trying to show that when a man thinks he's caring for a woman, he is in fact patronizing and manipulating her. That there's not much difference between chivalry and violent abuse,' said Neil, whazooming straight over Marc Linsey's beautifully coiffed head, and mine too, if I'm an honest bunny.

33

Neil's cheeks were burning and his heart rate was creeping up past the safety zone. 'Neil,' I wanted to say, 'you are not Oliver Sachs. You are, or were, a reasonably successful television comedy actor. All this talk of violent abuse does not sit well, and what's more, you're confusing the man with the chequebook.' As my brother Tony would say, if you're in a hole, stop digging.

'So there's no murders but he fixes the fridge of this woman he's never met?' said Marc, who was more used to editing books about homoeopathy for pets or cellulite in the Royal Family.

'Fuck you,' said Neil, 'fuck you.' He was breathing heavily and was obviously nursing some deep creative angst which he was incapable of sharing or even communicating to us. And then – worst scenario – he was up and walking. He was walking and finishing his glass of wine as he went. He was leaving the dining room. Agent's nightmare. People you want to bring together fall apart. A chasm opens, money falls down it, but worse than that, feelings are hurt, pride is bristled, niceness is deflowered, deals crumble, pillars tumble. A crashing, creaking, awful sound.

'Neil,' I called, 'it's OK.' But it wasn't.

I had a brief few words with Marc, who said he understood, although I doubted that, bunged some cash on the table for the bill, and hurried out into Soho after Neil, who had sloped into the Coach and Horses pub opposite. I bought him a drink.

'I'm sorry,' he mumbled. 'I fucked up your deal. But they want me to turn out some sexist crap like Jeffrey Archer. I should've just done some Christmas joke book off the telly like Harry Enfield.'

'No, it's my fault,' I said, trying to enjoy a half of lager. 'Maybe you're right, Marc isn't the right editor for you. He's just into quick, easy bucks, I know. I shouldn't have got you into this in the first place. Look, go home, think about it. I'm sure something will occur if you give yourself time.' Trouble is, some people – and I'm not necessarily saying Neil is one of them – are afraid of success.

A second-grade-venue tour of an Alan Ayckbourn play had come into the office that morning and I wanted to get back on the phone to see if there might be something in it for Neil. Get him away from all this, back on the boards, clearing his head, earning some dosh. Maybe things weren't going so well for him at home in West Hampstead where he lived with his therapist partner, an older woman, American. He looked as if he needed some sex. I didn't want to see one of my favourite clients suffering from spiritual anxiety, or doing a Dennis Potter on me. Oh dear. 'Twas ever thus.

'Look at that,' said the taxi driver, momentarily drawing my attention away from Jeremy Planter's photocopied contracts. 'I don't know why they bother. We're all gonna die anyway.' I glanced at the traffic but had missed whatever piece of road manœuvring had prompted his doomy remark. I decided to agree with him nevertheless, since he was undoubtedly right, philosophically speaking.

The earlier contracts were mostly buy-outs. Royalties and repeat fees are sadly, more often than not, things of the early seventies. Since deregulation and the mushrooming of the independent sector, even things like video sales and spin-offs are usually covered by an upfront fee. Gone are the days of artists and writers retaining rights over their work in perpetuity. The market has been so swamped by poor-quality cable and satellite product that broadcasters just cannot afford any more to encumber the sell-on potential of their properties with obligations to the originators of the material. However, the later three contracts were full of juicier stuff. As an artist grows in stature and pulling power, one can negotiate better terms, committing the hirer to increasing cash releases, shortening decision times on second and third series options, lessening the number of showings available, that sort of thing. Though I say so myself, Planter's last three contracts were minor masterpieces, studded with sparkling caveats and buyback clauses. I had even managed to achieve a twenty-eight-day option renewal on *Planter's Revenge*, which meant that the powers-that-struggle-to-be would have only a month from next Saturday, when the first episode of the new series went out, to make up their minds about whether to recommission. I wondered how fast a worker this Bella/Samantha/Chrissie woman would turn out to be.

The taxi driver slammed on his brakes suddenly, sending the sixteen pages of the *Planter's Revenge* contract spluttering to the floor.

'Wanker!' shouted the cabbie out of the window, and then, over his shoulder to me, 'Why not just drive straight to the crematorium, eh?'

'Quite,' I said, picking up the contract and putting it in order. I should have taken the time to staple it.

'Look at them all, hurry hurry hurry. Wankers,' he said, and I wondered if he was in the right job. Grave-digging perhaps might have suited him better, or lighthouse keeping. Grumpy old tart.

Bloody Jeremy Planter, such a ladies' man, such a chap's chap. There was a time when I would have found it amusing to be out with Jerry. To chat up the hopefuls in the VIP lounge of some joint like the Limelight or Browns while he was snorting coke in the toilets or getting off with some young floozie. Vicariously, I could experience the dubious joys of the debauched life, and yet return home suffering nothing worse than an alcohol and Silk Cut hangover, conscience clear. This was in the days when Liz still asked me where I had been. Always the straight guy of the double act, the Ernie Wise. Never the one who got laid, but somehow maybe the one for whom it was all being performed. Maybe Jeremy was latently homosexual, maybe he fancied me underneath the braggadocio. Maybe his appetite was purely a show with an audience of one: me. If that was the case then I had played into it. I had laughed at his antics, who wouldn't? They were funny after all. No, not just funny, absolutely hilarious. He was the best, after all. He was the king fish. Of a small and insignificant pond, it has to be said, in the wider picture of things, but the king nevertheless. More outrageous than Barrymore. Slicker than Jonathan Ross, sexier when on form than, oh, I don't know, Billy Connolly, Albert Finney, Chris Evans, whoever you find sexy. More modest than . . . well, no, actually, that was a joke, not modest at all. Jerry had always been exciting to be with. The line between work and pleasure was non-existent with him. Needless to say, normal hard-working women hated him. They knew what he was up to. But he seemed to hold an endless fascination for that certain celebrity-notching type of woman, and, strangely enough, for us blokes. It was as if he could live out our most fearsome fantasies for us. Could epitomize our biggest dreams and worst night-mares. He was exhausting. And I might have to let him go.

The one contract not to be found in Jeremy Planter's file was a client/agent agreement. This is because I don't think they work. Naomi disagrees with me over this. In fact she more than disagrees, she thinks I am a 'head-in-the-clouds girlie pushover' on this issue, 'a pussy'. Whether to bind a client to you by contract is the one area in which the 'Mullin' and the 'Ketts' form two distinct armies in the agency, with the battlelines firmly drawn up along the 'and'.

Traditionally there are no such contracts. It's not the music business, thank God, and an agency can never talk of 'signing' a new artist. An artist is free to go at any time with an understanding that any money from already negotiated contracts will continue to be filtered through the original agent. On the face of it, this puts one in a rather insecure position, but it must be remembered that without a binding agreement, the agent is also free to drop the client at any time if he or she becomes boring, for instance, or unemployable for whatever reasons. Usually alcohol. And, of course, it can be difficult sometimes to get a client, especially a younger one, to sign one of these agreements. But my main argument against them is that once a client has signed to you, they expect more. They do less for themselves and they are constantly whingeing that you don't do enough for them. The mutuality is soured. Rather like marriage. People who have been living together quite happily for years decide to get married and then split up shortly afterwards. There's nothing like a marriage contract to reduce a healthy sex life to a bi-monthly obligation, is there?

Naomi Ketts is keen on client/agent agreements, I suspect, because she dreams of selling the agency on one day, of being bought out and retiring, although the thought of her without her daily dose of show-biz animosity is inconceivable. She can't even manage a long weekend, let alone a holiday in Greece, without at least three faxes to agonize over. She is the sort of woman who eats stress for breakfast. It's her roughage.

This disagreement between myself and Naomi first reared its ugly head when we, mistakenly in my opinion, took on Debbie Sarchet. You may remember her, she had a brief flirtation with the media in the late eighties. A part-time model with a rich daddy, whose main claim to fame initially was giving blow jobs

37

to rock stars in the toilets of briefly fashionable nightclubs. After a one-season stint presenting some low-rating 'yoof' show, she announced to anyone who wanted to hear – which, as it happened, turned out to include most of the British press – that she had really wanted to be an actress all along, was taking acting classes – though how often was not clear – and would shortly be moving to Los Angeles because the English 'hate success'. She was the kind of person who sees fame, rather than talent, as the currency, and I couldn't stand her. However, the women in the office thought she might amount to something, and Tilda actually admired her, so for about five months, she was one of ours.

My point is that if we had actually signed her, as in made her sign a contract with us, we might still be stuck with her now, which even Naomi agreed would be a nightmare. However, during those few months, Naomi, I think, got a taste of that eighties cliché, the 'money for nothing' bug, the pot of gold at the end of the rainbow, the massive share-option yuppie dream. She wanted to live happily ever after.

This was because a week after taking on Debbie Sarchet, we got a call from her modelling agency, Studio Visage. She had retained them, which was OK by us because we know doodly-squat about the fashion world. They wanted to know if we would be interested in taking on various other clients of theirs. We started getting Studio Visage Z-cards in the post. A Z-card is the modelling equivalent of a Walker-print. Instead of the standard actor's full-on head-and-shoulder shot, a Z-card will have a glam shot: something in a bikini, or if she looks exotic, some leopardskin or fishnet; plus what I call a Chanel shot – something grown-up with classy aspirations – and a fresh-face shot. The hair and make-up will be different in all three shots and the girl's measurements will be printed down the side.

Likewise the boys will have a shot with a shirt on, a shot without a shirt on, one with hair gel, one without hair gel and occasionally an outdoor shot on a motorbike.

We giggled and joked about these arrivals at first, and the sexier boy ones ended up plastered all over our walls. It being an office peopled entirely by women, the sexy girl shots went straight into the bin, and I had to pretend not to notice. Tilda was particularly into the model boys, though, and I suspect she harboured serious yearnings for some of the hunkier guys. I bet she took some of them home for private perusal. Anyway, when, amid an unwarranted amount of publicity, Tilda managed to get Debbie Sarchet half a line in an actual American movie shooting in London at the time, the Studio Visage wooing really began in earnest. Would we like to go to a meeting with them? Could they take us all out to lunch? For a couple of months we wasted time farting about with them, while they toyed with ideas, first of a merger and then of buying us out. They must have looked only at our most successful client list, done a few sums and reckoned it would be nice to expand into films.

Of course, when it was explained to them that to run an agency like this you have to have a ratio of at least three low earners to one star and they realized that we have to do a lot of dog-work for over 100-odd clients, they backed off a bit. What really sent them packing, though, was when, to their amazement, it was revealed that we have no actual contracts with any of our clients. Anyone is free to piss off at any time.

This they could not buy. I was relieved. They were awful people who had no understanding that this is a very personal business. Bigger is not necessarily better, and you can't force a director or employer to take someone on. It's all about relationships with people. It's about loyalty and intimacy. But by then, Naomi had seen the figures. I mean, financially speaking. And they were, it has to be said, impressive. There must be a lot of dosh swilling around in the glam biz but I didn't want to hang about watching Mullin and Ketts turning into an artistic laughing-stock, however many copulating holidays in Barbados I could have afforded in the short term.

One or two of the pics of the model boys stayed up on the cork board alongside Tania's animal rights posters, though. Debbie Sarchet married some pitiable thirty-year-old muso millionaire and scuttled off to Los Angeles, occasionally appearing nowadays in women's magazines – as you must no doubt know – with tips for young mothers on exercise and dieting and, of course, breastfeeding. Although whether it's possible to breastfeed through a silicone implant is tactfully not gone into.

Strange that all this seems so clear to me when it comes to the agency, but at home I seem to have adopted the reverse policy, having signed the ultimate ever-after agreement with Liz. I often wonder why I married Liz, why she married me. My three-reasons-for-marrying-Liz joke: I fancied her, I fancied her and I fancied her. I suppose I figured that to stand a sparrow's chance in the happily-ever-after stakes it would be best to marry a woman I fancied a lot rather than one I liked but only half fancied, since as a man I might be tempted to become a bit frisky and spoil everything after a couple of years. Actually women are as likely to be unfaithful as men, but we all conspire to remain silent on that. However, with previous girlfriends I'd kept other doors open, had a roving eye even, but with Liz it was different. She had a way of looking into my eyes as if I was the only person on earth who could save her, and this used to – still does – make me tumescent. That and the needy quality in her voice. As if that very inability to cope in her, which has now become untenable, irritating, was initially the main attaction. Vanity, all vanity of course; who am I to save anyone? But that look and that plaintive sound made me feel right, like I had a place. Somehow I got it into my head that she needed me. I wanted to be useful.

As the taxi came to a standstill on Hammersmith Broadway, the cabbie took time to reflect further on the absurdities of life.

'There's people dying everywhere, you know. Sarajevo, look at that, and did you see the programme about Burma on the telly last night? Diabolical.'

I hoped that the traffic was not going to snarl into a gridlock as it can so often in this part of London. The thought of sitting here for forty minutes with Mr Morbid did not fill me with any joy. I wondered how long it would take to walk from here to the Planters' house in Chiswick. Too long, probably. It was already quarter past two, and I wanted to be out of there before Susan and the children returned. I put the contracts back in my bag and took out the estate agent's details for my mother.

The noise of a thousand engines turning over in their stationary vehicles on the Broadway was throbbing inside my head. A traffic helicopter passed by overhead, but the sound of its propelling blades stayed with me. I suppose Neil James was right: thinking I could look after Liz was a kind of abuse. Being the right man for her had turned me into some kind of Roman emperor. *Mea culpa.* And now she was breaking free of her bondage with centurion Bob Henderson from over the Alps and I wouldn't have the time to suppress this insurrection because the bleeding empire needed constant maintenance.

The Planters had a nice and big house in Chiswick. Jeremy's success was not yet long-lived enough to have warranted a move to hugely grander surroundings such as Shepperton or Henley, but they had had an extension built out the back and an extra floor on the top with dormer windows and a sort of half-balcony.

I knew the house well; I had been there on many occasions. Sunday barbecues, late-night chats in the kitchen with whisky. But I had never been there alone before. I knew the downstairs toilet with the framed posters, photos and cartoons of Jeremy's early work, but I didn't know the upstairs en-suite bathroom adjoining their bedroom, for instance.

Jeremy wanted me to collect a couple of the natty suits for which he was renowned, two of his awards, a golf club and three of the funny wigs from his very first TV show. It was a peculiar set of requests and seemed more like the props list for a *Hello* magazine photo-shoot than an inventory of requirements for life in a 'love nest'.

In the living room, among the framed mantelpiece photos, there was even one of me – well, one in which I featured – a hot day in their garden with a slide and a swimming pool. I had my shirt tucked into tight jeans. Cripes, it must have been some years ago, before Liz. Nowadays, in the summer, I wear linen or silk shirts, untucked, to cover the weight gain, and those jeans have long been used as oil rags.

I caught myself in the Planters' mirror. Women put on weight when pregnant but then they get the chance to lose it if they breastfeed – fifteen hundred calories a day, that – and, if they're like Liz, they go to aerobics and yoga to stay slim. Or maybe it was Bob Henderson who was doing that for her.

Silly blokes like me spend nine months empathizing, eating all the Haagen-Dasz ice-cream with their wives and then have to cancel all exercise as they buckle under the strain of supporting three people. The blob in the mirror stared back at me. I turned to the photos again. Some had been removed from their frames, no doubt recently by Susan. On the table were a couple of photo albums and a box of photos. In the bin were some photos torn in two. Susan had been going through the memories then.

Susan is good-looking but, in life as in all the photos, she lacked that vanity, that desperate need to be looked at, that fear, even, of being judged on her looks – which Liz has in buckets – which attracts men like a blood-magnet. Which makes a woman beautiful to the mindless-dick part of a man. Most of him, that is, as the girls in the office would have it.

There were a few photos in the box of a Planter holiday, presumably before Polly was born, sun and swimming pools. Jeremy of course larking about in every shot, always aware of the camera, no matter what – true pro. But Susan, who didn't feature that often – presumably because she was the one who remembered to bring the camera and use it – even when wearing a bikini, with tanned skin and tousled hair, looked – how can I put it – wholesome, nice, at one with herself, drinking no doubt just enough to be merry and then going to sleep, turning down the second cup of coffee, eating the right amount of salad. Not that she is fussy or prim: the sofa cushions were not overly arranged, breakfast had been left unwashed-up and even the duvet in the bedroom was not pulled tight but rolled back. Jeremy did not deserve her.

I had the awards, the wigs and the golf clubs but there was a problem with the suits. In the wardrobe were only Susan's clothes, sensible clothes, nothing too expensive, no men's shoes in their shoe rack, but on the floor several empty coathangers and some shards of linen and bits of thread. It looked as if Susan had been at his stuff with the pinking shears. There was one tie which had been snipped in two. The suits, no doubt, were already in pieces in black bin liners like the chopped-up remains of murder victims. Now I felt like the secret prowler in Neil James's unwritten masterpiece. A chubby little bad-luck elf silently prowling through this woman's house to change the course of events, as if Neil were my alter ego, as if he were writing my life.

The Planters' wardrobe light was on the blink; it flickered and died. I looked up and saw that its junction box was hanging loose, not from Susan's attack on Jeremy's garments. It had

42

obviously been like that for some time, the plastic around the terminals had melted and browned. Shoddy work. I followed the badly stapled cable back to the skirting by the door. Whoever had done this loft conversion was a cowboy. I tried the bedside light and the main light switch. It was warm, even after the couple of minutes I'd been there. Dreadful job. The landing was no better. No doubt the electrician had overcharged as well because of Jeremy being on the telly.

I have to be careful when it comes to wiring. No one, not even Liz, really knows about me and wiring. It's something I had to walk away from, something about growing up, being a man if you like, getting away from my father, proving myself.

You see, I actually have no qualifications to be in show-business at all, no right to be here. I wasn't born into it, I didn't do media studies, I didn't even work my way up in it, I was a spark really, just a lonely little crappy spark. You can't have people in this business getting to know that and continue to wear the Armani suit. Not that I go for Armani; Hugo Boss does for me. I did have a stint working in a rep theatre once, and even went on stage a couple of times. It's OK to be a failed actor-agent, the biz is replete with them. It's not so good to be a failed electrician-agent. It's not lovely, it's not stylish. The 'teccies' don't come to our parties, they lead their own lives and have their own lunch, usually in the pub while we all scoff the location catering on the bus. The 'teccies' eat big breakfasts with black pudding and bacon while we have orange juice and script meetings. I have buried it, it's gone.

But the house was empty, so I traced the cable back to the consumer unit and checked the main fuse box. The wiring was a joke and probably dangerous. The under-sink cables in the bathroom had not been properly earthed and there was virtually no sheathing around any of the cabling where the plasterboard flushed against the joists in the cellar. It denigrated the whole place.

There was a sadness in the quiet air. It came off the curtains like a dog kept indoors all day. There had obviously been crying here but no evidence of rows and tantrums like in Liz's and my home. No taped-up windows or kicked-in cupboard doors. No dents from thrown objects on the wall plaster. No scuff marks, no scuffles. Just a kind of suffering peace. On the coffee table were the five packs of cards with which we had all played Racing Demons last time I was here, ten-year-old Dave going apoplectic at the concessions being made for his younger sister, Polly.

Downstairs the fridge thermostat turned itself on with a gurgling noise like the low-key chant of a Japanese Noh play. Some hot-water pipes cracked into life. The house was readjusting to my prescence, to the opening and closing of doors. If there were such a thing as an aural microscope it would reveal myriad undersounds in ordinary silence, as those who live alone must know. Maybe that's why Liz used to keep the television on all day while I was at work.

One handy thing about old Planter, despite his professionalism, was his complete lack of application when it came to matters financial, contractual or administrative. The escritoire, when I opened it, was bulging with disorganized correspondence, receipts, scraps and scribblings. There was an unpaid-in cheque from Granada TV, which should have gone through us. Naughty. But it was only for a guest appearance on a kids' show, about £140, so I let it pass. Undealt-with fan mail and charity requests. Quite a few angry letters from Reg Simpson, the designer on the last series, whom Jeremy had had fired. Luckily no letters from other agents, but mixed in with the whole bundle were hundreds of paying-in slips from Mullin and Ketts, dating back to the previous tax year. Obviously Jeremy's bookkeeper had not been for a while, or maybe taken one look at this mess and resigned. The payslips showed all sorts of different monies received: voiceovers, occasional overseas and video sales, one or two little repeat fees, a radio chat show. No very large sums but an adequate cash flow ticking over. I thought Jeremy was earning a lot more than this; I'd check with Tania on Monday. In the past I would have been aware of all these minor transactions, would have recognized every fee and commission. But that was before the agency grew and I had learned to delegate; also, of course, before the arrival of Grace. Nowadays it was impossible to check every single item, there just wasn't the time, and to be honest, I couldn't see the point in it any longer.

I copied out some of El Planter's figures and addresses into my spiral-bound notebook and reinstated the confusion in the escritoire as I had found it. I watered the plants and left.

Dear Guy,

I know it will most likely be you, Tony's not really up to it, is he? I'm writing this just to help you deal with all the paperwork and everything when I've gone. You'll find my will and all the information, solicitor's addresses, etc. in my middle drawer. All my notes and everything are in the brown filing cabinet – key is on the smaller of the two rings in bottom right. Classes and text books, etc. I have put in the big cardboard box. You can throw them away, or hang on to them, it's up to you. They might be useful for Grace one day if she ever shows an interest, although all will be probably out of date by then. Tools and components you can have, Guy, if you need them. You know where they are. Look after your mother for me. I've done my best. I know it's not often been enough. You make sure she doesn't want for anything. I didn't get round to renewing the junction boxes in the kitchen. Make sure they're properly earthed with fire-proof cable. There's some 5ml in the utility room cupboard. I wouldn't want her to start a fire inadvertently.

And that was it. The sum total of wisdom passed from father to son. A whole generation's worth of progress: 'There's some 5ml cable in the utility room cupboard.' I refolded my dad's last letter and put it in my jacket pocket. Not much of a symbolic chalice, but it was all there was.

I like the flannelled sound of distant traffic you get in the back rooms of the terraced streets of suburban London. It is more calming to me than the quiet of the countryside. The muffled roar of a jumbo jet grew out of it and petered away again as it descended over Kew on its way to Heathrow. I could hear my watch ticking again.

I remembered the day when I had been taken by my father with my younger brother, Tony, to visit a friend of Dad's in Brighton – it was some seaside town – and when asked by his friend, 'How's your wife?' he had replied in an apologetic sing-song voice, 'Disappointed.' They'd both laughed and at ten years old I hadn't been able to understand why. I was clutching some comics that my father's friend had given us to keep us amused while they talked. I decided to save my comics until I got home and so I read Tony's to him instead. When we were leaving, my father's friend asked for the comics back. They had been a loan, not a gift, so I never got to read them. That was a day of learning about disappointment. I must have been cross with Dad for not explaining to me about the comics. The thing that irritated me most of all now about his posthumous letter was that he'd assumed, correctly, that there would only be me there to sort out, and hence had only bothered to address his remarks to me. My mother wouldn't touch it and Tony, he was right, was not really up to it, although there had been some improvement in his condition in the last couple of years. He was actually managing to hold down a job now, working for the Hammersmith and Fulham parks department.

Looking through my father's drawers, cupboards and filing cabinet now was another disappointment. I could find no dark secrets which had been nursed by him over the years. No encoded secret agents' telephone numbers, no hidden stash of porn. In fact, the only evidence of a sex life at all, whether shared with my mother or otherwise, was a packet of Durex which I found filed in a buff envelope folder neatly under 'D'. Well, they would be, wouldn't they? They were some years past their sell-by date but that was fair enough, I suppose. He had had a prostate op in 1989. Going through his drawers and finding the Durex stirred a memory of myself and Tony — we must have been eleven and nine at the time — first finding Durex in his bedside table and counting them, then returning a week later and counting them again and giggling. The game lasted several months, kept alive more by Tony, who has always had an over-fascination with sex. One problem was that occasionally my father bought a new packet and we couldn't be sure whether he had put the remainder of the old into it or thrown them away. This mucked up our counting system. But even with this setback, we calculated that Mum and Dad must have been having sex about once or at most twice a month. 'If you can call it sex with your father', as my mother would say.

I wondered now whether he had known about our boyish game and this is what had prompted him to keep his Durex in his filing cabinet in the study instead of his bedside table. This must have made spontaneous lovemaking impossible, since the study is a flight and a half of stairs away. Maybe he took to decanting the Durex singly or in twos from the study each month. Certainly Tony and I never found this squirrel's store under 'D'. We were never allowed in the study on our own.

Feeling like an eleven-year-old again, I looked through the other entries in the 'D' section of his filing cabinet for some clue. There was 'Dunstan's', the school at which he had taught for twenty years before my mother had encouraged him to be more ambitious and take on the headship of a posher school in Devon, where he had lasted one year before being made redundant, something from which neither he nor the rest of my family had ever fully recovered. There were various other names, friends, newspaper cuttings, none as full as the Dunstan's file. The Durex nestled in their buff envelope folder all to themselves. There was, I suppose, one mystery, also in 'D': an empty file which had the unexplained title of Doris. Doris and the Durex. Sounded like an educational film about AIDS.

I carried on checking through his bank statements. All seemed predictably in order. But as my eye went down the columns of figures, my mind ranged over the possible connections between the Durex and Doris. Had my father had a secret lover called Doris? Or was Doris an acronym for an undercover organization of ex-schoolteachers? 'Dunstan's Old Rascals Illicit Sex'? My grandmother's name was Mabel, my father's sister was called Auntie Rose, so it couldn't be either of them. I know that my parents had been wanting a girl when my younger brother Tony had arrived, so he'd been a disappointment from day one. Could Doris be the name of the daughter they never had, and had my father put his contraceptives out of reach of the bedroom in the superstitious belief that their proximity to the empty Doris file would somehow enhance fertility?

As I moved on to his insurance papers, I lingered in my mind on the word 'disappointment'. There was no file under 'D' for this, but it seemed that my father's life had been a series of disappointments. Not least of all me. Giving up stability and qualifications to go razzamatazzing with glitzy folk, sleeping with fly-by-night actresses. Whatever next? He'd had such hopes for me as a child. I had been the one to learn all his tedious skills. I was top in physics, his subject, at secondary school. But then, just when he thought he'd got me right, off I waltzed into the glamour.

Plentax is a large electronic components company, mostly involved in armaments. At the time, I justified my leaving so abruptly with adolescent idealism, feeling rather noble that I was turning my back on that happy band of men – and it was almost exclusively men at Plentax – who design and make parts for the sonar devices used in the search mechanisms of various types of torpedo. My own personal contribution, long since computerized into redundancy, of course, was to weld the miniature DC4 resistors on to ceramic plates, which formed part of the microcircuit, which would cybernetically monitor the torpedo's progress through the water to its target. But really, I just couldn't take the numbness working somewhere like Plentax, where desensitization is as traditional as soldiers marching in a parade ground, as necessary as medals for bravery. But emotional numbing seems to be an essential part of earning a living, and I didn't know that in 1976.

I imagined, if it had been Liz that had died and not my father, what I would find among the chaos of her shoe box full of memorabilia. Billets doux from Bob Henderson? A diary splodged with tears and splattered with descriptive passages of stolen afternoons with him, wet gussets and hard members like in some magazine fiction? I couldn't help but have the thought that Marc Linsey would like that steamy stuff to find its way into the pages of poor Neil James's nov. I could feel a headache coming on. The neat left-right compartments of my brain were jumbling; I needed vortex reinforcement.

My mother came in with a cup of tea for me. She put it on the desk. I thanked her, even though it had milk and sugar, neither of which I take. I long ago gave up connecting with her on dietary matters.

'What do you want me to do with his cricket things?' I asked. 'Shall I give them away?'

'Oh, you keep all that, Guy, you're a boy.'

'I don't play cricket, Mum.'

'Oh, don't you? Was that Tony? Give it to Tony then.'

'I'll hang on to them for him. If I make a list of everything I find, then you can tell me if there's anything you want.'

'Oh, you're just like your father, making lists. I don't even want to come in here.'

'That's what I'm saying. You can just tell me, and I'll deal with it.' I was trying to make things easier for her.

'Just leave me a pair of his socks.'

She left the room. I was thankful my father hadn't left a video message or anything embarrassing like that. Definitely not his style. A pair of socks would be easy and couldn't give one any Californian-type messages of advice from the grave. After putting various insurance policies and bank letters into my bag to be photocopied, I closed up and went to the kitchen to pour away my cup of tea and go. I opened and closed the fridge door. I always do this in my parents' kitchen, it's a sort of reflex action. I was unaware of even looking at the contents. Some vestige of childhood insecurity.

'All these years I've been having penetrative sex, or rather not having it because of your father, and now they tell me that I've been wrong all along and I should have been having clitoral stimulation,' said my mother. She was sitting at the kitchen table looking through out-of-date colour supplements. My mum comes from that generation of women who never expected to find the right man, but rather to spend a life comfortably complaining about being stuck with a barely adequate one. As if her successes and shortcomings were his responsibility alone.

'Who told you, Mum?' I asked.

'That nice man with the silvery hair and the creases down his trousers.'

'You've been watching too much daytime TV, Mum.'

The Saturday papers were on the sideboard, unread.

'Anyway, your father wouldn't have been able to find my clitoris if it'd been the size of a tennis ball, you know what his sight was like.' She sighed and poured herself more tea. 'There's something about one of yours in the papers today if you're interested.' She indicated the sideboard.

'Mrs Planter's Revenge!' A fairly obvious shout line, which

can't have exercised the wit of the copywriters over-much. A picture of Jeremy in an open-neck shirt with a frocked-up tartlet under his arm on the front page, half a paragraph, and then: 'Full story on pages 4 and 5.' I resisted the temptation to feel intoxicated by the quantity of coverage. A double-page spread. Inside, a picture of Jeremy and Susan in happier days taken at some première do, two or three pictures of pretty girls who might once have been fondled by Jeremy, and a picture of Susan in dark glasses earlier in the week, leaving her front door with Dave and Polly in tow. Across page 5 was a recently posed reclining photo of an ageing bimbette in corsetry, and an interview with her. They'd dragged up Selina Barkworth – Jeremy's four-year-old affair – and bunged her a few quid to say how Jeremy had been in bed. I scanned the piece. Evidently he'd been a five-times-a-night animal who was also tender, kind, gentle and, inaccurately for those who know him, generous. They'd also done a backsearch on the computer for embarrassing Planter quotes and found a couple of corkers: 'My family means more to me than anything' being one from 1993, and 'Susan is not only my wife, she's also my best friend' the other, more recent, from a *TV Quick Guide* interview.

From a glance through the main copy, it was clear that Susan must have talked to them. Most out of character, and possibly foolish. There are no winners when it comes to the press, or lawyers. She of all people should know that, being a solicitor herself. Poor woman, she was losing it.

It was turning into one of those weekends where everything seems to be conspiring against one, and try as I might, I couldn't do what Barbara Stenner, my dearest, oldest client would have advised, and see it all as a spiritual manifestation, a karmic gift on my path to enlightenment. I felt bad about Jeremy and Susan's son Dave. I know being a godfather doesn't mean all that much these days, but what was the point of having one if he couldn't keep the rats and repomen away from the door?

'What do you do?' A woman was crammed up against me with a paper plate piled with bits of raw cauliflower and guacamole.

'Well, actually, I'm an agent, sorry. Mullin and Ketts.'

'Oh, God. I hate my agent. I joined her six months ago and

she hasn't done anything for me. Nothing. I mean, six months! I haven't been up for anything! I think they have such an easy life they don't bother with you unless you're known or in a soap or something.' Actresses are not renowned for their sensitivity and tact.

'Well, the whole business is slow at the moment, it's very hard . . .' I was standing in the kitchen near the only decent bottle of wine.

'That's exactly what my last agent used to say. He was completely useless too . . .' Maybe she thought that this badinage would endear me to her enough to offer her something.

God, I hate going to parties in Islington. I always seem to be the only male not wearing an Afghan hat. In the pubs and on the streets everyone looks at you in that judgemental way peculiar to N1. One wrong item of clothing, one chance remark, and you are branded on the politically correct blacklist. And of course if you drive as opposed to cycle, you must be very careful not to incur the Islington sneer. Your car should not be, as mine is, a Vauxhall Cavalier, or a Sierra or suchlike, which is low on petrol and runs OK, but looks, well, salesmanny, Milton Keynesy, eighties-ish. Classic Saabs which belch black fumes on to the run-down Georgian house fronts are OK, of course. Everything must look run-down, in fact, while costing more to maintain than it does in, say, Wandsworth or Tooting. I say our car was OK, but to compound the awfulness of the weekend, it was at the mender's with an ironic wiring fault. Yes, I should have fixed it myself like a proper hubby, but it had gone wonky in the week when in Liz's care, so I hadn't interfered.

'Have you tried writing off for work yourself?' I tried to continue a non-inflammatory dialogue with the cauliflower-scoffing actress.

'That's what a bloody agent is for, isn't it?' she said.

At Mullin and Ketts we get, I'd say, thirty to forty letters a week from actors who want to change their agents, who don't think their current one is 'right for them'. I prefer clients who talk to me if they're unhappy, rather than whinge behind my back at parties and then secretly write to someone else imagining glorious new scenarios. If you don't know something's wrong, how can you go about fixing it? Actually, Liz left her previous boyfriend, Andrew, to be with me. Another sign I failed to read. It's worth remembering that if they can do it *for* you, then they can do it *to* you, whoever said that. Actually, I think it was my father who said that. In which case, I take it back.

I asked why this actress had left her previous agent, more out of personal vacuity than out of any genuine interest.

'I mean, when I was at the British Shakespeare Company I found out that I was on less than what the younger men actors were on, I couldn't believe it. I mean, it was so totally sexist. And my fucking agent didn't seem to give a fuck. He just told me they were all playing much bigger parts than me. I mean, as if the number of lines was what it was all about. Soooo fucking petty.'

Being in the British Shakespeare Company, as a woman, and probably one of the only two or three in the minor touring company, and not a leading woman at that, not even the second leading woman, she probably didn't have very much to say, or do, in the actual plays. It was Shakespeare on a shoestring after all. No doubt she made herself Equity dep.

'I mean, there I was getting less than some boy just out of drama school, and I came out of drama school ten years ago.'

And it shows, I thought. Liz's friends. Best to keep quiet.

'Yes, it's just luck not talent,' said Liz, joining us.

Well, it's luck *and* talent, I thought, and an ambitious killer instinct, and above all an ability to get on with people one way or another, something this woman with the cauliflower obviously needed extra tuition in.

'Anyway, it got sorted out in the end, but it's disgusting, women get treated so badly in the theatre.'

Agreed. Agreed. We pride ourselves at Mullin and Ketts that we negotiate very hard for parity between the sexes. It's true, women are often still paid less than men, even in this business, and we adopted a sort of 'favoured nations' policy early on, which helped us gain a reputation as a new up-and-coming agency. But it's not just that. I actually believe in equality, although of course I wouldn't say that in so many words for fear of inviting a visit from Dorothy Derision. In theory, if we had equal wages across the board, then I'd be allowed presumably to have some time off to spend with Grace, or with Liz even, were she interested. In practice, it doesn't seem to work like that – I did try to bring Grace into work a couple of times when she was smaller, but people start to lose faith in your business acumen with puke all down your lapel.

'Yes, but don't you think that if you want to have equal pay, which I agree with you is essential,' a male voice here, 'women should be accepting equal responsibility? It's fine to want to share some power or even have it all, but with that power goes responsibility ... I mean, men are still legally expected to support families ...'

I let Liz and the cauliflower woman continue their *Late Show*-type discussion with whoever the poor misguided bloke was. Josh Baines I think, the fringe director. A man with alimony and several children to support, no doubt.

Bringing Grace to work really made it hard for Naomi Ketts. I mean, she's forty-three this year and after fifteen years in the biz and a string of crappy relationships with unsuitable men, she must feel cheated. She desperately wants a baby herself, I know – well, we all know, it's pretty bloody obvious – and it's hard enough for her, seeing the picture of Grace on my desk. Knowing Naomi Ketts as I do, though, I suspect she would have liked the baby, but not the life-long commitment to the adult it would turn into. Mustn't bitch, though, I think she dealt with her envy of Liz very well, considering. She's only ever once openly expressed it.

It was when Liz was going through the old post-natal depression. The dreaded and denied PND. No one, especially me, was allowed to mention it, let alone suggest she go for some kind of help. It was pretty self-evident however. She would ring the office, sometimes three or four times a day, on my direct line. There would be a couple of seconds' silence and then a scratchy crocodile of a voice would whisper, 'I – can't – cope – Guy. I – can't – cope.' Sometimes Grace would be crying her head off in the background and Liz would scream at her, 'Jeeeeeeeesus Christ. Shut up. Shut uuuuuuup!' Which of course made Grace redouble her efforts. These were difficult calls to handle, finding a tone that was both genuine and soothing for Liz and yet, at the same time, nonchalant and cheery so that the women in the office would think I was neither some kind of wife-beater nor a hen-pecked patsy.

It was during one of these calls, when Grace must have been about six months old, that Naomi Ketts lost it. A coffee cup hit the wall, some ten-by-eights were flung across the floor and Naomi was heard to say something like 'That fucking lazy bitch. Why doesn't she try working for a living!' before storming out of the office into Old Compton Street for a cool-down, cappuccino and maybe a Danish or two. I sympathized with her sentiment but it's not true to say that Liz doesn't work at all. Giving birth and bringing up a baby are hard work, and she does do the occasional fringe show.

One thing I knew tonight, however, was not to enter into this kind of conversation under any circumstances, least of all when out as a couple. Any moment now someone would say, 'Have you read *Men are from Mars, Women are from Venus*?' and then we'd be on to the whole subject of the differences between men and women. Are there any? Are they fair? Does this mean we can all start shagging again?

'Have you read *Men are from Mars, Women are from Venus*?' said Josh Baines, walking into it with hobnail boots.

It's difficult for an agent to be married to an actress. Particularly one who is not so often in work. Out-of-work actors and actresses have on the whole, amongst themselves, one main subject of conversation, and it is us, the agents, and how awful, crap, money-grabbing and lazy we are. How we do not do enough for them. They do talk a bit about plays and films, and how certain other actors are 'not right for the part' or simply 'can't do it', but this soon leads them back to how on earth these lucky actors were given the part in the first place, and from there to talking about agents, and how crap, money-grabbing and lazy we are.

I looked at my watch. In half an hour or so it would be time for me to start rounding us up. 'We have to go because of the baby-sitter.' Useful things, baby-sitters, on a night like this. Liz would probably want to stay longer, but two cabs from Islington to Fulham is too expensive so we'd definitely have to leave together this time.

It had started to go wrong the moment she gave birth to Grace. During labour a lot of women evidently scream, 'You put me through this, you bastard, it's all your fault!' Liz didn't, but it was as if she let this thought linger over the ensuing years. As if she nursed a resentment at me for the pain of childbirth, and the ensuing tiredness and depression and, of course, what it had done to her acting career. And how annoyingly dependent having Grace had made her on me. Breadwinner, macho man, two thousand years of oppression – all my fault. The more I tried to help, the more this resentment grew.

It would be wrong for me, or anyone at Mullin and Ketts, to take on Liz, even though professionally she uses her maiden name, Garnet. I am far too close to tell if she's really any good, for a start. It's complicated because I don't think she's a crap actress, I just fancied her more than I found her work exciting. As an agent, if you meet someone you fancy, you have to make a decision: whether to fuck them or represent them. This is why straight male agents – of whom there aren't many, actually – end up living with bad actresses. And then came Grace, and suddenly we were no longer two autonomous individuals. No, suddenly we were catapulted into 'me Tarzan, you Jane' time: I get the money in, you do all the home stuff. Difficult for us, because Liz is a good two inches taller than me. Definitely a no-win situation, bringing up a kid with a partner and no little trickle of private income. Liz resenting me for being out in the world, having a job, having a willy even, and me envying her time with Grace, the fact that she's provided for, the way she's out of the heart-diseasing marketplace. It'd be nice to share it out more evenly but somehow, in this country, no can do. Sometimes I wish I was Swedish. Mind you, their comedy is crap.

On Sunday, the stress of having a weekend off continued unabated. I had suggested we get off the bus and walk the rest of the way home after dropping Grace at her mother's for the night. To my surprise, Liz had agreed. Surprise, not just because she hated walks but because her usual stance was one of contempt for anything I might suggest, on the grounds, I assumed, that it had been suggested by me. We were walking along the towpath at Fulham. It was Sunday, and the calmness of the trees in the breezeless evening made it possible to ignore the heavy traffic noise from the main road, and Putney Bridge, from which we had just descended. We could talk more quietly now, the playground sandpit was empty of children and beginning to lose heat. It was May 1st, I think. A few young couples played showing-off games along the thick black wall, beyond which the river ambled slowly at depth, while the twinkling reflections on its surface danced hyperactively in the fading light.

Away from the road now, I felt more courageous about speaking to her, I felt I could broach subjects, ask questions. I could forget the bruising attack of the traffic noise, which was now a distant throb.

'So what did you want to talk about?' she said in a tone that did not exactly invite a warm response.

The evening was such that I let fear of her customary aggression subside in me.

'Us,' I said as a joke, but managed to hang on to my thoughts enough to formulate them into something which resembled coherence, while keeping the Bob Henderson factor temporarily at bay. 'I would like us to run our lives differently.'

'I don't want my life to be "run" by anyone,' she replied as I could have predicted.

Instead of trying to rephrase my thoughts, try a different track that would be acceptable to her, thus apologizing for my impulse, I felt unusually motivated to continue in my own way. The trees and the river had given me that space, even if Liz had not.

'I know you are not happy with me. These days I feel like I can't do anything right.'

'You don't even try any more, Guy. Do you?'

I knew she was referring to the fact that I'd stopped making the beds. I always used to make them, but then she would remake them afterwards, neater, with the top cushions at particular angles. After a while, observing this ritual of hers, I stopped bothering.

'Look, it would take me three hours to make the beds the way you do it. We can't afford the time. And anyway, I don't feel the need to be so incredibly, unbelievably tidy as you do.'

'You don't have to look at them all day, Guy.'

'I could give up the agency,' I said, feeling righteous. We'd been here before.

'Bollocks,' she replied. 'It all has to be so stated with you, doesn't it? So self-conscious. You can't negotiate for happiness, you know, I'm not a deal.'

I felt the clanging bell of shame calling me again. D for Dong. D for Liz's disappointment in me. We lapsed into a silence in which she no doubt returned in her thoughts to her Bob and their times together, while I muffled the hammer of the bell and breathed deeply. The air smelt of beech sap. I tried putting my arm around her. She let it rest there like a yoke while she trudged on like some large pained ox. Hugs and cuddles between us had long ago become the arena for savage disagreements, she maintaining that I saw them only as precursors to sex, whilst I – well, no, she was right there too, I suppose. Clang. 'We can cuddle as much as you like afterwards,' I can recall shouting at her through some intervening door or other. Hugs which led nowhere with Liz seemed to me like having diarrhoea with a cork up your bum. It's funny, because at work I spend half my time hugging people, I really do. It goes with the job. But today, down by the river, I just wanted it to be alright between us. That, and her to tell me about Bob Henderson of her own free will.

'It'd be good if we could manage to talk, don't you think?' I said.

Whether rightly or wrongly, I interpreted her simple lack of response as a tacit agreement. By now, we were approaching the football ground at the gates of the park and soon we would be on the streets again.

'I need a sign,' I said. 'I need something to make it clear to me. A sign.' I fantasized her breaking down in loving tears and telling me that Bob Henderson was a one-night mistake who had come in under three seconds from a penis so small she'd gone to the opticians the next day.

From the corner of my eye, I had been watching a small flotilla of mallards as they meandered alongside us. They had split now into two groups of three. The two brown females with a pair of males each. Both drakes fussed and fought, each trying to be the one to keep up with their duck, as she changed direction in a coquettish attempt to shake them off. I had learnt, when with Liz, to observe things like the birds and the bees privately, to avoid her comments about anoraks and trainspotters.

In the water, about ten yards from the shore, on the receding tide, stood what looked for a moment like a heron. I remarked on this since herons are not common on that reach of the river.

'It looks more like the bottom of a tree,' said Liz. And as usual, she was right. It did look more like a tree. As we strolled closer alongside it, we looked again and for a moment I thought I could see quite clearly that it was the face of a bearded man, still in the water, his body submerged beneath him. From his mouth came a string of what looked like seaweed, but could have been heavy saliva, vomit and twigs. He exhaled hugely, like a snorting seal, and then gracefully and slowly disappeared beneath the surface.

We stopped and waited for him to come up for breath. I scanned the river ahead in the direction of the stream, trying to calculate his speed in the undertow and so predict the area of his re-emergence, but the river remained flat with its sparkling ripples like dragonflies on the surface. Nothing. I ran in the direction of the flow, looking for some trace of him. A hand, an arm, perhaps his head again, further downstream. I climbed the thick black wall and scrambled down to the shore. I made my way back up towards the bridge, skipping across the driftwood and plastic detritus like a horse doing dressage. My feet were splashing in the shallows now. A couple of teenagers on the top of the wall stopped their kissing to look at me. I shouted to them to look for the man and to point him out to me if I missed him surfacing.

By now I was knee-deep in water and the ground beneath me was lumpy and unpredictable. I would dive in but could not know where the man was. The river was unyielding. He had disappeared. I looked back to where Liz was. She had walked to the steps and was standing at the top of them, calling after me, but I couldn't distinguish the words. I slipped, as the bottom beneath me descended too rapidly on an incline, and for a moment, I felt the huge power of the undertow of the river, my feet bicycling madly into the freezing black.

The water rushed to my shoulders, its coldness hitting me like a shot of iced Valium, and I was spun around. I must have travelled for some yards before sinking first one foot and then the other into the mud, which squeezed me to my knees. Breathless, and having swallowed some of the Thames, I hauled myself to the shore once again, and stood shivering and muddied.

The teenage girl was alone on the wall now.

'Are you OK?' she shouted down.

'Yeah,' I piped back, in that high pitch that comes from extreme cold on the testicles.

'My boyfriend's gone to call the police,' she yelled.

'Good. Did you see the guy?'

'Naaa.'

I needed to keep moving and ran back to where Liz was standing at the top of the steps. There was a strange man in a shiny yellow shirt hovering just behind her on the path as I came up the steps.

'I can't get rid of this guy. He asked me if I was alone and if I would like to go for a drink,' she said to me as I joined her.

I didn't have the energy to do anything about the guy, and he hung around, a few yards off, like the second male mallard, looking Liz up and down. I leaned on the wall and gasped for breath.

'You're filthy,' said Liz. 'You've probably caught some dreadful disease now.'

I thought of Liz watching me from the top of the steps as I was pulled away momentarily by the river and wondered what her feelings might have been, if any. Whether she would have willed me further into the stream to drown. Whether if I subtracted myself from her life she would be happy at last, free to fly away to the arms of Mrs Henderson's hubby. Maybe it wasn't a bearded man I had seen, maybe it was just the roots of a tree, and I had merely tried to throw myself away for Liz's sake like in my dreams with Grace.

'I've got to keep moving,' I said. 'I'm frozen.'

She helped me up, being careful not to get any mud on her new suede jacket. As we neared the gate to the park, a fat policeman in a flat chequered hat came towards us with a waddle in his walk, like a goose from Toon Town. The guy in the shiny yellow shirt quickly took another direction and made himself scarce.

'There was a man in the water.' I said to the policeman. 'He had a beard and then he just disappeared under the surface.'

'Oh, yes, yes, yes,' he said. He was followed by a younger policeman who had a crackling radio receiver. 'Probably drunk.

They wander in, don't know what they're doing, don't care. Spook, was he?' I do not expect your average friendly bobby to be anything other than a rampant racist.

'No, I think he was white, actually.'

I pointed out to them where we had seen the man and turned down the offer of a blanket, since we lived nearby and I was not in the mood for hearing a racial diatribe from a cartoon duck in a uniform.

'Could have been drowned already up at Richmond. We get a lot of them. Might have been in the water for days.'

'He sort of breathed,' I said, 'and then just disappeared completely. If I could have seen where he was, I would have gone in.'

'Lucky you didn't, son,' said the round policeman. 'You'd have lasted about one and a half minutes in there, with this tide. It's a treacherous bend in the river, you know. People don't realize that. We get it all the time. He could have been dead days ago and drifted all the way down here. Lucky you didn't.'

As we hurried back to the house, Liz was quiet. At the front door she said, 'There's your sign.'

I was getting out of drenched clothes in the front hall.

'What do you mean?' I said.

'You wanted a sign. To make things clear. There it is. Don't go jumping in to try and save drowning things. It was probably just some driftwood anyway. You'd have got yourself killed, you bloody arsehole. Like the policeman said.'

She got me some towels. Old ones that didn't matter, with trailing threads.

'Who was that weirdo in the yellow shirt?' I asked.

'You see?' she said, putting the heater on for me. 'You go and get yourself killed and I get hit on by some mad rapist in the park.'

She was right about the sign. It was a completely foolish thing to wade in, thigh-deep, to try and save an unknown bearded man who had probably drowned some hours or even days before.

Liz's parents separated when she was seven, so she had to learn about loss and secrets and lies as a child. A good training for grown-up life, it would seem. Sometimes I feel that having

60

parents who did not divorce puts one at a serious disadvantage. I, whose parents had stayed together until death parted them three weeks ago, walked out into the large world with the body of a grown man and the emotional cunning of a newborn goose. Maybe this was why she was able to avoid telling me about her Bob. She felt comfortable making separate compartments out of her life: sex in one place, work in another, children another, security a fourth, and so on. She felt at ease with the deception necessary to keep the whole train going. I think of her now as one of those toy snakes made from slices of bamboo which are joined with wire – each segment a separate entity but the whole thing moving with a frighteningly real slinkiness. People like that never seem to suffer the consequences of their actions, can always shift the responsibility down a couple of segments, causing no more than a gentle ripple in the whole body, which is often mistaken by mugs like me for attractiveness. I asked her again about our lives together, hoping she would volunteer the truth. She assumed I was pressurizing her for sex again.

'I couldn't possibly sleep with a man I didn't respect. Surely that's obvious,' she said.

'Why do you feel you need to look up to a man before you can have a relationship with him?' I was diving in now with pointless abandon.

'I said respect, not look up to,' she said, right as usual, and started to make herself a cup of coffee without getting a cup out for me, or asking if I wanted one too.

I had followed her into the kitchen, the only neutral space in the flat.

I supposed I would have earned her respect more had I been more decisive, had I either dived straight into the water, thereby heroically drowning myself in the effort to save him, or been more realistic and known that the guy was a goner, and phoned the police myself. Instead, I had run about a bit, tripped over, got myself wet and failed to get rid of the weirdo in the yellow shirt. This is what I imagine she meant by respect. I had not looked like someone you could respect. I had been ineffectual, clumsy and covered in Thames mud.

'That's not what I meant,' she hurled back at me, and then, a phrase very often heard, 'you stupid, stupid man.'

61

It was amazing how we could talk in what I thought was English, and have apparently wholly different meanings for words, an entire vocabulary of misunderstanding.

I found myself contemplating that I had not made any allowances, in my breakdown of the hours of the week, for time spent arguing, and wondering whether a fair apportionment of rowing time would be an appropriate element to take into consideration. And in whose column ought it to go, for luvviedom's sake?

Either way, Liz would still be the one with free time at the end of the week, because she seemed to have a remarkable ability to decide when a row was finished, whereas I, on the other hand, am incapable of leaving things in a state of conflict and need to put things away neatly. I can't just switch the computer off. I have to have everything saved as what it is, with a dated safety copy.

No doubt I exacerbated the situation by standing outside whichever room she was sulking in and demanding to know who Bob Henderson was. I shouted at her for a few minutes: things I would regret later. She locked the bedroom door – it was the bedroom this time, I think – and the sound of smashing furniture emanated.

'Why don't you just go and see a prostitute?' she yelled through the tantrum. 'That's all you're after!'

I decided it would be best to stay overnight at the office for a while.

THREE

IT'S VERY UN-ENGLISH isn't it, to reveal information about money. The English economy works on an arcane gentleman's agreement that sources shall remain secret. Nevertheless, it seems relevant to point out the fiscal realities behind Mullin and Ketts here because I have no inherited wealth and these are the figures I have to bear constantly in mind in every contact I make, in every conversation I have, whether assessing a young actress's earning potential or contemplating education or health matters for Grace and Liz.

I know this may make me seem grubby, small-minded, like some Dickensian clerk, but that's tough cookies, I'll have to put up with the drop in image credibility in order to clarify my position, as much for myself as for any purpose.

At Mullin and Ketts we have ninety clients, forty mine, forty Naomi's. The remaining ten are looked after by Tilda, who is our trainee. These clients bring us in approximately £150,000 a year in commission. We pay Tilda £12,000 out of this, or more if she exceeds her targets. The office costs us £35,000 a year in rent and expenses. Our theatre tickets, travel, stationery, etc. come to about £20,000 a year. Joan gets £9,000 and Sarah, who is part-time, gets £3,000.

This leaves Naomi and me about £25–35,000 a year each before tax, although of course, if we have had a bad year, like '93, it's a lot less, and at the beginning, we ploughed everything we could back in, to get going. We have no formalized salary agreements because it depends on the state of the industry. I tend to have more high-profile clients than her, although she does have a couple of soap stars and a commercials artist who earn well. I do have a few directors and one or two clients who write

– or, like Neil, fail to write – scripts and books, but on the whole I deal in performers. Everyone knows the best client to have is a dead writer; you just collect. But at Mullin and Ketts we have no such luxuries, it's very much a hand-to-mouth existence. Sometimes it's been my clients who have seen us through the hard times, sometimes Naomi's. There's no real way of controlling it and every day is a worry. We could collapse at any moment.

At the building in Meard Street, we have four rooms, well, three and a half really. There's Naomi's office, my office, the main room and a sort of kitchenette the other side of the stairs which has just enough room for a camp bed in it for overnights when working late in town, and it was here that I stayed some nights when things were becoming fraught between Liz and me. A couple of times I've even gone back home to bath and bed Grace and then if Liz wasn't going out, I've come back up to the office. Couldn't really get any proper work done obviously, because most people have gone home. A call to LA was always a good excuse, though.

A night in the office was a strange affair. Really nothing to do but phone. There were no real books or anything in there, and, anyway, being so near to work made concentrating on anything else almost impossible. I sat worrying about Susan Planter and decided to check Jeremy's income slips since they'd been in such a mess at his home. That would be useful. There were definitely a few irregularities, our fault. I made a note to get Joan on to it in the morning. And one rather large late payment, again our fault. Our expenses book wasn't being filled in properly any more either. Any one of us could have been driving around in our own chauffeur-driven limo for all that was down on paper. You have to do everything yourself, it seems. Lucky that the office girls don't know what my real nickname is, what it was at school, I mean: Muggins.

I became agitated and decided to leave business for the night. I cracked open the emergency champagne and poured myself some into a coffee mug. I'd replace it in the morning. I stared at the phone. The ventilation system from the Chinese restaurant three floors below was humming, and in another fifteen minutes the tape loops from the strip-joint next door would start up again and then I'd be done for. 'We're gonna make this a night to remembaaaa . . .' over and over again. Somehow, in the day, with all the women in the office and the buzz of deals and the banter, the sound of Soho did not intrude into the consciousness. Once everyone was gone, though, the noises crowded in as reminders of the harshness and cheapness outside. The loud woman next door was screaming at her man again, 'Don't come back here! Go to her! Fuck her! Go to her!' This seemed to be a nightly ritual followed by noisy sex. Occasionally this pre-coital slagging match would include the sound of kitchen utensils clattering against the wall. Once I heard gunshots down the street, but there was nothing about it in the papers the next day.

Grace was playing near the river, too near, she was toddling still and in her sun hat and a nappy. By now, I'd had this dream, or a version of it, so often that I knew, even asleep, what its outcome would be. It was almost a ritual. I looked around for the wooden danger sign. Sure enough, it was to my left. 'No bathing: dangerous water', it said, but it was broken and there were weird symbols painted on it as well. That was new. Grace looked behind at me, before putting her foot too close to the edge. In that moment when I would have found myself falling into the shiny blackness of the water in Grace's place, there was a heaving sound. Suddenly, Neil James was there, coming out of the water like a corny special-effects giant. It was Neil, or the drowning man at Putney, or both, they were the same. Neil's beard had grown to Biblical dimensions and horrible green stuff was coming out of his mouth and nostrils, just like the drowning man. Neil held me back, his presence preventing me from throwing myself over the edge for Grace. Neil submerged exactly like the drowning man had done, taking Grace with him. Leaving the surface black and rippling and shiny. I could not see Grace. She was gone. I awoke as if landing from a great height. Bloody Neil. Getting into my dreams now and messing them about.

I lay in the grey dawn on the creaky camp bed with the cold street lighting intruding across the ceiling. Maybe Liz was right, I should go to a prostitute. Have a bit of in-out. Get rid. Maybe that was all there was to me. Maybe she would respect me if I was like that, if I was more honest about being like that. I could live down to her expectations and she could relax into resenting my mobility. Like proper mummies and daddies. Once when driving through Bayswater with Grace in the back baby seat, I stopped at the lights and, turning round to talk to her, my move was mistaken by a skinny leather-mini-skirted streetwalker for interest. She hadn't seen Grace in the back there. She approached the open front passenger window and stared in at me with stark, drug-glazed eyes and said, 'Fancy a blow job?' before she noticed Grace. As the lights changed she gave us both a look of such hatred that had I believed in the evil eye, I would have asked the garage to exorcise the car next time it went in for a service.

It was six thirty, I might as well get up now anyway. The morning dust cart had started its grinding mere yards away in Dean Street, and it was making the windows rattle in their frames. I could go and have coffee somewhere Italian and look as if I was the kind of guy who had breakfast with important American producers.

They wouldn't even see Neil for the Ayckbourn tour. I'd had to spend some minutes obliterating self-doubts, and think positive. The biggest kick you can get as an agent is persuading someone to see a client they wouldn't normally have thought of for a job. This has to be done with great skill. Maybe you have an actress who is commonly perceived as a light comedienne, who normally does cute and cuddly – a Felicity Kendal, say, or a Penelope Wilton – and she wants to develop her range, and you know she can do it and she's ready – kids grown up, or recently single, for example – and there's a role in a TV film as an alcoholic having a breakdown, or a politically active barrister, or an AIDS victim wife, or whatever. You must enter into casual talks with the casting director, going through all the obvious choices for the part, rounding up the usual suspects, and subtly deriding them with remarks such as: 'Yes, so and so could do it, but we all *know* she could do it.' Late on in the conversation, almost as an afterthought, with self-deprecating innocence, you must pong in the name of the client you have in mind, as in: 'Well, we haven't discussed Felicity, or Penelope or whoever, because no ordinary person would even have thought of seeing her for the part, but God knows, if anyone's brave enough to give it a try then you are.' You must help them to think they had the idea. You must facilitate their adventurousness.

I've never been proud about flattery. However outrageous it becomes, however much it might be denied, people inevitably place flattering remarks on a reserved shelf in their minds, a special inner mantelpiece for the Oscars, but nothing could persuade this lot to consider Neil. I even tried telling them of his recent weight gain in the hope that they would see him for the side-kick dickhead part, but zilch. They already had what they wanted firmly fixed in their minds, and for some reason, Neil it wasn't. I couldn't push it too far because I was in the midst of negotiating the finer points of a contract with them for dear old Barbara Stenner to play the lead part in the same tour, and we hadn't yet discussed her billing, touring allowance and days off. I didn't want to queer Barbara's pitch. It was a depressing phone call all round, especially since I'd had Barbara on the phone earlier saying she'd rather not do the tour at all. 'The last thing on earth I want is to take this tired old pair of tits round the provinces again,' as she had put it.

One has to be careful how one suggests things to Barbara. 'Darling, I've got something which I'm sure you won't be interested in but I thought I should at least run it past you' was how I'd put it to her the week before. She'd been a Rank starlet in her youth, so the 'darling' was appropriate, nay, obligatory. 'How would you feel about another Ayckbourn tour, darling?'

'Darling, do you even need to ask, darling?' she'd replied, as I could have predicted.

'OK then, darling, I'll get out the Big Fin,' I said, meaning I'd ask them for far too much money, like a proper shark. I got her a grand a week, which is actually piss these days, but she had accepted it, as I knew she would, because at least it wasn't insulting, and films, TV and class theatre had long since slipped from her grasp, sad old thing.

Barbara Stenner was my first name client, and as a rookie agent I was proud to get her, so I've sort of hung on to her ever since. Her faded glamour gave trad credibility to the agency early on. It meant we had the official stamp of show-biz on us, and it meant I could go to first nights and meet other folk who'd been around for aeons, and have a forage amongst them. She was my bridge. She spent her life now doing revivals in the home counties, her recognizable face on posters from Guildford to Exeter.

Having her and keeping her meant endless negotiations over holiday entitlements, dressing rooms and cars to pick her up; also long conversations about the healing power of crystals and astrological rebirthing, and having to attend one or two Buddhist chanting sessions in Primrose Hill. But she was worth it. She was a good stick, was Barbara, with a proper deep actress's voice, which she'd got through a combination of diaphragmatic muscularity, vocal cord fatigue and gin, due to many years of shouting in the evening for a living. Her famous pout was so exaggerated that by now she had become incapable of saying her s's. What came out instead was a sort of soft shushing noise rather like the gentle trickle from one of the bonsai fountains in her very Japanese garden in Barnes.

But what to do with Neil, that was the poser. He could have done with some of Barbara's old-fashioned thespian resilience, or maybe he should be going to one of her chigang yoga classes for mind-spirit balance. Something. A visit to West Hampstead, where he lived, was probably on the cards at some point to see what he was up against. His partner was a lot older than him, a therapist, but what kind I don't know. Maybe this was where the trouble lay.

I see this business as rather like a massive kindergarten full of all kinds of children whose feckless parents have abandoned them to go for an extended skiing holiday in Gstaad. There are sporty kids, team players, loners, bullies, sensitive, creative ones, but they all need individual care and attention, and they all have to learn to play with each other. On the whole they get bored easily, and it's my job to know when to get out the finger paints and when it's time for a nap. When to hug and when to be strict. But no one hugs their agent, no. One gets accustomed to being ignored and treated like a toilet roll even by one's own, it goes with the territory. Doug Handom, for instance, was very unhappy on that first film, and was ringing me hourly from LA saying, 'Get me out of this, I've made a mistake, get me out, Guy.' I said, 'Look, you signed a contract, why don't you see how you feel in a couple of days, if you still hate it then I'll see what we can do. Wait until Friday, I'll speak to you then.' He never rang back on Friday. I had to ring him. When I got through, he'd completely forgotten our earlier talk. 'Oh, I'm fine now, it's fine,' he said as if I was mad, which was great, of course, that it was fine, but he hadn't bothered to let me know of his change of heart and I'd been worrying like a fruit bat. Mind you, I could worry for England. Not that anyone would know. Despite the banter, and despite my current nickname, which is Muffin the Mule for some reason best known to the women in the office, I am actually quite a fragile petal underneath it all. No, but seriously, I couldn't look after all these people if I didn't care.

Onwards and upwards. At least staying over at the office cut down on travelling time, enabling me to get an hour or so in before the women clattered in at half nine. Trouble was, I'd already had about seven cups of coffee by then and was a bit hyper.

He's a good boy, Doug. Well, actually, he's a very bad boy. He took that first feature role when Denise was pregnant with their first child and then stayed out there among the Candyfloss Cowboys. I was very careful not to influence his decision at the time, of course, just let him know that the offer was on the table and left him alone to talk with his conscience. Unfortunately for Denise and the baby, Doug's conscience was obviously not very articulate that weekend because he was on the plane to La-La-Land by Sunday night. It all worked out all right in the end for Denise, though. She now lives in Crouch End with a much kinder and more reliable guy, Charlie Bennett, another one of my clients, as it happens. Not that I was instrumental in that. They just happened to both be working in the same production at the National, directed by Stephen Cranham, another of mine. The women in the office go wobbly in anticipation of Doug's twice-yearly visits now.

I know I refer to those on the other side of the Atlantic too much and in too unfavourable a light. You will have to allow me that, it is pure envy. In the States, the entertainment industry is second only in revenue terms to the arms industry. It's huge. One of the reasons we see so many American films over here, almost to the exclusion of everything else, is that the Yanks bought all our cinemas, so nowadays we have a home audience who understand the dialects, mores and myths of American culture better than they do their own.

I wish I was like Doug Handom. I wish I was like Jeremy Planter. I wish I was Bob Henderson. Ruthless. Not a ruth between them. That's what impresses the girls, they're not attracted to losers. Liz wouldn't have given me a second look if I hadn't had some air of potential success about me. And powerful women seek out more powerful men, not pushovers. I know, I get an earful of it every day. The women in the office are fascinated by men who win, in the same way that boys ogle boobs. Today, though, would be a day away from the quadraphonic sound of women talking into telephones; I had to go to Birmingham.

Working out the railway pricing system these days requires advanced qualifications in statistics and the laws of probability.

The man in the ticket booth at Euston patiently explained to me that if I bought a ticket for the 3.50 train as opposed to the 3.32, it would cost me £60 more. If I returned within three days, a return would be cheaper than a single, provided I stayed over a Thursday night, and I could travel first class for an extra £5 as long as I was going north-east and not westwards. He kindly advised me to get a Weekend Saver as opposed to a Supersaver Weekend.

On the platform I asked another man, this one in a uniform, whether the train was going to Birmingham and whether I could travel on it with a Supersaver ticket. He told me he had no idea because he worked for a different rail company. Still, at least the shareholders have holiday homes.

The journey itself was pleasant enough, except for a man three seats away who called his wife on his mobile to report the train's progress every twenty minutes: 'Yes, we're leaving Watford now and it's 15.58, so I might be five or ten minutes late, darling.' Then, 'Hello, it's me. Look, we're already at Milton Keynes, so I may be three or four minutes early after all.'

Jeremy Planter was shooting a summer special sketch in a hospital on the outskirts of Birmingham and it was time I saw him face to face, preferably with Harry, his producer, there and, probably unavoidably, with this Bella Santorini woman. I had ascertained her name by now from a shooting schedule. The sketch was not a hospital sketch, one would use a studio for that. It was a sketch set in a police station which required some offices and a long corridor.

Defunct or half-defunct hospitals are used all the time nowadays as film locations. They are the cheapest big buildings available since health authorities are so starved of resources. Sometimes they still have a few patients knocking around in them, sometimes just old fluttering noticeboards and medical debris. Semi-derelict institutions are perfect for film crews and the art department can easily bung up a few false walls to turn them into schools, police stations, government buildings or even, in one BBC drama serial last year, airport departure lounges. The location in Birmingham – St Mary's Infirmary for Mental Care – must have been still in use as some kind of home for patients, because as I walked down the vast Victorian corridors following the 'Film Unit' signs, folk in cardigans with mad eye-contact greeted me with that overfamiliarity of the institutionalized. Unless they were crew members breaking for lunch.

A brief whispered conversation with Harry to the side of the set in which he told me – as producers always do – that the rushes were looking especially good, that this series really was looking to be the best yet, established my right to be there, so I hung about for half an hour or so watching Jeremy go through a routine which involved a plumber's-mate plunger getting stuck on his forehead. In a tea break we made contact whilst Jeremy was being fussed over by the make-up artists and I arranged that we would meet at the hotel and have supper together. I checked in at the hotel and got on the phone in the last office hour available.

At half six, when I was showering, the hotel phone rang and I padded across the floor, dripping, to answer it. A beautiful and steady female voice came out of the earpiece.

'Hello, Guy. It's Bella. Bella Santorini? I'm just calling to let you know they're running late. Jeremy won't be able to get back for another hour or so but I thought it would be nice if you and I met up for a drink? It would be great to get a chance to talk to you. You must feel a bit out at sea and I know Jer won't have explained anything about what's been going on. You know what he's like.'

'Erm, yes, I do.' I laughed gormlessly.

I was a little thrown, not just by the directness of what she was saying and the consideration she was showing but subliminally and more powerfully by the calming tone in her voice, like a slow-bowed cello.

It was hard to imagine that I was speaking to the hostess of a TV game show. I'm very affected by the timbre of someone's voice, very vocally aware, especially of women, and it always surprises me that the voice is never listed in those monthly magazines' 'What Turns You On?' round-ups, in which men and women both lie by putting 'sense of humour' top of the list. I dressed and went down to the lobby.

'I know it must look awful what we've done, Guy, but please believe me, we have agonized over it a lot, thought about it, talked it through, and honestly, it's not what it seems. I don't want you to think I've taken this lightly. I'm not the sort of person who goes around breaking up homes and families for a pastime.'

She was drinking a camomile tea. I had a vodka and orange to calm my nerves. Her skin was naturally iridescent, her teeth perfectly placed, her hair was clean and simply brushed. No make-up on, and a plain cotton frock covered her small, healthy body. Her posture was good but not overly self-conscious. Nevertheless, definitely an ex-dancer. She could not have looked more different from the picture of her draped over Jeremy's arm on the front of last week's papers. She quietly exuded confidence, I was stumped. There was nothing about her which might cause the word 'bimbo' to come to mind.

She continued in her assessment of the situation whilst I nodded or shook my head where appropriate, like a back-seat puppy. Also, she was not that young, only a bit younger than Susan I would say, mid-thirties. Her dancing career must be reaching its close. She was looking for something more stable. I guessed and she told me that the Bella was short for Arabella, the Santorini merely an invention; her real surname was something double-barrelled. A home-counties girl with an education and ponies and a doting father who was a surgeon in Surrey, no doubt. Classically trained but too wise to stay in the ballet beyond the age of twenty-five.

'We have tried to explain it to Susan, believe me, but in the end it just seemed the best thing to make a decisive break. I know she's very upset at the moment and I hope things calm down in time. It's too early for me to meet the children yet but it's important that they stay in touch with their father. Maybe you can help there, Guy. Susan can't keep them away from him forever.'

According to Arabella, the situation had been going on for a lot longer than I had been led to believe by Susan. Jeremy and she had told Susan about their affair over a year ago. So, uncharacteristically for Jeremy, the whole thing had been discreet, considered.

Susan Planter was also behaving uncharacteristically. As well as savaging his clothes as I had seen, she was evidently threatening to deny him all access to Dave and Polly, she was talking to the papers and now she had been committing various acts of petty revenge, like ordering alarm calls through the night on his new phone number. Worst of all, she had evidently put an ad in the massage section of a local paper with Arabella's phone number in it, the wording of which went something like 'Domination and golden shower my speciality. Call Bella if you dare.'

In fact, the more I heard, the more I developed a sort of sneaking admiration for Susan Planter's inventiveness. She was certainly not taking this like a humble politician's wifey, and, I must admit, I laughed inside at all these revelations while expressing only deepest concern. Maybe I should have been an actor after all.

A waiter arrived and Arabella signed for our drinks, making steely eye contact with him. She smiled and he smiled back gratefully. I cannot put my finger on the quality she had, possibly a sort of queenliness, which brought out the chivalrous in men. She was not a flirt and I can imagine that guys would be more likely to offer to do her favours, carry her bags, take her across the road, make her something useful, than to get leery. I could sense that any attempt at a pick-up line would be met with dignified incomprehension, against which most men would shrivel. Her attention was flattery enough and in the hour or so

73

while we waited for Jeremy, her confiding in me and her frankness made me feel special. She had the opposite of an actor's charisma, which is all surface and is why great actors are so often disappointing when you meet them in real life. She was the genuine article, she didn't have to perform to pull focus, the focus seemed naturally to be on her. I tried to imagine what it would be like having sex with her but somehow drew a blank. She seemed too self-contained to come across, or maybe she just wasn't my type. I wouldn't have thought she was Jeremy's either, but then . . .

When he eventually arrived, it was 10.30 and Jeremy was bushed. The dining room had stopped meals, so we stayed in the lobby, where we sat in the giant sofas, upholstered in those overly traditional materials typical of hotels which were converted in the mid-eighties, too many patterns, too many fabrics, too much matt silk finish on the walls.

Arabella managed, with some determination, to secure a salad and soup for Jeremy which weren't from the room-service menu. I had a bar-snack sandwich, she had nothing but more herbal tea. From the first minutes, it was obvious that Jeremy was different; he didn't order a drink for a start. He seemed to be happy to let her dictate his eating habits, organize his weekly timetable and remind him of his early call, telling him when he should go to bed.

However, none of this infantilized him. He seemed to accept her suggestions with trust and enthusiasm. In the past, when drunk, if reminded by his wife Susan that he had had enough, he would have ordered another bottle, made a joke at her expense, talked too loudly and made sure that his role as one of the boys was re-established. His showy loudness ensuring that punters in bars and restaurants would be in no doubt that they had been in the presence of a celeb.

But this new subdued Jeremy was a surprise. In the two minutes when Arabella went to the phone, he looked at me with the grateful eyes of a labrador and said, 'Isn't she . . . w . . . wonderful?'

I agreed outwardly, because that's my job, but I couldn't think of a reason not to agree for real as well.

'She's certainly not what I was expecting,' I said.

'You mean you thought old Jeremy's been thinking with his
. . . d . . . dick again and got it caught in the m . . . mangle this
time.' His face puckered up comically at certain consonants.

'Well . . .'

He didn't touch the bread roll and left his soup half finished,
pushing aside the tray. He sat back, his whole body visibly
sinking into a contented relaxation, difficult on these designer
sofas. It was as if his Tinkerbell had waved her wand from the
other side of the lobby and he had instantly gone floppy.

'I j . . . just want to see the children, Guy. I know it was s . . .
stupid of me to p . . . p . . . put it about like that, but Susan and I
h . . . h . . . haven't had s . . . sex for four y . . . years. She went
off me after P . . . Polly was born. What was I s . . . supposed to
do?' All of this sentiment was very unusual coming from Mr
Happy Telly. I didn't know what to say.

'Will you talk to . . . S . . . Susan, Guy? I mean, she's upset at
the moment I know, but soon it will be time for us all to move
on, you know. Draw a line in the sand and walk over it.'

A most un-Jeremy-like phrase, which I assumed he had
picked up from Arabella. It was all a bit fairy-tale like. When she
returned, they touched lovingly but not sickeningly so, not for
show. I had never seen Jeremy actually warm and relaxed in the
company of a woman before; come to think of it, I had never
seen him warm and relaxed before at all, only energetic and
attention-seeking. I wondered how it would affect his work, but
as if by telepathy, Arabella pre-empted my concerns.

'Don't look so worried, Guy, it's time he moved into a
different market area anyway. The *Revenge* show won't last
forever. He's got to stay one step ahead of the audience
expectation. Did he tell you Harry's leaving? He's been offered
Head of Comedy at Granada.'

A goodly piece of goss, which of itself made my trip to
Birmingham worthwhile. Thank you, Bella.

I talked with her of Jeremy's career plans as if he weren't
there, and he seemed happy for us to do so. Evidently he was
tired of having plumber's-mate plungers stuck to his forehead.
He was tired of his famous suits. He was tired of game shows
altogether. He wanted to develop his range, his talent. He
wanted to grow artistically and he and Arabella were aware that

this might mean a drop in income for a year or two. They had worked this one out. In order to see Susan and the kids alright, he would do a couple of large-venue farewell tours to large audiences for large money. Simultaneously, the agency was to seek out classier work for him, some acting, some Chekhov, a detective series, maybe, with the long-term intention of writing and directing himself in his own movies.

So, she was a businesswoman as well, this double-barrelled dancer woman. She seemed to have achieved what many women dream of, I am told: first get your man, then change him, and Jeremy was certainly changed.

'It's time you went for your zizz, Planter,' she said, and he got up, apologized to me for having to get an early night, said his goodbyes and followed her to the lift. Beauty with her captive Beast on a thin silvery lead.

On the train home in the morning, I went for the full cardiac breakfast, along with all the other fat cats in suits.

If you eat slowly enough, you can sit in the first-class dining car for the whole journey on a second-class ticket. As the shadows from passing trees flickered across the tablecloth, I ruminated on the night before. It'll never last and love is blind and he's hooked and other cynical envious snippets percolated through my otherwise positive mood as I half read the *Independent*. The two of them seemed genuinely, nauseatingly happy. They had been seeing each other for at least two years. Apart from awful feelings about Susan and the kids, where was the catch? Maybe there wasn't one. Maybe I could afford to relax a bit.

I confess I was excited at the prospect of testing out the reactions to Jeremy in the world of serious drama. It's much easier to sell a personality, or even a newscaster – providing he or she is famous enough – as anything than it is to get a proper actor work. The money-making tour shouldn't be too difficult to set up. Naomi knew two or three promoters who would jump at it. Yes, I was excited. I ordered more coffee. My little expenses trip had definitely borne fruit.

'How to have a happy balanced relationship that lasts. The five magic ingredients that you should look for in a man that turn a passionate quickie into the real thing: 1. Sense of humour;

2. Sensitivity; 3. A caring side; 4. Self-confidence without arrogance; 5. A wizard in bed.'

I had put the *Independent* down on the seat opposite so that I could get my feet up without taking off my shoes and was flicking through the pages of *Metropolitan* magazine looking for the small piece by one of my clients. I got it at Birmingham station, happy for an excuse to actually buy a copy. I am fascinated by women's magazines and could read them for ever, but unfortunately have to restrict my perusals to doctors' waiting rooms or lobbies of production companies.

'You're a modern woman with a schedule from hell and it's easy to put yourself last. It's time to invest in yourself. Do it now!' This was the copy-line underneath some glossy pictures of a new range of blushers.

'Look at your life – if something is wrong, make it right. Work out an ideal future – then live it!' A picture of a beautifully turned-out young woman in a suit dictating a letter to a male-model secretary, also no doubt wearing blusher but his more subtly applied. And over the page, an advertisement for a rather small new hop-about car. 'For too long women have been relegated to the back seat when it comes to buying cars. We're here to tell those car manufacturers that we want much more than just somewhere to put the shopping.' A beautiful model with unbelievable hair and even more unbelievable glasses swinging her £900 handbag near the open door of a pristine mauve automobile with a natty name on the numberplate. Through all of these wonderful ironic and aspirational pages, I managed to find my Jenny Thompson's piece. It was actually a location diary of her time filming in Prague last year, but they'd bunged 'Start getting your own back. Every woman deserves an adventure' across the top of it in heavy print. Referring, no doubt, to the adulterous subject matter of the film Jenny had been working on and not, I hoped, to her personal life. Also, this month's edition of *Metropolitan* was supposed to be themed. The overall concept being infidelity, or 'Why having a fling is a good thing' month. So I suppose they needed to tie it all in.

Jenny's article was OK. A bit dull but they paid her quite well and she seemed to be getting more and more of these kinds of offer. I discussed it with her and she thought the idea of getting a regular column somewhere would be, in her words, 'amazingly brave'. So this was just a station on the way, as it were.

On the other side of the spread from Jenny's piece was another picture of two anodyne models. This time the chisel-jawed man was looking into the middle distance while the pouting female gazed sadly at his left ear. This to illustrate an article by an evidently eminent psychologist which had the shoutline 'Staying faithful to an emotionally unavailable man. How to handle it so *you* win.'

I speed-read the first few paragraphs and found myself being hoovered into the world of victimology, where relationships are the altar we must worship at, where marriage is about winning and losing self-respect, where words like empowerment and independence and emotional maturity and cherishment are the sacrament and lack of emotional openness is the deadly sin. There was a tick-box quiz at the end, to find out on a score chart whether 'Your man is worth staying faithful to'. This kind of stuff affects me like a cinema-sized pack of Opal Fruits. You want a couple of them for a small sugar hit and end up chewing your way through all forty and thinking the movie was crap because you came out with a headache and a confused bowel. I read through the tick-box quiz, wondering what mine and Liz's score would be.

'You've got a new boss who's making your life hell. Does your man: a) Give you advice and then threaten to ring your boss on your behalf? b) Get angry and go down to the pub? or c) Listen to your problem and produce tickets for a weekend in Paris?'

My mood began to deflate. The scenery became more urban again. The sun went behind the batch of clouds. The train slammed into a short tunnel.

'Ladies and gentlemen, we shall shortly be approaching London Euston.' The microphone-happy steward made his last announcement. The men in suits began packing away their computers, mobile phones and ball-park budget brochures. I dawdled with the magazine. The train stood for some minutes, awaiting a free platform to enter. A couple of outbound trains whacked past the nearside window but we didn't shift. I started to go through my diary of events and calls for the day. I toyed with merchandising possibilities on the Planter tour and wondered which of Naomi's promoters would be the best to approach. I fiddled with my Psion but it was no good. Underneath it all was the jumpy feeling. The feeling that must be avoided. The one that has no name but a hell of a presence. The one to do with Liz and me. I do not have the language for this. There is no dictionary of terms other than that supplied in buckets by magazines like this one, over whose cover I had now spilt coffee in what I supposed must be some kind of Freudian slip of the elbow. The black liquid ran towards my lap as the train noisily lurched back into action. I mopped at it with a serviette. The coffee had first splashed on to the summary of this month's leader articles — 'The best sex I *ever* had. Women confess' — and had now dribbled down over 'Free with this issue! Four available men!'

Walking up the platform, my mind had become a quagmire of 1990s mag-speak. There is no doubt that Liz feels disempowered being with me, I thought. It is humiliating for her that the money in our bank account comes only from me. That we get round it taxwise by saying she is employed by the agency. She hates to be thought of only as Guy's wife or Grace's mum, and not as a person in her own right. It must be awful for her, I thought. Talk about emotionally unavailable. I'm almost entirely unavailable. I have to work so hard to support us all and when I do get back home, there's Grace. It must be degrading for Liz, knowing that the car she drives is officially a Mullin and Ketts company car. She must feel that she doesn't exist. No wonder she used to hide the child seat in the boot. No wonder she needs to get out of the house so often. She must feel like a prisoner. I have disempowered her, that's what I've done with all my privileges. I must be part of the backlash conspiracy against women. No wonder she's ended up sleeping with Bob Henderson. Poor thing.

As I reached the taxi rank, a more familiar feeling surfaced; resentment and anger at Liz. Just because she felt disempowered, it didn't naturally follow that I was empowered, did it? Didn't mean that I was doing the disempowering, did it? That I was some irritatingly confident father figure, basking, wallowing even, in my authority? An easy life inherited through gender.

There's room for two people to feel they have no choices, you know. I would love not to have to work so bloody hard, etc., et bloody cetera. But I put it out of my mind. I wouldn't want to be accused of being a misogynist, as well as all my other well-recorded faults. I suppose I have trouble buying the idea of a misogynist conspiracy. Maybe that's because I've never had the time to pursue a competitive sport, but shouldn't a conspiracy have meetings and special signs? And aprons?

'Largo factotem della citta largoooo.' The cab driver was a very large man who barely fitted behind the wheel. 'Tra la la la la la la la laaaa.' He was in the chorus of the taxi drivers' choir and had played several leading roles in his local operatic society, including Nankipoo from *The Mikado* and Rossini's Figaro, the opening aria of which he was now giving me a rendition. I wish I hadn't told him I was an agent. Or maybe this was a treat he bestowed on all passengers. He offered a running translation alongside the sung Italian version.

'Basically, he's saying like he's a pimp and a gigolo and everyone in Seville comes to him if they want a bit of an erotic ding-dong, a bit of how's-yer-father, right? He hears all the gossip while he's doing his haircutting and that, and he passes bits of it on, and his name is Figaro tra la la la la la la la la la la.' He burst into baritone again: 'V'e la risorsa, poi del mettiere, colla donnetta, col cavaliere!' His Italian accent wasn't bad. 'Oh yeah, 'cos they were all at it, you know, them sixteenth-century Italians. Donnetta, that's like a young dolly-bird, and cavaliere, that's some feller who wants to stomp her one from behind. Personally I think I was wrong for the part, being a big fellow, even though as you must know Figaro is usually played by a big fellow. Oh yeah, I had to stick on the old beard and everything, really tickles. But I think it'd be better if he was played by a little feller, you know, he's a sort of camp sort of hairdresser sort of a bloke. Someone like Peter Stringfellow. But he couldn't reach the notes, you see.' He started to sing again. 'Stringfellooo, Stringfellooo, Stringfellostringfellostringfellostringfelloooo.'

After the habitual exortation to cheer up it might never happen, I paid the fare, declining to tip but taking his phone number on a cab card which he pressed on me. I binned it when he was round the corner.

'Am I blonde with big tits?'

'Well, you did bleach your hair that time when you got back from Ibiza, and I would have said your breasts were definitely of the more-than-adequate type.'

'Guy! Look at me! Am I blonde with big tits?'

'No.'

'Then why are you trying to fuck me?'

The news of Jeremy's new career plans had not impressed Naomi Ketts.

'The man – if we can call him that any more – has less acting talent than a mollusc, and he couldn't write or direct his way into or out of a paper bag. He's a frigging game-show host, for frig's sake, who's poking the totty! Your client, Guy. Your problem.' End of conversation.

We had these kind of days every now and then at M and K. But I suspect Naomi's somewhat hostile and OTT outburst had more to do with her irritation at having to face my shaving things by our coffee sink than with any of Planter's high-flown new ambitions.

It was a few days after Birmingham, and my little sojourn in Meard Street looked like turning into a full-scale siege. By the end of the week, I could no longer pretend that my overnights were for business purposes, and, except for Tania, the women respected my reticence in not coming forth with any explanations. If things were bad at home, that too was my problem. Much as they may have secretly disliked Liz, she was the woman after all, and in any confessional they would take her side. Tania, on the other hand, pestered me with love and advice. She left me the phone number of a cranial osteopath by whom she swore, and tried to convince me that I should cut out dairy products.

On Friday after work I returned home to Fulham to see parked on the driveway by our front sitting room window a very recent model Porsche with the cherished number plate BH 123. All silver and shiny and clean and glistening in the early-evening light. Sitting there like an overfed shark. No rubbish on the floor of this car. No sweet wrappers, no kids' toys. No ice-cream stain on the baby car-seat. No baby car-seat. Porsche, the car designer lauded and subsidised by Adolf Hitler. Porsche. Sitting there on my front drive under the large elm growing out of my front fence, with a humourless and complacent smile on its radiator grille, while Grace slept inside the house.

Some time during the next week, while Liz was out, I went home and packed a proper load of things to bring to Meard Street. I admit it, I did check through all of Liz's drawers, but found no incriminating sexy diary, no extravagant receipts, no raunchy polaroids with which to hurt myself. I also went through the mail. There were various bills to pay and policies to renew. Liz never does any of that. Maybe there was more to Neil's right man story than I had thought. Here I was prowling through this woman's affairs, making sure her premiums were up to date and none of the roof tiles had fallen off. I again had the feeling that Neil was writing my life. I must pay him a visit to find out the end of the plot. I slunk back to Soho with plastic bags of bumf.

It was a hot Monday night with many sirens in it, I couldn't sleep, my feet seemed to have swollen beyond endurance in the claggy heat. I prowled around the office again slurping a mug of 'poo and then, when I'd had enough of fidgeting – and taking a couple of scripts and a copy of *Broadcast* with me – I nipped over the road to the Jade Tree to eat.

The crowded street was full of hard staring faces like a bad acid trip, or at least what I imagine a bad acid trip would be like. My younger brother Tony would know more than me about that, of course. I made a mental note to call in on him and see how he was. He didn't have a phone, which meant one had to take time out to see him. This seemed to have left Tony with a much more trouble-free existence than us normal people. Bastard. Sometimes I wish I had his mental problems; everyone accommodated Tony. He hadn't been to see Mum since my father died. He never really got involved in family things. That was my job.

Out of the Soho fog of strangers there was a face I recognized; Simon Renman, the producer, coming out of a tacky strip-joint. I smiled at him and instantly wished I hadn't.

'Hello, how are you? How are you coping with the twins?' I said without realizing that he would have preferred a cursory nod. Sometimes my memory for people's personal details is a disadvantage.

'Oh, hello, Guy,' he said tensely. 'I'm researching a script about strippers so I have to, you know . . .' indicating the dive behind him. He paused, lost for words. I hadn't asked.

'That's your excuse and you're sticking to it,' I said with the nearest I could get to a boysy chuckle.

'Sorry?' he said.

'These are my Y-fronts and I'm sticking to them,' I said, compounding my error and embarrassing the spunk out of him. He was lying about the script research then. He was guiltily haunting the wank palaces, and I'd caught him at it. So the rumours about his marriage must be true. He sloped off into the multinational night leaving me certain that I must keep any trouble between myself and Liz under wraps. It's a tricky old biz, show-biz, and anything that puts you at a disadvantage – anything – may be taken down and used against you, and don't say trousers. I was already logging his domestic troubles in my mental file under 'Well Sorted Films', the name of his production company. Not the right time to invest, I fear.

After a meal which was too fatty for ten thirty at night, I returned to the office and rechecked everyone's desks, emptied the bins, straightened the noticeboard, that sort of thing. There was one new message on the answerphone.

Kemble Stenner, now there's a good name. Worth representing just on the strength of it. Nice voice in the message. Was a child actress for years. Must be all of twenty now. I looked her up in the *Spotlight* and the photo was pretty gorge too. Barbara's granddaughter, although brought up mostly by her dad, who was a producer I think – big in the seventies – and a series of second, third and fourth wives of his. I don't think Barbara had seen her particularly from one year to the next, and her mum was Sandra Peters, of whom the less said probably the better. I don't know if you remember *Crofter's Way*? Yes? Well, Sandra Peters was the token totty in that, you know, the one with the plastic hair? Yes. For five years, and then nothing. Except for a couple of embarrassingly drunken appearances on *Blankety Blank* or *Celebrity Squares* or whatever it was at the time. Wise move of young Kemble to take Grandma's surname and not Mum's.

Kemble Stenner, and a bit of a stunner! And from the answer-phone message, funny and pushy and clever to boot. I made a note to return her call in the morning.

I sat on the small cane sofa we have by the window at Mullin and Ketts, partly because it was the only non-work piece of furniture in the place, and partly because I'd bought a cigar and I didn't want to fug the place up and have to explain myself in the morning. I looked at the phone. It looked back at me. Grace would be long asleep by now, so no point in ringing Liz again. She had evidently had a reasonably good day but had scribbled in wax crayon on the bathroom wall. Personally I can live with her extempore murals, but I'd promised to do something about it next weekend. I suppose it'd be different if she'd graffitied the office.

Another siren two-toned by. I sat in my underpants smoking my cigar and drinking the rest of the champagne and flicked through my phone book. My own phone book, which is a much smaller affair than my Mullin and Ketts one. I sat with the phone in my lap, looking through my black address book. We didn't even have a radio in the office. I suppose the phone is more important than sex, especially since AIDS. No wonder British Telecom just made ten million profit. It was too late now to ring anyone out of the blue without appearing to be a lonely old pervert in the middle of the night, which is what I suppose I was. There was an uncomfortable buzzing in my brain which I wanted to put an end to through conversation. I would have liked to ring Lottie or Maggie, or even Lesley: girlfriends of mine prior to Liz arriving on the scene – two actresses and a dental hygienist – but you can't just call someone up like that at midnight after years of silence, can you, and expect to be taken on board as a normal human being. Actually, that's a slight fib when it comes to Lottie. I have spoken to her a few times over the last three years. Not to keep any doors open, you understand, just to keep in touch. Of course, I never told Liz. She would have found it intolerable, especially when pregnant, to know that her feller had any kind of a confidante of the female kind. 'When a man wants to talk alone with a woman,' I could hear her say even now, 'it can only mean one thing.' Or was that her mother who said that?

Barbara Stenner, she'd be awake, most likely hitting her second or third bottle of wine by now, and would love to drop everything for a long talk about the seven chakras of my kundalini and whether my energy paths were being blocked or what have you, but then the effort required to talk to dear old Barbara was always greater than the result. In any case, it's not my place to ring clients when I feel like it. That's not the deal. It works the other way round, they ring me day or night when they need something – usually help in making some decision or other, like whether to go to Manchester to do a nice part for no money or stay in London and wait for lucrative but unrewarding pap to arrive. They are, most of them, under the illusion that I am sitting on invaluable information about what the future holds for them. I was through to the end of my little book now: Malcolm Viner, he was a nice bloke, old, old friend of mine, was an actor once but had given it up to go on to pastures sensible. I dialled his number but felt foolish when the ringing started and hung up. What could I say to him now? 'Hi, Malcolm, just wondering how it's been going with you for the last decade. Oh, me? I'm fine. I'm just sitting in my office in my underpants for the hell of it and suddenly thought it would be a good idea to wake you up and have a chat about the early eighties.'

I flicked through the entertainment listings guide on the little coffee table, through art, comedy, film, even poetry events. This is how punters find their way into the stuff I sell. I never use it, of course. I go only to things with clients in them. The last thing I want to do on an evening off – although I haven't had one of them since before the Old Testament was written – is go to be entertained. Bit of a busman's holiday, that. I can't even watch a video at home for pleasure. It drives Liz to distraction, but to me the most interesting thing about a film or a TV programme is the credits roll at the end.

Soul Connexions. I started to browse the phoneline lonely hearts columns, and it afforded me some momentary amusement working out the meaning of the repeated phrases and abbreviations, giving me the sort of satisfaction one gets from solving the *Guardian* Quick Crossword in under three minutes. 'Profess. educ. e-g. M. 30s. WLTM sim. for f/ship poss. ser. r/ship must like mountains, *The Fast Show*, travel. Veg.n/s. SOH.' 'Profess.

educ. M.30s' meaning forty-two-year-old bloke with a couple of A levels and a job, 'e-g' meaning easy-going, but actually meaning frightened of commitment. 'WLTM sim.' meaning would like to meet someone with a similar problem. 'Mountains and travel' – a reference to his desire to go walkabout as soon as anything develops. 'F/ship poss. ser. r/ship' just a straightforward lie to make sure he gets more than one reply, and the *Fast Show* reference a rather pathetic attempt to demonstrate that he is one of the very few 'veg. n/s' – vegetarian non-smokers – who has an 'SOH'. Sense of humour featured very often in the women's requirements but not half as often as tall: 'Grad. F. hedonist WLTM *tall* solvent M. for walks, dining and frolics. Must have SOH.' 'Rubenesque redhead WLTM caring M.30 + *tall*.' 'Rubenesque' meaning obese with dimpled buttocks. 'Slim hourglass F. 20 likes arts, eating out and more. WLTM *tall* M. any age.' In fact, as I scanned the column, I could find only two entries where the woman had not written 'tall' as a criterion for meeting a member of the opposite sex. Depressing reading if like me you happen to be five foot six. In the men's column, there was no 'must have big tits' abbreviation, MHBT. This is the nineties after all and if all we want is BTAA – big tits and arse – we can buy the *Daily Sport* or any tacky toilet-paper tabloid.

Some entries were simple and obviously rather cheap: 'OK guy, Nottingham area' or 'Asian bi F. WLTM guy 20s.' Others were virtually incomprehensible – 'Mary, 40, seeks righteous Joseph to sit under lemon tree and make shining star noodles' – or had a poetic slant: 'Jazz librarian WLTM his concertina.'

An entry caught my eye: 'Gorgeous shapely babe, Newcastle, will give all for right man . . . No dickheads, please!' No serial killers either, or anyone suffering from Roman Emperor Syndrome, presumably.

I dialled the Soul Connexions main number. A recorded woman's voice answered like the speaking clock: 'Hello and welcome to Soul Connexions. Please press the star button on your telephone. To hear the message line of your choice, please press 1. To leave an advertisement, please press 2. To go to the main menu option, please press 3.' A different woman's voice came on, this one with all the stresses and inflections in the wrong places, like an air stewardess announcing turbulence. 'To

86

hear the message – line of your – choice, please press – the corresponding number on – your telephone now.' And then, 'You have chosen message line number . . .' and the computer-ized numbers came out individually, each with its own placidly banal and soothing emphasis. Then a third woman's voice came on the line. This one was a real person. This was gorgeous-shapely-from-Newcastle's message.

'Erm, hello, it seems really strange doing this but they say you must describe yourself, so . . .' Long, embarrassed pauses. '. . . So, well, I'm twenty-nine and I'm quite petite, slim, and I see myself as having a sense of humour but I have got a serious side, and, er . . .' She was talking slower and slower, it was excruciating. 'Er . . . if you can hear rustling paper, it's because I've written some notes here . . . in case I forget who I am . . .' She must have found that funny when she thought it up but now, talking into the disembodied digital void, she lost confidence in her own joke and it fell flaccidly like old lettuce. She went on.

'. . . And in case you're wondering why I put the ad in, I reached the point where I got fed up with waiting for the right man to materialize out of thin air and I thought it was time I did something about it, so . . . this is it, really . . .' Christ, she was about as exciting as a supermarket queue. 'I like walking and being outdoors and sitting by the fire and talking and I like eating out in restaurants . . . and they say you've got to say the sort of thing you're looking for . . . so here goes . . . well, he's got to have a sense of humour and be tall and . . .' I held the receiver away from my ear, as you would when an elderly relative calls to witter on. My cigar had gone out so I relit it. I took another gulp of 'poo. I checked back with the babe from Geordieland. She was drawing to an end in her own good time. '. . . Just someone I can have some fun with, really . . . and that's it . . .' Click. Back to the plastic tones of the option menu hostess. 'To hear this message – line – again, press 1 – to return to the main menu – press 2 –' Could be an interesting torture to hear that message line again and again. I'd crack after a couple of goes.

I was surfing the option menu now. I pressed other message line numbers, most were as sad as gorgeous-shapely but some were bizarre. 'Well, I'm fifty-two, my work is as a detective superintendent in the police force and my husband left me two years ago and I'm looking for someone who likes Elvis Costello, Chopin and Vivaldi but not Sting or Beethoven, who could bring me out of myself a bit.' After six or seven goes at this game, the buzzing in my head started to return; I was getting bored. These people and their stories were drab, they'd had their fifteen minutes of fame and they'd blown it. There was nothing I could do for any of them.

Suddenly, the hot night cracked with a massive roll of thunder overhead. No rain yet, but the sky was bursting. I went to the window and looked out. A lightning flash and then almost immediately another crack of thunder. This time a sudden vomiting of water from above and people in the street rushed into shop doorways to hang about for a few minutes with the homeless who were crouching there. I closed the window – the rain was flying in past the sill on to our fax machine.

I returned to the sofa. I was a player now. I flicked through to the back of the entertainment guide to where the hot chat-line numbers are listed after the rubber mini-skirt and French maid outfit ads. 'One to one! The horniest, hottest girls!' 'Wet talk!' 'Thirty-five seconds of sexy mouth!' 'Oral exams!' 'Come in my crack!'

More air stewardess voices with option menus. I punched in a request number. Tania would be able to clock all these 0891 numbers when the itemized phone bill came, but my Captain Sensible side seemed to have gone loco. It's lucky we weren't yet on the internet, or I'd be entering deviant and expensive porn web-sites in Las Vegas by now. I was suddenly connected to a recorded scenario with the front dialogue lopped off, like when you get through to a cinema information number and they're already going through the showing times, and you have to wait for the tape to go round to the beginning to find out what's on.

An Australian male voice was plodding through a turgid script. Worse than *A Country Practice*, if you can credit that.

'. . . and you were a very bad girl going out in that short dress when I told you not to. I'll have to put you over my knee and spank you now.' He was joined, if that's the right word, by the voice of a woman straining to sound husky.

'Oh, that makes me so wet when you do that.' Then the sound of someone wearing rubber gloves slapping a block of wood. Then the woman's voice again. 'I've been very bad and I need to be punished.'

Acting, surely, is about convincing someone, anyone, that you believe what you are saying – as any of the voice artists on our books will tell you. I need not go into the wherefores of why the owner of this voice was not, nor ever could be, an actress. The Aussie bloke was back.

'I'm going to have to pull your knickers down and spank you again.'

Well, it was entertaining. For about half a minute. I put down the phone. My friend the phone. My constant companion over these last ten years. It had let me down. No, I had let it down. I was ashamed. The phone looked back at me from its cradle like a hurt puppy in its basket. All those things Liz had told me about myself – that I was arrogant, that I had no feelings, that I didn't know how to express my feelings, that I didn't understand feelings, that I was only interested in sex, that I was only interested in possessions, that I didn't know how to treat a woman properly, that I was cheap – all were real and true. I was seeing myself through her eyes. Her refracted interpretations had won the territory of my self-respect. The thunder had receded some miles away by now, but the stagnant air had begun to move. Outside in Soho a wind heaved up Shaftesbury Avenue. I got up and fetched the Yellow Pages. I couldn't stand it in the office any longer.

Outside the chintzy-curtained window were the branches of a streetlamp-lit chestnut tree, thrashing in the wind. The heat had broken, and the air currents were angry. I sat on a small candlewick bed, waiting for the courage to take my trousers off as I had been told to do. There were clean towels everywhere and a Spanish bullfighter print on the wall.

On the TV, there was a video of a frenzied blow job to the accompaniment of soft, irritating music. On top of the TV, on a chintzy doily, stood a painted souvenir donkey from Madeira. At last she came in. She was wearing a cheap lacy all-in-one and a silk-mix dressing gown open at the front. She was bigger than me.

'Stormy night, eh?' she said with a grin. 'And we're going to be pretty stormy too.' The wind outside was rattling the sills and driving stray soft drinks cans along the pavement. The chestnut tree outside fought with the storm in a tussle of swaying and yielding.

She sat on the bed beside me.

'Ooooh, you are very disobedient,' she said, referring to the fact that I had taken off my shoes and nothing else.

'Well, I'm nervous,' I said. 'I've not done anything like this before.'

'Aaaaaaah. They all say that. Now, give us a hug,' she said, and pulled me to her, her painted nails on my shoulders, one hand still hanging on to the children's Snoopy glass which contained her vodka and coke. My drink, in a Mickey Mouse tumbler, was sitting on the small bedside table under the table lamp from Tenerife. The carpet was threadbare and a lacy shawl had been draped over the main light, giving the room an amateurishly theatrical ambience. The tassels of the shawl jogged with the force of the gale outside. Her free hand rubbed between my shoulder blades, where the tension lives like a knotted pair of tights. It was soothing.

'Do you like titties?' She asked, and peeled down her Marks and Sparks lacy top. Well, of course I like titties, I thought. I'm just not sure about having them so large and so present right now. I felt like a child and she seemed to think that was good.

'You have to tell me what you like,' she said. Even if I had known what I like and had the words in my mind to describe it, I wouldn't have been able to speak. I imagine that Jeremy Planter, if he ever found himself in a situation like this, would be able to be very decisive and clear about what he wanted. 'Stand over there at an angle of forty-five degrees to the chair, flutter your eyelashes and say, "Oh my God, I've never seen such a big one",' he would say without a moment's pause. I have no idea what I like. That never comes into it. I aim to please, I suppose.

'Do most men tell you what they want?' I asked.

'Some do,' she said, and started to unbutton my shirt. Inside she flicked her painted nails over my nipples for a bit and then started to unbutton my trousers.

'Unless I'm doing the old "dommo." Oh yes, I'm good at

giving orders. 'Cos then it's more like a performance, you know, it's like acting. I've got all the boots and whips and everything but they have to say that's what they want beforehand, like, so I can prepare, and then it's straight into it the moment I get into the room.'

She spoke with a straightforward Brummie accent. She was mixed race. Quite dark-skinned but not black like Joan in the office. What's known in the biz as 'BBC brown'.

Although they would issue a statement to deny it – introduce a packet of measures to stop it, even – the broadcasters seem not to employ black actresses, other than to play the odd one-line junkie/whore/single mother with attitude. No, when casting the larger roles, they tend to go for the more acceptable, lovable and cliché-sexier mixed-race type, hence the expression 'BBC brown'. I don't know why we don't all admit it and shove it on their CVs.

This unwritten code does not apply to men, however. They're allowed to be macho black – like my Simon N'quarbo, does very well on telly – thus making the TV industry appear both sexist and racist at the same time. It's as well to know these things when digging around for clients. And don't let any directive, equal-opportunity employer pamphlet, memorandum, conference bullshit convince you otherwise. The woman in front of me would have stood a chance, had she been an actress and had she so wished, of playing the token female doctor in some worthy drama series about vets.

'Come on, off with your things, mate,' she said.

I obliged.

'Do you get the same guys coming back again and again?' I asked.

'Oh, yes. I've got several very regular gentlemen. They're the best. Mostly married men, you know.'

'I'm not used to this.' By now I was lying naked on a towel on the bed and she was tickling my thighs and balls. I was vaguely tumescent but hardly on the verge of anything. A dustbin was blown over outside in the back yard and its clatter made me start. She soothed me again with her stroking. She was working so hard, I felt sorry for her. What kind of a client was I?

'You've got a very big one,' she said. I laughed. I didn't bother to say, 'I bet you say that to all the guys.'

'I should know,' she said. 'You could be a black man. It's true what they say, you know.'

'Is it really?' I said, trying to be polite.

'And I'll tell you another thing for free. The Chinese? Very small.'

'But it's what they do with it, isn't it? Well, so I've been told,' I said.

'Naaaaa,' she said, and then, 'You could come on my titties if you like.' Over her shoulder, the video came to an abrupt end and the screen hissed with snow and crackle. She got up to turn it off and came back with a condom packet which she tore open with her mouth.

Luckily I was hard enough for the rubber to fit on and she unfolded it expertly to the bottom, kneading me all the time like a cow's udder. I needed to keep talking and she didn't seem to mind my questions, so I asked her how many clients she saw in a week.

As she wiped the condom with a tissue, she told me she had ten regulars, any number of others and that she worked for several different agencies. I enquired how much commission an agency would take, and was surprised to hear that sometimes it was as much as fifty per cent. I'm obviously in the wrong business.

'But some girls I know, the really pretty ones, like, they can get a thousand pounds a night.'

She said she would give me her number before I left so that I could get in touch again if I wanted to and she could avoid paying commission. I thanked her. For a few seconds, she put her mouth around my cock, condom and all, but then returned to kneading it.

'Do you feel like coming yet?' she asked sweetly. I wanted to, if only to participate fully and help her to feel that she was doing her job properly. I couldn't find an answer, though.

'No hurry,' she said, and sitting back for a few moments, she offered me more vodka and coke.

'We've got lots of time, you can relax with me.' We both looked at our watches at the same moment. We caught each other's eye and laughed.

'So you've got a lot of pressure at work, have you?'

'You could say that,' I replied.

The chestnut tree outside was still struggling with the wind; bending and swaying, its flexibility being tested to the limit. I've always liked trees, they cheer me up. The absence of them from the Shaftesbury Avenue area is one of the main drawbacks to working round there. There's Soho Square, of course, that's got some ash, and the Soho church graveyard with its little trimmed hedges and plane trees. I was brought up in the suburbs, you see, so although I'm pleased that I got out of there and made it in the big city, as 'twere, I do miss them. It's OK down in Fulham tree-wise, in fact, London is one of the most tree-ish cities in the world. One of my earliest memories is of the noise of poplar trees swishing in the wind around Adam's Pond in Kingston. The myriad dark leaves tinkling together as they flipped over in graceful waves to reveal their pale undersides, as if they were being blow-dried by a massive hairdryer in some giant-sized shampoo advertisement for lustrous hair. Very sensual. Because trees are sexy, they just take a very long time getting round to it.

The first so-called London plane tree, for example, was imported and planted in Barnes in 1680, just one tree, and look at them now, the commonest tree all over London. They've been at it for three hundred years. And they're not so hung up on gender roles as us humans either. Sometimes there's male and female trees, sure – like the two big ailanthus trees of heaven on either side of the Fulham Road, the male growing achingly towards the female, ever closer each year, only to be cut back to make room for double-decker buses – but sometimes, like elm trees, females can go on replicating themselves for a few generations until a seed of male elm arrives on the wind or in a piece of squirrel or bat shit to stir up their genetic mix. Essential if they're to adapt, evolve and perpetuate themselves and avoid being overrun by other, more virulent strains with quicker, randier ways of spreading themselves. I've often wondered how – after being blown halfway across the country – the seeds and fruit and flowers and pussy willow catkins of trees know when they've found the right opposite number with whom to procreate and have lots of little saplings. There are no shocking divorce rate figures to worry about with trees. Recently, it seemed as if – despite our initial attraction – Liz was in fact deciduous, whilst I'd turned out to be coniferous and our little Grace offshoot was to be one of those mutations which gets eaten by a wandering deer before it gets to be one foot high. I wonder, if men were like trees and every spring they all had a massive communal wank into the sky – letting the wind blow their millions of chances at immortality hither and thither – whether my Grace seed would have found its way to Liz's Grace bud or whether all the Grace-type buds would have been reserved for pips from the genus Henderson, tall and mighty broadleafs with big conkers in the autumn. Was me being with Liz just a mistake? A genetic flirtation? Were we destined never to be broadcast? Never to enter the *Pocket Users' Guide to the Sex Lives of Trees and Shrubs of the British Isles*?

Someone must have come in from the street downstairs, because a draught rushed under the door and made her shiver. I felt a twinge of cramp in my left foot. It was OK, though, I'd left my socks on. There was a man's voice on the stairs and then a door slammed.

'You need a break,' she said, pouring the last of the vodka into our funny glasses. 'You're a very tense man and I should know, I've seen some very tense men.'

'I'm missing my kid,' I managed to say. 'I don't see enough of her and there doesn't seem to be a way around it all.'

'Aaah, you poor man. It's very hard on men these days, isn't it? They get a rough deal, I think. I don't know what I'd do if I couldn't see my daughter. She's the only reason I do this. And my trips, ooh, I like my little trips.'

She told me about her holidays in Tenerife and all the things she got up to when drunk. She showed me her scars from gashes over twelve years old, inflicted by her man in Leeds before she'd walked out on him taking only her daughter, a bin bag of clothes and her Yorkshire terrier, Scraggy, who had now passed away, God rest its soul.

'He was always telling me what to wear. "You're not going out in that!" you know, that sort of thing. He told me I was ugly, I was ugly, and after a while I looked in a mirror and I *was* ugly. So I just upped and left, had enough.' A bitterness entered her voice momentarily when describing the father of her child, but was blown away briskly by another gust of wind outside.

94

'Still, you've got to move on, haven't you? Just draw a line in the sand, walk over it and never look back.' Second time I'd heard that recently.

'I wish I could do that,' I said. Feeling sorry for us both now. I wished I had some scars to show her, but all I have is a vaccination one on my left shoulder and a mole removal one somewhere around my lower back.

By now, we were lying squished together on the bed, quite cosily. The pressure on me to perform seemed to have subsided. I was limp but it didn't matter.

'Does this often happen to you? I mean, do lots of guys come in and sort of, not actually . . . you know?' I asked.

'Oh, yes,' she said. 'It takes all sorts, you know. Some of them just want to tell you their problems. I'm like some therapist, really. There's a lot of very lonely people out there. I mean, you get some right psychos, you know, who want to do horrible things to you, but we don't like them. Soon sort them out. You're lonely, aren't you?'

'I don't have time to be lonely,' I said.

'Anyway, we're not just going to talk, are we? We're going to be very naughty tonight.'

My half-hour was nearly up, but for some reason, in the last five minutes I became aroused and achieved an orgasm into the condom. I felt relieved that I had not let her down. She wrote her number on a piece of card and I was on the street in seconds with my collar turned up, looking for a cab.

There were none, and wind-broken branches were strewn along the pavement. There was a sharp, hot rain in the wind which buffeted me from the front and the back. I was pissed now but the strength of the storm alone was enough to make me totter like a drunkard. I kept walking, not really heeding in which direction. Small broken branches and twigs from all the Conduit Street chestnuts were scuttling along the ground like terrified crabs.

By now I'd turned into Park Lane and the wind and sheet rain had not abated. The traffic was minimal and there was nobody out walking. No one was this foolish. There were massive branches strewn and blowing across the dual carriageway here. Hyde Park, the other side of the road, looked a tangled mess. In

95

the morning, there would be big clearing-up to do before the rush hour.

In the grassy central aisle of Park Lane, an old ash tree had fallen in its entirety, impacting on the metal crash barrier and twisting it into nonsense. It lay half on and half off the road, pointing away from me like a fallen Don Quixote. Where the tree had stood was now an earthy crater some seven feet across, churned up by the snapping roots. The massive upturned underside was exposed to me, a round inferno of twisted limbs, a gorgon's hairdo turned to stone, and at its centre, the dark central avenue to the heartwood of the tree, like an ancient and mythical vagina, a hole which had sucked up life from the ground for two hundred years.

Back in the hollow safety of Meard Street, as I tried to sleep, the wind still rang in my ears like the aftermath of a rock concert.

FOUR

'OH, HI, GUY, I thought you were one of Karen's patients.' Neil ushered me inside, past the double downstairs room and up the stairs without any further explanations as to why he was wearing a mauvy-pink frock, full make-up and pendulous earrings.

I followed him up the stairs of the rather grand house, past some portraits of what I assumed must be the great and the good in the world of psychotherapy and into his tiny attic room, which was a maze of piled books, stray paper and unwashed coffee cups. There was a mattress on the floor with a rumpled sleeping bag flopped across it. He still hadn't shaved and there was a row of empty vodka bottles along the windowsill. The rest of the house had seemed well kept, bourgeois, even, but in here it was a poet's den.

'Shall we go for a drink?' he said

'Well, it's a bit early for me, but, sure, fine,' I said, and then, 'Love the outfit. Do they go in for that sort of thing down your local?'

'For you, Guy, I'll change.' The frock came off to reveal purple silken French knickers. He slung on a pair of waisted blue slacks which zipped up the side, and a voluminous cream blouse with floppy wide lapels. The earrings stayed where they were, dancing as he spoke. 'It's not really fair, is it? A woman can go out in anything she likes. She can wear a skirt, a suit, trousers if she wants, make-up, no make-up, but if you're a bloke . . .' he was wiping his face with an old tissue now, '. . . they just assume you must be a poof.' Complete weirdo more like, I thought, with two and a half weeks' growth on your chin. Still, he did seem to have had a bath. We must be grateful for mini-mercies.

I'd never known Neil had TV leanings. That's TV as in

97

transvestite, not television. I wish he'd told me, it could've been useful.

'Also, since Karen started her own therapy practice, she's been using the downstairs rooms as her clinic, and we get all these uptight neurots visiting through the day. I'm supposed to keep in the background because they're not meant to know anything about the therapist's home life, you know, in theory. So I just see if I can't fuck their brains a bit by wafting around in a dress at the top of the stairs every now and again. It's a laugh. Drives Karen mad.'

Client-led, that's what I am. That's the basic principle behind my work. It was high time I paid that visit to Neil. He was obviously going through a hard time, and there must be something I could do about it. Unfortunately, he didn't have the neat physique of a Julian Clary, nor the vampish poise of an Eddie Izzard. He just looked, well, garish, unhinged. His decline must be my fault. I wasn't looking after him properly, too involved in my own stuff, no doubt. And besides, I couldn't face going back to the camp-bed room for another night and staring at the phone. I couldn't vizzog it. As far as my attitude to the state Neil was in went, I've learned not to let anything judgemental so much as flicker across my face. My opinion on literally anything is the least important part of the equation. For example, I don't even know any more whether I actually like musicals or detest them – whether I prefer classical drama to soap opera. My field of operation need only concern itself with what may or may not work – for instance, I might have a client who can tap dance and sing, so I will be excited by the latest five-person show looking for a theatre in the West End, or I might have a method-trained serious young student of Acting with a capital A, so I will be thrilled that the BBC are doing a season of studio-based American drama. I do not prize one over the other. My personal taste jury went out a long time ago, and stayed there. I am lucky in that my own likes and dislikes do not really trouble me. It's about people, and people change. Like Jenny Thompson, for instance. Started out in agit prop and political theatre, wouldn't touch anything unless it was changing the world, done for charity or written by David Hare. Now, eight years later, she's writing diary pieces in *Metropolitan* magazine helping women with their sex lives, and doing stills sessions in designer clothes for Sunday lifestyle sections. And good for her. So if Neil wanted to grow a beard and wear a purple frock, my job was to follow wherever he led, waiting only for the right moment to pop questions about possible bankability.

In this game anything is not only possible but preferable. Well, almost anything. Child pornography is obviously out, in fact all kinds of pornography are out, although nowadays one has to be quite flexible about definitions.

For example – neat little anecdote, this – I had an enquiry call for Annie Schuster, a brilliant voice artist, ex-client of mine. An American woman on the end of the line wanted to know if Annie was available for filming immediately on a daily-rate basis. I said yes, depending on the rate of course. It was very good, so we proceeded. Then she explained the work might involve nudity, I said a tentative yes but asked for a little more information.

'Well,' said the woman, 'it involves a certain amount of *action*.' This word said with emphasis. But the daily rate would obviously go up, the more action Annie was willing to provide.

I took her number and said I would check with Annie first. Thank God. Because as I punched up Annie's number, it took only a second to realize it was the same one. Annie had been doing a Rory Bremner on me. Agents beware. Annie's not the most in-demand voice artist in the biz for nothing. She was just having a laugh and testing me out at the same time, to see what kind of a company she was working for. Luckily I passed the test and she stayed with me for several years before leaving to marry an Italian record producer and have children in the Tuscan hills.

So I had to think positively about this new Neil in front of me, this bearded apparition in 1950s Doris Day casual wear. It was just a question of adaptation, flexibility, inventiveness. Obviously he was no longer in the running for a nice eight o'clock slot sitcom. Nor appearances on daytime telly or any of the more 'civilized' fairways of entertainment.

I would have to think again. Find some niche, some artistic bunker in which he could hole up, be happy and earn us all a living.

A one-man show perhaps? Edinburgh in drag? Maybe he'd

like to direct? In the early days he'd been so eager to please. He'd let me help him with his image, his hair, clothes, audition technique, and his attitude to authority – always an important one, that. Now he had developed a wilfulness and a rather alarming bluffness.

We sat in the pub in silence for a few minutes, me feeling awkward and flimsy in my linen jacket and tie, Neil with a creased brow, glaring at the beer mats on the table.

'Can I have one of them?' I asked him as he lit a third Silk Cut.

'You don't smoke,' he said.

'I know, but I feel like one right now.' I had to find some way of crossing the bridge between us.

A man with a sheepish grin came over to our table and hovered a moment over Neil.

'It is you, isn't it?' He loomed, recognizing Neil from *Every Other Weekend*.

'No, I'm his bad twin brother,' said Neil. I smiled nicely at the guy.

'What? You haven't got the kids this weekend, then?' said the guy, as if he was making the most original and hilarious joke in the history of comedy.

'It's not real. It was a television programme, you know. Fiction. Stories. I don't actually have any kids.'

The guy laughed as if Neil's reply had been equally hilarious.

'You lot. It's just a job to you, isn't it?' he said, with smug reverence. 'So, you got anything else coming up? Or just . . . resting?' Why does the word 'resting' cause such amusement to members of the Great British Public?

I thought it appropriate, at this point, to slide into the conversation, if you can call it that.

'They may be repeating the second series of *Every Other Weekend* on UK Gold this autumn, if you get that?'

The guy ignored me completely.

'What's the beard for then, getting ready for a new role, are you?'

'No. This is the real me,' said Neil, and at last managed a sort of half-smile. He jiggled his earrings. It was enough at any rate to satisfy the guy, who wandered back proudly to where his friends were, at the bar. They all turned and smiled across the room at us, nodding and thumbs-upping at us.

'Didn't even offer to get us a drink,' said Neil. I started to inhale the ciggie. What the hell.

'So how's the writing going?' I dared to venture.

'I've had to start again from the beginning,' said Neil.

'Oh, shit.'

'You were right, it was all bollocks, so I chucked it all away.' Oh, God.

'Oh, that's not quite fair, I didn't say it was *all* bollocks. I think there was an awful lot of really good stuff in there. It just maybe needed a little bit of reworking,' I squirmed.

'Too late now, I've binned it all and started again,' said Neil. 'I want to write something about the difference between men and women, more like a sort of self-help thing.' Oh, no. RFA. Double RFA. Sound the submerge hooter! Men in orange overalls slide down fireman poles! Neil helping people! Abandon ship!

'Maybe you need a break from it, Neil,' I said. 'Think about something else for a month or so and then get back to it with a fresh brain?'

'No,' said Neil. 'I couldn't do that.'

A woman from the gang at the bar came over to our table.

'I'm sorry, but would you mind signing this for my daughter?' she asked, putting a beer mat and a biro on the table.

Neil obliged automatically, and while he was writing, she added, 'Could you put, "Get to bed *now* or else . . .!"' The nearest thing Neil had to a catchphrase in *EOW*.

He did, and handed the mat and pen back to her.

'You can say you've been recognized now,' she said, as if offering Neil charity, and returned to the group at the bar, who nodded and thumbs-upped us again.

'I've got about five thousand words but I can't work at home, the phone keeps ringing. Karen's got patients coming in and out all day long and her teenage son is coming back from university next week. If I had the money, I'd get a room somewhere and just write.'

Before Grace, I would have instantly offered him my own flat during the day. Now, not possible. We had more drinks and I smoked another cigarette.

But I didn't leave without telling him what I thought, however tactfully I may have put it.

On the way back to Soho I made a note to ring Bill Burdett-Coutts about a possible Edinburgh booking for Neil. I felt sure that, if the gig was there, he'd rise to the occasion, he'd have to.

All the phone conversations I had at work the next day seemed to be happening in a place other than my head. I could participate and function perfectly well, listening, responding, thinking even, but the old aeroplane was on automatic and air-traffic control had gone AWOL. Inside my head there was a dank, dead acoustic, like the 'thunk' a spoon makes on the side of a bowl of whipped cream. It was as if I was underwater and Guy Mullin was up there above the surface, gabbing on and on in some untranslatable patois. I made it through the day like this. And I made it over to Susan Planter's in Chiswick, where I'd been invited for dinner *à deux* and a chinwag about the evils of Jeremy.

'And how's Liz?' Susan asked.

'Oh, she's very well. Very well indeed.'

'And Grace?'

'She's fine. Fine. Starts big school in September.'

In fact I hadn't seen Grace for six whole days. The longest time ever. She could have grown a shoe size or forgotten all about me by now for all I knew.

'Liz picked the right man in you, Guy.' Susan Planter ran her hand through her hair and refilled her wine glass. I took the pasta off and asked her where the strainer was. I was meant to be talking to her while she cooked us supper, but it was turning out to be the other way round. She was looking considerably the worse for wear. Poor love.

'You're so dependable, Guy. I still can't get used to you smoking, though. It doesn't look right somehow.'

Her complexion was in revolt at the stress of the last fortnight and she had unsuccessfully tried to plaster over the bumps with a thick base. A translucent pre-foundation would have done the trick more effectively but it would have been wrong for me to mention it. She was wearing an old sweatshirt and cardigan – comfort clothes – the sort of stuff you pad around the house in after getting over 'flu, or when your husband has just gone off with another woman.

Polly came to the kitchen door in her Paddington Bear pyjamas.

'He's pushing my bed, Mummy, and I can't go to sleep.'

'Tell him to stop,' said Susan, and then shouted up the stairs, 'Dave! Stop pushing Polly's bed.'

'I didn't. She left my computer things on the floor.'

I poured a glass of water and gave it to Polly. Susan gave her a peck and she went back upstairs.

'I have always thought of you and Liz as the perfect couple,' said Susan, getting in my way as I stirred in the pesto sauce from a jar.

'Here. Why don't you put all this on the table?' I loaded her up with the salad bowl and things. I had to get her out of her kitchen, or this meal would never arrive. I did manage to get her sat down, though, and bringing the pasta in, we started to eat at last.

'So what's she like, this Arabella?' It didn't look as though Susan was actually going to eat much tonight. She poured herself another glass of wine. Luckily, I'd brought a couple of bottles. Since I was eating, I could measure my reply through mouthfuls.

'She's sort of ordinary,' I said. 'Not too bright – but I see what you mean, she seems to have got her hooks in.' I had to be careful neither to build up the other woman too much nor talk her down unrealistically. Susan told me another story of some misdeed of Jeremy's. How he'd once forgotten her birthday, or one of the kids'. Then another: the time he'd left her stranded at a BBC do and taken the taxi home without her.

It was as if she was sorting back through her diary of memories, setting in cement all the ones in which Jeremy had been a bastard so that she could now justify to herself all her feelings of loathing towards him. It wasn't making her any happier, though, and her words were beginning to run into one another. I opened a third bottle, for myself more than for her. She was beginning to berate all things male. I didn't like to see her turning into another 'what's wrong with men' bore, so I tried to steer us back to the here and now.

'He doesn't care about the kids, how could he, so why should he get to see them now?' she slurred.

'Do they ask for him?' I said, and lit a Dunhill. The machine in the pub next door where I'd gone for a quick drink so as not to be too early had run out of Silk Cut.

'Dave does but he'll have to grow out of it,' she said.

I found it hard to imagine the Susan I knew sneaking around in the night to squeeze Superglue into the locks of Jeremy's car, as Arabella had told me she had.

'Arabella Planter.' With disgust, Susan rolled the name around her tongue with the wine, which was acrid and cheap. 'Mrs Arabella Planter.'

'They're not intending to get married, I don't think,' I said.

'Ha!' she said. 'Not and have clothes to stand in.'

'You are being careful who you talk to, though? I mean, in the press, aren't you?' I said, clearing away the plates. She'd hardly touched her food.

'Why should I be?' Susan followed me back into the kitchen, where she took an opened family-sized bar of chocolate out of the cupboard. She offered me some but I was stuck into the wine now.

'You can't trust any of them, you know that. Did they offer to pay you for that interview you did the week before last? Because once they've paid, they can say what they like, you know.'

'How much do you think it's worth?' she asked, and laughed.

Publicity and the press isn't really my bag. I'm not that good at it and I find it tacky, but I said, 'Two or three thousand at this stage, possibly a couple more if you can bung in a sexual perversion or two.' We both laughed.

'I suppose I could invent something, but the trouble with Jeremy was, he was useless in bed, after the first two months, that is,' she said, gobbling the chocolate.

It was important for her, at this stage, to have him locked in the drawer marked 'Cad', and he'd been a cad, no doubt about that. She should have known, though. Didn't her parents tell her? 'Have fun with the cads, but marry a dad.'

'I just think you should try and keep it under control, that's all,' I said. 'For everyone's sake. For Dave and Polly's sake.'

'What if I did an interview for money? You'd take ten per cent of that, would you?'

'Look, I'm not Max Clifford. This isn't my scene. I don't want either of you to get hurt any more than is inevitable. It's difficult for me, I like you both.'

This was a mistake. Susan was not in the mood for a balanced appraisal of the trickiness of my position.

'Mrs Arabella Planter,' she said again, with painful relish. 'Dave and Polly Planter. Every fucking thing Planter. I should have given them Christian names like "Beloved First Wife", or "Betrayal". That would have given the fucking bitch problems at cocktail parties. Here are my stepchildren, Betrayal Planter and Beloved First Wife Planter. Ha!'

Her laugh was gluey and set her off coughing because of the chocolate. She caught herself in the mirror and sat up straight, tucking in her waist and pushing out her tits.

'I suppose she's got a perfect figure?' she sneered. I decided to remain silent.

'He's not even a good game-show host, he's just a Catch-phrase Charlie.'

'It's an unfair business. You don't necessarily need talent to get to the top.'

'You do need to be a complete bastard, though, and Jeremy fits that bill.'

We were sitting on the sofa together now. It was quite warm and relaxed and, as usual with Susan, not sexually charged. My leg could be alongside hers, for instance, without either of us particularly being aware of it, without any subtle flicks of eye contact. To try and join in with her mood a little, I told her about the list of names I'd seen on the wall of the casting director a couple of months before, in which Jeremy's name had appeared in heavy print. When I'd asked what the heavy print meant, I was told it meant 'book 'em even if they're crap'. There are a select few artists who get all the offers because, in theory, they put bums on seats. Everyone in the business knows that they're crap but everyone also knows it's a business. This is why you see people like Mick Jagger trying to act in films or tennis players making pop records. Or, indeed, why someone like my Neil was hired to write a novel.

I thought Susan would be pleased to hear that Jeremy did not have the respect of his peers, but this was another mistake because, of course, it was a measure of his success and popularity and power.

'I hope his new show plummets and he ends up having to do

sports links for local radio,' she said. 'I know that would be bad for you, Guy, but can't you afford to have one client's career go down the toilet in a humiliating way? You could arrange that, couldn't you, just for me?'

This wasn't put seriously, and we laughed. She leaned her head on my shoulder, fanning the smoke out of the way. Dave came in. I don't know how long he'd been standing at the door.

'Is Guy staying the night, Mum?' he asked.

'No, of course not, Dave, go back to bed,' she said, and instinctively pulled away from me. 'He's got his own family to go to.'

Actually I would have liked to have stayed the night. It was warm. I could have curled up on the sofa or put cushions on the floor. Anything rather than go back to the office, where the flashing light from the strip-joint on the other side of the street wheeled across my ceiling every other second and where the noise of the street crept into your dreams.

Thoughts of that and of Liz, and then of the gap where Grace should be, escaped into my body, making me cold. Susan seemed to mistake this for some kind of sexual frisson, and she shivered and got up to close the door. She wouldn't risk an intimate chat with me if she thought I might respond physically to her.

I got up and made leaving noises. Dave obeyed his mum and went back upstairs to bed, though no doubt not to sleep until he had heard me leaving. Quite right. Seeing me off the premises at ten years old. Territorial. Proprietorial.

I called for a cab and said Fulham, changing the destination to Soho only when I was in it and Susan had closed her front door behind me. I was drunk again. The mini-cab driver was completely silent. His car radio calling out jobs was the only noise between us, and outside the roads were almost empty. It must have been quite late. My head lolled against the seatbelt strap.

Once, as a godfatherly thing, I'd taken Dave to the Natural History Museum to see the moving dinosaur models. Grace must have been a baby at the time because it had just been me and Dave one Sunday afternoon. Like most children under eight, he knew more about dinosaurs than any adult does.

Dinosaurs is standard nursery school project fare. After the dinosaurs, we got lost trying to find the exit and an ice-cream, and found ourselves wandering through the primate room with models of gibbons, chimpanzees and gorillas from floor to ceiling. There was one model which fascinated Dave. It is only small, about a foot in diameter. It is of a group of orang-utans sitting around a rock.

The king orang-utan has a few of his wives sitting around him but one of them, one of his wives, is just the other side of the rock. He's looking at her, she's looking back at him over the top of the rock. Unbeknown to the king, and hidden behind the rock, is a young male orang-utan, shagging the wife as she smiles at her husband. The little label by the side of the glass case containing this model explains that it is in the interests, genetically speaking, of the female to have as husband and protector the biggest, strongest old orang-utan, the king. He will fend off predators whilst she rears her young, his mortgage was paid off long ago. So he's the best bet as a permanent mate, he's the king, he's big daddy. But it is also in her interests, genetically speaking, to have sex with younger, more genetically varied males. This of course must be kept secret from the king, lest he kill her adulterous offspring. It is in the genetic interests of the male orang-utans to sleep with as many of the females as is possible. If not by being king, then through affairs behind rocks.

I had to pretend to Dave that the shagging orang-utans were from another family down the way, just visiting from the land beyond the rock, so there I was, perpetuating the myth of the family with my godson.

Funny things, genes. I wonder if our behaviour is really dictated to us genetically, as it is currently fashionable to think. As the mini-cab bumped up over the Hogarth flyover, I imagined what it would be like to be a digitally reincarnated gene.

'Hmmmmmm. Which gender is the body I've found myself in this time? What's my ammunition? What balls, what racquets?'

'Well, you've landed in a female this time, so you've got a limited number of food-rich, high-investment eggs which, if fertilized, are going to take two years of your life, so it's quite labour-intensive. So you've got to find a good specimen worth mating with who's going to stick around and help bring up the kids, and fight off enemies. Oh, and can he have a nice bum, please?'

Apart from the bum, Susan was right, Liz had picked the right man in me. A right mug. The thought made me angry. So what about my genes? The ones who found themselves in my male body, poor bastards.

'Well, you've got sixty million chances a day to replicate yourself, so go for quantity of women but make sure they're fertile. Thin waist and wide hips would probably be a good indicator. Oh, but there's one problem I forgot to tell you. There are seven billion other guys around like you, who want to have access to the limited supply of eggs, and they are all going to try and stop you replicating. Same as you're going to try and stop them. So there may well be a few wars. Also, even if you do manage to get a woman pregnant, if you don't hang around to help her bring the kid up, these other guys may move in on her and kill your kid. All part of stopping you replicating. More room for them and their issue. So your best bet is probably to find a good one as a wife and then shag around in secret.'

Either way it seems we are all genetically programmed for infidelity. Better not let Liz know, she'd think that lets her off the hook.

Half an hour later I was lying on my back on the camp bed in Meard Street, staring at the ceiling, when the buzzer went.

'Hi, gorgeous. It's Kemble Stenner.'

I buzzed her up. In the minute or so it took her to climb the stairs, I put my trousers back on and tidied up a bit. Closing the curtains on the now rather sordid-looking kitchenette which contained my campbed.

'Hello,' I said as she breezed past me into the main office area, carrying an already opened bottle of red wine. 'Did you ring earlier?' I asked.

'No. Saw your light on. Thought I'd ring the bell. See if you fancied a drink.'

She went to the window and peered out through the blinds. The buzzer rang again.

'Oh my God! He saw me coming in here. Don't answer that,' she squealed. 'Pleeeeeeease.'

It buzzed again, more insistently. She sat down on the floor by the window and took a slurp from the wine bottle. She offered it to me. The buzzer went again.

'Ignore it. He'll go away in a minute.' She giggled. 'Nice wine, though – it cost him sixty quid.'

I took the bottle and drank from it. It was bloody good.

'Well, it's nice of you to pop round on the off chance. I'm Guy Mullin. Er, how do you do. Lucky I happened to be working late.' The buzzer went again, this time more insistently. 'Is everything alright?'

'Oh, yeeaah,' she said, stretching her vowels like a teenager. 'He'll give up in a minute. He'll probably call me in the morning, or try to give me something again.' She took a mobile phone out of her bag. 'He gave me this last week. Good, eh?' she said, while dialling. And then, into the phone, 'Look, fuck off, OK? Leave me alone.' She switched the phone off and popped it back in the bag and, laughing, took the wine bottle back off me.

'Who is he?' I asked.

'Oh, just some bloke. Record producer. Took me to Silverstone last week. I met these really interesting guys, they let me drive one of the cars. I smashed up a whole fence and a hot-dog stall. It was fun.'

She got out an empty packet of ten Silk Cut and chucked it on the table. I offered her one of my Dunhills. We lit up. I didn't know what to say. She noticed the Z-cards of model boys plastered on the corkboard and went over to it.

'Ffooaarr!' she said. 'Oh yes, we like him! Gorgeous. Look at those thighs!' Then she noticed a recent Walker-print of Doug Handom on Joan's desk. 'Oooh. Doug Handom, I'm in love with him. I'd like to tie him to a seatless chair and use him as a gear stick.'

'Yes,' I said, 'he seems to have that effect on women.'

She picked up the photo and put it in her bag.

'Can I keep this to have a wank to later?' And I thought women were meant to prefer erotic literature.

'Yes, of course,' I said, 'we've got hundreds.'

From the street below, a man's voice was shouting her name up at us.

'Kemble!?'

'Don't answer,' she said, and then, 'He wants me to go away with him next weekend, but I'm not sure I want to go to a hotel in Monterey with him.'

'Is he your boyfriend?' I asked, and she looked at me as if I was about seventy years old and needed putting in an institution.

'So,' she said, sizing me up, 'you look like you need a damn good shagging.' And she walked towards the kitchenette and pulled back the curtain. 'Working late, were you? Kicked out by the wife and sleeping in the office, more like.' And she laughed like a ten-year-old. There seemed to be many extra decades between us.

I smiled along with her, trying to hide my embarrassment.

'Well, it's difficult sometimes to . . .' I mumbled, wondering whether her observation about my needing sex had been a suggestion, or merely a statement of fact. It's true, I must have looked as if I needed a damn good shagging, but I wasn't sure whether I needed one with her. If that was indeed what she had in mind.

She went back to the window and peeped out. She was wearing tight black leggings over her skinny legs, a skimpy T-shirt and a man's leather jacket, far too big for her. Another gift, no doubt.

'Good, he's gone. I'm starving, do you want to take me out for a meal?'

I reflected to myself for a moment. Yes, I did want to take her out for a meal. That would be fun. To get out of the office. I put on my jacket. I could be one of those tom cats who dines in several different households every night.

Out in the street, she linked her arm in mine, as if we were old friends, and rested her long auburn hair on my shoulder. I stood up straighter. Feeling uncomfortable with her uncalled-for familiarity and yet secretly enjoying the warmth.

'By the way, I don't do sex,' she said cheerfully. 'Not with people I like.'

'And you like me?' I asked, trying not to sound disappointed, which I suppose I wasn't really.

'Oh, yeah. Anyway, you're old enough to be my father.' And she snuggled up closer. 'Not that that's made any difference in the past.'

I steered us past the Soho House and the Groucho and anywhere where biz-folk might be. I didn't want anyone to get the wrong idea, or the right idea come to that. I didn't want anyone to have any ideas. I just wanted to be with company. There was a frisson of excitement too, I suppose.

We went to a little-used Lebanese, off Broadwick Street, which was just as well, because Kemble Stenner's sense of fun extended to throwing bread rolls at me and saying lewd things in a very loud voice.

'That was so good, when you went down on me yesterday morning. You've got an amazingly long tongue,' she shouted, as the waiter brought us our starters. Men at other tables goggled at us. Throughout the meal, we were on the edge of being asked to leave as Kemble pushed harder and harder to embarrass me out of my skin.

It was as if she was testing me, auditioning me for some role which I had no idea how to play. I kept smiling and quietly sat through all she threw at me. When the bill came and I put my card on the table, she said, 'Thanks, Dad, that was great. I won't tell Mum I've been seeing you.' Maybe she was auditioning herself. She was certainly being very funny. I kept laughing and smiling and we shared a cigarette. She took all the mints from the saucer and blatantly shoved them in her bag.

'Aren't you going to spank me then?' she said as we were leaving.

'I would never hit a woman, my angel,' I said, playing along.

'I bet I could make you.'

Did she want me to get angry with her, shake her by the shoulders, tell her to behave herself? I wasn't going to. For some reason, in my present state of mind, I found her antics entirely engaging and I followed her back to my own front door.

'Can I stay the night with you?' she asked, in a pouty, little-girlish way.

'Well, there isn't much room, as you saw,' I said.

Upstairs, we finished the wine and smoked more.

'Do you want me to be your agent?' I asked. 'Because I'm very happy to take you on. I mean, you don't have to do all this, you know. I think I could get you work.'

'Oh, I'm giving up the business tomorrow anyway,' she said casually. And then, 'Do you want to see my tattoo?'

'Well. That depends . . .' I started, but she'd already pulled down her leggings to reveal a rose on her left buttock. She wasn't wearing any knickers.

There is a certain breed of actress, known in the business as a 'no-knickers actress'. Their performances are usually strident and assertive, with a lot of saliva-spraying. Sometimes, when in a Greek tragedy, for instance, they will actually wear no knickers, but generally the term refers to their brassy and worthy approach to their work. Kemble was not of this type. She was simply not wearing any knickers.

'It's very nice,' I said. 'Did it hurt?'

'Yeah. It was agony, but I'm used to pain. My stepdad used to beat me up on a regular basis. Oh God, I think I'm going to be sick,' she said, and raced to the toilet. I followed her to the door and listened while she retched rather unconvincingly. When she came out I rubbed her puny shoulders and made her a cup of tea, which she never drank.

Despite my best intentions I found it hard to lie on the camp bed squashed up against a naked twenty-two-year-old and not get an erection. She folded herself around me and pulled the unzipped sleeping bag up tight around our shoulders. I lay there, stiffly, wondering what to do. I kissed her ear.

'Can't we just cuddle and go sleep?' she said. I'd love to do that, I thought, but erections and sleep don't go together. The blood is confused. I lay there for a bit longer, listening to her breathing. She had fallen asleep, spread over my chest. I tried to sleep, but inside my scrotum the two sperm factories had received the message to manufacture and they weren't going to stop now. I wondered how many millions had been created since Kemble had whipped down her leggings to show me her tattoo. Counting sperm is not a recommended soporific, they somehow lack the placidity of sheep. Especially since, as has now been discovered, not all sperm are the same. There are sprinter sperm, the ones who race straight up the tube for the egg, ready or not. There are slow-burn sperm, who hang around the darker fallopian corners for a few hours, waiting for a later opportunity. And there are rear-guard killer sperm, who don't go for the egg at all, but lurk at the entrance in case another man's sperm should happen by, in which case they explode themselves, kamikaze-style, killing their rivals. Sperm are, in fact, rather like an army, or a football formation. Thoroughly chap-like. I wondered what kind I would be, were I a sperm. Not the right kind, I had no doubt. Not the one who scores the goal. I wondered whether sperm are aware of what kind of sperm they are anyway. At least my erection was gone by now. With great delicacy, I extricated myself from the camp bed and from Kemble's embrace, and tiptoed into the office. I rang for a 7.00 a.m. alarm call. She'd have to be out by the time the women arrived. I tidied up the office and curled up on the sofa.

'I just didn't think it was going anywhere. I woke up one morning and thought – I'm not in love with him any more, so what's the point?' Maureen Beauley slammed the door of her bright-red VW golf, and started it up with the keys which she'd casually left in the ignition. 'He never really loved me properly, I mean, he was a great guy and everything, sweet, but he didn't know how to really cherish a woman.'

Why do women always tell me their stuff? What is it about me? Or do they tell anyone and everyone, and I'm one of the few who actually listens to it? As she changed gear aggressively, the tight skirt of her green business suit slid up the lining slip a couple of inches to reveal the top of a stocking and a quarter-inch triangle of white thigh. I clocked it in a blink of my eye without letting my neck muscles move an iota. She noticed that I'd noticed nevertheless.

'Yes, I see,' I said. 'I understand. Do you think he even knew what loving you properly would be, or did he just not care?' I could have said, 'Wwwoooooaaa! Stockings! Nice!' or words to that effect, but I'm not made like that, and anyway we were supposed to be looking for a flat for my mother. It seemed inappropriate.

'I just want to be loved by a man above all else. To know that I come first. I think most women do. And I was earning more than him anyway, so . . .' She jumped a light and hung a left without indicating. Someone hooted at us. I gripped the seat-belt holder; she was driving much too fast. 'What did you think of that last one?' she asked.

'Too many stairs.'

'Yes, and it needed a lot of work. I think they'd come down, though, if you wanted to make an offer.'

I sifted through the estate agent's details. All with small glossy photos pasted on the front. All virtually identical, rather like a casting directory.

'And what about your son? You said you had a son,' I asked.

'Oh, he comes first. Always. I love him more than anything. Here we are.'

We pulled up outside a terrace of houses with double front doors. Cottages built originally for the river-dock workers at Hammersmith. Most have kitchen extensions now and a small yard out the back. After fumbling with her huge assortment of keys, she opened the door and we entered the ground-floor flat, which had piles of junk mail in its narrow front corridor. This one was unoccupied, a recent conversion. The builders had tried to stretch a two-bedroomed self-contained granny flat out of what must once have been a living room and pantry, so the rooms were tiny and wedge-shaped and smelled of emulsion paint still. Most of the doors, when swung open, missed the opposite walls by only an inch or so, making one have to step back and round before entering, like a lovers' gate.

Maureen Beauley and I were squeezed close together in the corridor momentarily and entered the tiny front room with its authentic mini-fireplace still intact, although unusable in this now smokeless zone. She watched me looking round the place in silence, occasionally putting in remarks such as: 'I don't know what the service charge is on this one.' I wondered whether she was expecting me to make a pass at her. Her beige silk blouse was certainly unbuttoned to reveal a slice of bra. I wondered if it was one of the things about her job that she got to have dubious sex in other people's houses whenever she wanted. Or whether men making erotic suggestions to her was actually the bane of her life. What did she want? She seemed to be signalling something, but not in a language I understood. Women dress, I am assured by Liz and by others, to please themselves. It is nothing to do with catching male attention, that is merely an inconvenient by-product. Jeremy Planter would most likely have done it already with the breezy estate agent in every room. He would have known the right thing to say.

I've never been very good at reading signals. Sexual signals, I mean. Through my early twenties, when I suppose I should have been out rutting with the best of them, there were countless occasions when I only realized afterwards that I had been come on to, and was expected, as the man, to make a pass, or at least a suggestion of a pass, if only for tradition's sake. An incident – or rather, a non-incident – with a girl in a towel from the room opposite when I was a student springs to mind too often to haunt me as an example of a lost opportunity. The hint was there and obvious, she couldn't fix her lights or something, and knocked on my door half naked. What did I do? I fixed up whatever it was that was broken, and said good night. Presented with the possibility of passion, I spluttered like a rabbit frozen in the headlights to regret at leisure over the ensuing years. Why on earth this girl of my memory couldn't have done the asking, if that was what she wanted, I don't know, but as a man one is meant to be constantly up for it, a randy, thoughtless pumping machine, and therefore girls wouldn't have quite the same fear of rejection as boys. At least when it comes to casual sex. I've often had this argument with Liz. Me claiming that it's easier for a woman to go out and get immediate sex if that's all she's after than it is for a man. This is why men always make out that they're more interested in sex than affection, because sex is harder for them to come by. Whereas it's the other way round for women. That's the idea anyway. Someone should write a book about it. Oh, they already have done, haven't they? And done, and done to death. Another saturated market area for Neil to fail in. The point is that I don't see myself so much as sex on legs as a soft git with a permanent bewildered expression on his face like the sidekick to a TV glove puppet. Easy prey.

Of course, when I became an agent things changed quite a bit, and I got used to younger actresses ruffling their hair a lot in my presence, or laughing too much at my remarks, or just plain pushing their bodies up against me. In the first couple of years I did take advantage of this once or twice, with disastrous consequences. It's not good to mix sex and business. Maybe it's different in real estate.

I couldn't see Mum in this place. Mind you, it was difficult to picture her anywhere but in her own kitchen, reading out-of-date colour supplements or watching her TV with the sound turned up too loud.

'I just wanted to be touched – held, you know?' said Maureen Beauley.

'Well, quite. There's nothing wrong with that, is there?' I agreed vehemently as we pulled back out, too fast, on to the Fulham Palace Road.

'My little boy misses his father all the time now, of course. But he'll get used to not seeing him. He'll have to. His dad loves him to bits. Sometimes I think he loved his son more than me.'

'And you wanted to be loved above all else,' I said sympathetically.

'Still, children are very resilient, you know,' she said, as people always do when they mistreat them. If children are so resilient, I thought, how come the world is peopled with fucked-up adults?

'Yes,' I said, 'I'm sure you're doing the right thing.' As we stood outside the estate agent's office she gave me a professionally warm smile and said, 'Well, we've got your details, so we'll send you anything new that comes in, and as I say, that first one we looked at are in a hurry to sell, so I think they'd be open to an offer.'

Of course, I had no right to be depressed. Others have far worse problems than me. Neil, for a start. Half my clients, come to think of it. Everything about the day confirmed that I could make no claim on sadness. It was June and deliciously warm. The plane trees of Fulham were brightening like bells in the new light. You could feel their pleasure, hear their freshness in the breeze, almost smell the sexuality of their photosynthesis.

I could go and see my brother Tony. Apart from the funeral, we hadn't seen each other since my father died. I might find him in Bishop's Park where he sometimes worked. Trouble was, it was dangerously close to where Grace's first childminder had been, and I didn't want big whooshes of sad. I checked my mobile for messages. Simon Eggleston called to thank, and Barbara Stenner wanted to speak 'urgently'. For some reason I punched off the power button and put my mobile back in my pocket. I wandered down Queensmill Road without a sense of purpose. I became anxious at the thought of being off schedule, of being unaccountable. What was I thinking of, what was I doing? As I reached the river walkway by Fulham football ground it occurred to me. I was taking a walk, that was what I was doing. That's what people do, isn't it? They go for walks. Sometimes even just because they feel like it. Sometimes even during working hours. What a little 'aholic' I seemed to have become.

Leisure. Funny word. Leh-czha. Lejah. I rolled it around my mind for a while. When was the last time it had been there? Leisure. When? I thought about this. 1984. Yes, 1984, before Mullin and Ketts, before bloody Liz even. I was working for Anthony Sampson, the famous old-school agent. The type with a pocket handkerchief. I had a three-week holiday in Greece with my brother Tony and his girlfriend of the time. What was her name – Stacey, Tracy, Spacey? I had leisure and a job to go back to, as a commissioned trainee. Eleven thousand I made that year, and it seemed enough. Coh! Listen to me: 'In them days you could go clubbing, shag a few birds, pay off your mortgage, smart clothes, smart car, and still have change for the school fees and the wife's cocaine habit.'

I wandered along the towpath in the Putney direction. In the warm, girls were wearing cotton again and the river looked luxuriant: glinting silver diagonals emanating from the wake of a rowing eight. Spring had been grown out of, and the air was optimistic. It all made me feel, well, guilty. I could not come up to the mood of the day. I was aimless. There was no need to walk to the park, but like a headless chicken, I tottered down well-trodden paths. With Grace gone, the park would undoubtedly make me feel worse. The climbing frame train where she cut her knee, the now dried-out boating lake which we never did get to have a go on. The sandpit where some older kids had teased her and stolen her shoe. And of course, down towards Fulham, the spot where the bearded man had sunk so gracefully last month. I must have been mad coming here. A bicycle went past with an empty plastic baby-seat on the back. School pick-up. It was twenty past three.

Liz was right, I am an indulgent and self-pitying wanker. Stupid to come down here and look at all these things, sit on this bench. I bring things on myself. I set myself up to fail. How did I think Bishop's Park would make me feel, even on a day like this? What did I expect?

Some lads broke into a fight over a disputed goal in the football field beyond the playground. A dog barked and the irritating whine of a chainsaw suddenly stopped. Strange how, in its absence, one notices a noise which before had been there but blocked out by the mind. It started again. Damn, once you've noticed it, it really gets under your skin and makes it hard to think. I got up and walked towards the exit gate.

In the miracle of this day, which I spoiled with my presence, a flirtatious breeze invited the sawdust from the chainsaw to dance. Some of it stuck in my throat. The noise stopped again momentarily and then resumed. I was wading through brash now, large branches and sawdust strewn across the path which an old boy in a dark-blue donkey jacket was shunting into a heap.

Up in the branches, a pair of brown male legs in oily denim shorts braced themselves against the Y-shaped break of the tree, whilst among the leaves above, their owner wielded the whining saw like a TV magician showing you each side of a silk handkerchief. And that's TV as in television, by the way. The legs, though muscular and tanned, were scarred and lived-in. Not the legs of one of those model boys in the new jeans ads, or on the Z-cards. Older legs, a man's legs, tough, sinewy, bloody British legs. Not pumped up with steroids, vitamins or gym machinery. Men's legs must have been like this at Agincourt.

The old boy down below, clearing the brash, shouted, 'Cheer up!' at me. 'It might never happen!'

The saw noise stopped and the air thumped into a silence in my head. Broken only by the man above shouting, 'Tim-baaaaaah!' like a corny Tarzan. Well, at least someone was enjoying himself. It was my brother Tony. They'd let him loose with a chainsaw, the mad fools. After the remedial home in Kent, we were all pleased he'd managed to hold down a job sweeping leaves and picking up litter. Now he was limbering down towards me like a monkey on speed.

He flashed a pirate's grin at me, his earring glinting in the sunlight. Grace was not there to have this stuff explained to her. No one was asking me, 'Why, Daddy? Why is Uncle Tony cutting the tree off? What does timbaa mean? What did the other man say would never happen?'

He climbed down out of the tree with ease. Apart from his height, he was the nearest thing to a pirate you could ever see. He's concuss-yourself-on-a-door-lintel tall. Bang-your-knees-on-steering-wheels tall. Stoop-around-in-boats tall. Answer-lonely-hearts-advertisements tall. He could never have been a real pirate, not even a captain pirate, with the privileges and higher ceiling of the captain's cabin. Lofty was his nickname at school.

'Have the Tories reformed themselves into an electable party, number two?' said in an accent out of a 1950s submarine movie.

'What?' I said, gormlessly.

'Well, smile then,' he chirped at me.

'Oh,' I said lamely, getting his joke.

It was a fall from a tree that first put Tony into hospital. I must have been nine or so. I remember waiting with my mum in casualty for the doctor's results, and feeling that although it had been his decision to climb so high, it was my fault that he fell. As if my envy of him had been tangible enough to eject him from the branch. I still live with that ampoule of guilt. Mind you, the amount of LSD he took in the late seventies probably had more to do with his current mental state, and that had nothing to do with me.

The old geezer in the donkey jacket hustled me out of the way. I was standing on his brash. I apologized.

'You'll get over it, mate,' he said.

'What?' I said again.

'They're not worth it, you know, them women.'

Tony was unstrapping his harness. 'Fancy a cup of tea or an ice lolly or something, number two?' he said.

'Oi,' said the old bloke. 'You're not leaving me here with all this.'

'What do you want, Ted? Ice lolly? Cake?'

'Naaaaah,' said the old bloke. 'I've got me thermos.'

'Come on then, bollock-chops,' said Tony to me. 'I fancy a Mivvi.'

Even having a four-year-old child, I didn't know that you could still get a Mivvi. A slab of dairy ice-cream covered in raspberry sorbet on a stick. Grace always wanted Space Rocket Twirls, or Flintstone Icicles. I hadn't had a Mivvi, hadn't even heard the word, since about 1972. Childhood images of holidays in Newquay accelerated to the forefront of my mind. I wanted a Mivvi too. I wanted a Mivvi badly. I followed my big little brother across the park.

Despite his greasy denim shorts, he had on heavy boots and ski socks. He walked with the crooked gait of someone long at sea, or was this just my wishful thinking, my tendency to think of everyone's castability?

'So what the fuck's the problem, smiler?' he asked, as we climbed through a hole in the fence into the allotments. I couldn't think of a reply, so I just coughed and asked him how often the plane trees needed cutting back.

'Haven't the faintest fucking idea, pal,' he said, and we arrived at a small pavilion with a glass-covered noticeboard by the door. He went in. If this was the place dispensing Mivvis, we had entered a time warp.

An old woman in a pink nylon overall stood behind a tea counter. There was a small queue of people in cardigans, jolly fat women, people talking of plants in undertones. This was where the allotment-owners had their tea break. There were no advertising posters on the wall, though there was a signed ten-by-eight photograph of a famous television personality; Jeremy Planter.

'Seen Mum?' Tony asked.

'Yeah, I've been looking for a flat for her.'

'Oh?' Tony could never understand the logic of normal things.

'Well, it's a bit lonely for her, you know. In the house now he's gone.'

'Nineteen eighty-seven, that was a good year,' he said, as he delicately slithered the raspberry coating off his Mivvi with his tongue. I had bitten into mine from the top, not daring to attempt the denuding of the dairy ice-cream centre as I would have done as a child.

'Remember that, Guy? October the sixteenth, fucking hurricane, fucked up all the trees.' And he laughed with a shag tobacco smoker's wheeze.

'Terrible, though, the devastation. You know, we lost forty per cent of the trees in London. Forty per cent. So, how's the world of Thespeeenism, then?' he asked.

'Oh, you know, we survive.'

'What about the women, though, eh? You get to meet all the decent women, don't you, in your line of work. You can pick and choose, you can.' He laughed again and his face creased up like an old glove. I still couldn't manage a smile. I was off duty after all.

'What you doing down here, then? Shouldn't you be clinching deals, or relaxing by a pool with a pina colada or something?'

'Well, yes, I suppose I should, but I felt like a walk . . .' I said, feeling like rubbish in a bin bag.

When the Mivvis were finished, he got out an old rolling tin from a pouch at his waist, which had been painted with a yin-yang symbol, and rolled himself a fat ciggie.

I sat and watched as he lit it, and my look must have spoken to him as he inhaled the first curl of smoke. He pushed the tin across to me.

'I haven't had a roll-up for years,' I said. 'Or a Mivvi, come to that.'

'No wonder you look like a dead sheep,' he said, and laughed again.

I followed him back through the hole in the fence and we walked along the towpath together for a bit.

'How's your sexy wife?' he asked. I told him about sexy Bob Henderson. I don't know whether it's because he has a bit of his brain missing, but Tony comes across as a good listener. He lets you finish, anyway. I told him about the incident with the drowning man.

'Green Man, that's what that was,' he said when I'd finished. 'Fucking symbol of death and rebirth. The harvest. Oldest fucking symbol in fucking pagan folklore, that is. You should've done a Morris dance right there and then, Guido.'

'Well, I suppose I sort of did,' I said, remembering the silly run I'd done along the shore.

'And that wasn't bits of twig going into his mouth, that was a fucking new tree growing out of it. Symbol of fucking rebirth, that is, don't you know anything? Look under any church roof, look at the gargoyles. You lucky bastard, yuppying about in television, all mobile phones and fancy women, and one little

121

walk down by the river and the fucking Green Man himself floats by, easy as you like.'

'Is he giving you all that hippy rubbish?' said the old codger, ambling up after his lunch. 'He's been smoking that wacky baccy again, haven't you, Tony? Turns the brain, that stuff does. I tried it once. Nothing.'

'I'm Tony's brother, Guy,' I said. 'Pleased to meet you.'

'And you know what Guy means? It means wood man, man of the woods, in old language. You must be descended from a tree or something.' I never thought of it before, but Tony and Barbara Stenner would have had a lot to talk about. He buzzed on his chainsaw and wobbled it dangerously at me. 'And I think you need pollarding down to size, man.' He laughed like a maniac. I leapt out of the way of the whizzing teeth. He let the engine die, and hoisted himself up to the Y of the tree. 'Ever hugged a tree, Guy?'

'Erm, no, I can't say that I have.'

'You should try it,' and he wrapped his pirate's arms around the bole of the plane as if he'd just come back from a sea voyage and it was the first woman he'd seen for eight months. 'Aaargh. Lovely!' he said, and gave it a smacking kiss.

I looked at my watch, it was twenty to five and I'd said I'd only be gone for a long lunch. Must check in. What am I, some kind of basking snake? It had been a pretty dull day in Meard Street by the sound of it. But Liz had rung in to tell me the time of our appointment to see a counsellor. Yes, OK, we'd decided to go to a counsellor, it seemed like the only thing left. I wish she hadn't told Joan in the office, though. Joan would undoubtedly have told Naomi and Tilda and even Tania by now, who would probably start bringing me in special healing teas and books on relationships and treating me like one of her lost animals, and the others, well, who knows? Humiliating for me. I'm meant to sort out people's lives, for Jiminy's sake, to make people happy. It is my job, after all.

After this little excursion into Tony's *Lord of the Rings* world, I felt a bit better. Like I was on holiday. We've had holidays, Liz and I. I've made sure of that. But the trouble with holidays is that however much you relax while away, however many Stephen King books you read, the mail and the bills are still waiting for you when you get back. The well-being wears off much quicker than the tan. Usually before you've even got off the Gatwick Express at Victoria. Certainly before you get the key in the door.

The best holiday would be to tell everyone you're going away, pack, get in the taxi, and then turn it round, come back and secretly have a week on your own at home. A holiday in your dressing gown with order-in pizzas.

As I got into the taxi at Hammersmith Broadway, the sound of the chainsaw came back in stereo inside my head. It occurred to me that I ought to see a doctor about these noises. The taxi headed off towards Kensington and the West End. An hour or so left of trading time, and then the long Soho night. I leaned forward and slid open the driver's glass.

'I've changed my mind,' I said. 'Can you take me to Shepherd's Bush instead?'

Another thing about coming back from holidays is the resolutions you make to radically change your life. These also usually last a matter of hours. I was drifting into dangerously aimless waters. Cut loose from the moorings of home and family, I needed some kind of anchorage.

'Guy! Mate! Come in, how are you? Looking terrible as ever, you sad fucker. Come in.'

Malcolm Viner led me down the narrow hallway over cheap but insanely clean beige speckled carpet to a small double reception room wall-to-walled with the same. How did he manage to keep this place so clean? The cushions on his undersized sofa lay taut in their covers, arranged at diagonals to the arm rests. In home arrangements he would be very compatible with Liz

'Want a whisky?' He opened one of the glass-fronted built-in cabinets either side of the trim fireplace, and spent a couple of seconds selecting a bottle from the twelve kinds of whisky he had in there. Taking a couple of cut-glass tumblers from the symmetrical shelf unit, he poured me a large one, himself a very meagre one and sat down on his cane stool, urging me to the sofa.

On the bamboo and glass table were a pristine ashtray and the Sunday newspapers in a neat pile. He leapt up again.

'Unless you want ice?' he said. He smiled as if to say 'Even though ice would be sacrilege.'

'Is it alright if I smoke?' I asked. It didn't look like a cigarette had been smoked here for some years. Or anything else, for that matter. He kept his smile and sat down again. The cane creaked under his bum as he shifted his weight and took an almost imperceptible sip from his glass.

'Of course you can, Guy. I haven't since . . . ohhhhh,' he acted searching for the date, 'oh, must be three years now. Nerily, you know. Got to set an example. But you go ahead.'

'Thanks,' I said, taking a gulp of whisky that was bigger than his entire drink.

I'd gone and bought some rolling tobacco straight after my encounter with young brother Tone. I was living dangerously.

'God! Roll-ups!' said Malcolm with fake enthusiasm, and watched as I tore a strip of card from the pack of papers to use as a filter.

'You put roaches in cigarettes now, do you? Or is that a spliff you're rolling?'

I assured him it was just tobacco.

'Yes. Nerily's just at that age where you have to, you know . . . be careful, you know. I mean, she's nearly ten, and these days they get to know about these things much earlier . . .'

I made a messy job, with little sprigs of tobacco straying over the glass top of the table which I tried to brush back into the plastic pouch. They tumbled into the crack where the glass rested in the bamboo cane.

'Don't worry about that,' he said. 'God, we used to do all that on an album cover. Do you remember? I don't even have any vinyl any more. Gave that up too.'

I glanced across at the small, neat stack of CD player, radio and amp sitting dwarfed in the space under one of the glass cabinets, and finished my drink. Malcolm was up and fiddling with the window.

'You warm enough?' he asked, smiling. 'It's just . . .'

The early-evening air came in to remove my smoke before it had a chance to yellow the pristine paintwork.

'Tell you what, while I'm up, shall I leave the bottle out where you can reach it?' He reopened the cabinet. 'Or rather *a* bottle.' He laughed. 'That one we just had is a bit good. By which I mean it cost a fortune. Got it in Gilvannie last year. It's seventeen years old, would you believe?'

He found another bottle and put it on the occasional table, by my arm.

'That do?' he said, and sat again, creaking the stool.

'Brilliant. Thanks,' I said. 'Sorry about this . . .'

'You know, I suddenly had a thought about you the other day. You just floated into my mind, I know you won't believe that. And then you rang me the other night, didn't you? But you chickened out and hung up.'

'Sorry, did I wake you up?'

'No no no. Fine fine fine. So you and erm, what was her name, are no more, I presume?'

'I'm that obvious, am I?'

'No no no,' he said. 'Well, yes.'

I was at school with Malcolm.

'And you had a kid, didn't you? How old's he/she?'

'Grace. Four and a half.'

'Ah. A girl,' he said, with a gravity which was lost on me.

Malcolm had an exaggerated earnestness which many found intimidating, taking it for pushiness. His voice was always clear and resonant, with perfect diction, like a classical stage actor's should be. He'd always taken main roles at school, and after going to RADA had had a reasonably successful theatrical career in rep, with a couple of stints at the National. But somehow, apart from the odd episode of *Casualty*, he'd never really made it on telly. He was too plummy, too altogether actorly actually to be employed as an actor. After a few years working for nothing, trying to make his own fringe company survive, he'd had the good sense to get out altogether and was now, I discovered, a secretary in the civil service as well as being a part-time aromatherapist.

He bristled with a jumpy energy at all times, even, I remembered now, when drunk – which was rarely – or stoned, which used to be often. A very thoughtful man, but the kind of thoughts he had went in straight lines and never accelerated around corners. Decisive and athletic. Definitely officer material had he been that way inclined, although I wouldn't know how many Jewish officers there are in the British army.

125

He was also almost completely bald, and had been since his early twenties. He was a man who had made an early decision about his baldness. Not for him a flapping comb-over, nor even anything creeping over his collar at the back. What little hair there was had always been neatly cropped even in the seventies. He had a sensitive mouth and skin like polyester. I'd always liked him, despite the fact that his shirt tails remained resolutely tucked into his trousers at all times, unlike mine, which, even now, had been shuffled halfway up my back by the tidy cushions on his sofa.

'So, fuck,' he said, generally. 'Fuck fuck fuck fuck fuck. You still living in the same place together or . . .?'

'I moved out. I'm on the camp bed in the office,' I said, and a stack of ash fell on the carpet. I tried to rub it in a bit with my foot.

'That's bad,' he said, and then, 'Don't worry about the ash, the carpet's been sprayed. You seeing someone else?'

'Nope.'

'Is she?'

'Yep.'

'How long?'

'Dunno.'

'Kid's definitely yours?'

'Gotta be. I think so. Yes, of course.'

'She working?'

'No. She's an actress.'

'Fuck. And you? How is it these days in the high-powered world of entertainment? I always knew you'd make it big, you know.'

'Few clients playing up at the moment, but . . . what's new?'

'What's the bloke do?'

'Fucks her a lot, I presume.' I was tiring. 'He's a lawyer.' I opened the lesser bottle of whisky and poured myself a large slug. How long, I wondered, since it had last been opened? Malcolm must be the only person I knew, I thought, who could have twelve bottles of different beautiful whiskies for several years in his downstairs room and not even think of seeing how sick he could make himself by going on a bender and polishing them off at a sitting. I offered him a top-up. Of course, he declined.

126

'You hungry?' he asked, standing up again.

'Naa,' I said, although he could see through it.

'I've only got kids' stuff really, I'm afraid. I'm meant to have Nerily this weekend. Or at least I should do if her mother deigns to acknowledge my existence. Beans on toast or something?'

'No, I'm OK really,' I said.

'It won't take a minute,' he said. 'Talk to me while I get it.' And he went into the kitchen like his Jewish mother would have done, had he been me.

I gathered my smoking material and followed him through with the bottle.

'You still support Fulham?' he asked.

'I never did. What are you talking about?'

'You did, you used to support Fulham, you poor, sad, misguided fool.'

'I went to a couple of matches once. That's all.'

'And had the strip. And the sticker book.'

In keeping with the rest of the house, the kitchen we were in was spotless. Not a dirty cup in the sink, not even clean plates drying on the rack. All had been put away. We could have been in a shop window and there was just about as much room. I leaned on the worktop and watched him prepare crumbless toast.

The corkboard had on it photocopies of an activity weekend, and an events sheet from Nerily's school.

'Oh, that,' he said, seeing my interest in the noticeboard. 'It's been a major triumph getting the school to send me copies of Nerily's dates. You wouldn't believe the prejudice there is against single fathers.'

A photograph of Nerily, scrubbed and school-uniformed, was pinned to the frame.

'So you moved out? That's bad,' he said.

'Well, I still pay the mortgage and the bills, and I fixed the place up and everything.'

'And the little Princess Grace. What's she think is going on?'

'Nothing yet. I couldn't stay, though. It's pretty bad at the moment there.'

'Mmmmmmm. I can imagine.' He poured the beans neatly on to the toast and put the pan to soak in the sink.

'Obviously you can stay here if you need to. I mean, if it gets really bad. There's Nerily's room which is free most of the time, and the sofa sort of folds out. But you're not going to be left with much if you walk out, you know.'

'I don't want much. I just want to do the right thing.'

'Yes, you say that now, but what about Princess Grace?'

I wished he'd stop calling Grace a princess.

'Well, we share all that. Even when she was little.'

'She still is little, though, isn't she?'

'But Liz doesn't respect me any more. And that's evidently very important.'

Back in the main room, I tried not to spill beans on the carpet, or on the sofa, despite being sure that it too had almost certainly been sprayed.

With my mouth full, Malcolm was able to expound.

'In a way, splitting up with Geraldine was the best thing that ever happened to me, I mean, I was heading for a fall anyway. I wouldn't have lasted another year in your bloody business. Bloody awful. It was terrible at first but it just about works now. My main worry has been if Geraldine ever decides to go back to the States and take Nerily with her. Which technically, of course, she couldn't actually do, and Nerily's old enough now to make up her own mind. But we never married, you see, and she's refused to sign a Parental Responsibility Agreement, so actually I have no rights at all. You married, didn't you? That's one good thing. At least you could get a contact order. Not that they've got any way of enforcing it if she decided to deny you access.'

I sensed a stridency in his voice which matched the effort that had so obviously gone into the hoovering and dusting.

'Technically, you'd be abandoning. Mind you, you're legally the absent parent, even if you live next door and take the child to school every day. That's what makes me really angry.'

The cane stool seemed to be creaking of its own accord now.

'Did you know that until 1823 it was legal for a woman to kill her child if it was illegitimate? The Stuart Bastardy Act 1623.'

'Funny name, Stuart Bastardy,' I said. I was losing it. But Malcolm seemed to be charged with some zeal. This was obviously his favourite subject. As soon as my beans were finished, he zipped my plate away and rushed it to the kitchen to be cleaned. I stood limply in the doorway. He carried on talking while washing up.

'Do you know what is the demographic group most at risk from homicide? Mmm?' Malcolm was the kind of person who could use words like 'homicide' without sounding American. 'Children under the age of one, that's who. And fifty per cent of them are killed by their mothers.'

He dried the dishes too, and put them away. I almost wished I had had a more complicated meal. It would have given him more to do. His energy was draining.

'Listen, Guy, you have to be able to show that you are capable of caring for the child. That she's got somewhere she can stay with you. Moving out was a very bad move. I'm sorry, but it's true. Come and look upstairs.'

He trotted up the narrow staircase, stabbing each step with his wide feet. Upstairs were two small rooms. His bedroom looking out on to the street with a couple of sociology books on the bedside table, and to the side, a tiny child's bedroom, looking out on to the back yards of the adjoining terraces. Nerily's room was unrealistically neat as well.

'You have to have something to show the welfare officer, even though they lie all the time anyway. And remember to write everything down.'

There was a laptop computer on the child's dressing table. He flicked it on and clicked into a file.

'See?' He scanned through a list of dates. 'Every time I see Nerily, I log it here. And here, every time Geraldine messes up a contact arrangement for whatever reason. Which reminds me . . .' And, ignoring me, he put in a new entry, punching the keys with a delicate fury.

'I had the welfare officer round five times and they're really tricky. Doesn't matter what you say, though, they'll write a completely different report.'

'How often does she stay here?'

'Meant to be four evenings a month, and as of this year she can stay over weekends, but Geraldine's done her best to poison Nerily's mind against me. You know, last month she asked, "Daddy, why do you hate me so much that you won't let me go to America with Mummy?" Look . . .' And he flicked to another file on the computer. This one was headed 'Parental Alienation Syndrome'.

Down the various columns were subheadings: 'Domestic Proceedings and Magistrates Courts Act 1978'; 'Matrimonial Homes Act 1978'; 'Matrimonial Proceedings Act 1976'.

'You know, I spent eleven thousand pounds in solicitors' fees in the first year,' he continued, gathering momentum now. 'Nowadays I represent myself every time, which is better, because the judges have to bend over backwards to help you. I mean, they even try to speak in plain English. Unless you get someone like Coulworthy-Browne. He's a bastard. Hates fathers.'

'How many times have you been in court, then?' I asked.

'Oh, about nine,' he said, over his shoulder. 'Here, look at this, I've compiled a hit list of all the custody judges. You know, which ones are sympathetic, which ones are bastards. Judge Grantham!' He pointed out one name. 'God help you if you get Judge Grantham. Best to be ill that day and go for a postponement.'

I started to feel a bit sick. The coloured balloon pattern of the wallpaper was beginning to fall downwards. I closed my eyes and everything started rushing upwards and over my head. I opened them again and things seemed to plummet once more. I leaned on the door frame. I was having an attack of the whirlies. I'm not all that good with spirits. I gulped for air.

'There. Look at that,' said Malcolm. 'Children Act 1989. "No reason to discourage shared residence." No reason to discourage it! You should have seen Coulworthy-Browne's face when I read that out to him in court.' He laughed to himself.

'Did it do any good?' I managed.

'What? No, of course not. You can't win with those bastards. But someone's got to have a go.'

'Malc, I don't think I'm feeling . . .' I was holding on to the door now as well.

'Fuck! You silly cunt! You've gone white as a sheet! Why don't you sit down, I'll get you some water.' And he banged past me and rattled down the stairs, still talking.

'. . . Did you know that England and Wales now have the highest divorce rate in the world . . . Apart from California, that is . . .?'

I flopped on to the child's bed and sat there with my bottom lip quivering, taking deep breaths.

Some hours later, after the whirlies had gone, which took a lot of concentration and deep breathing, and after Malcolm had made me some alphabet soup, I accepted his invitation to stay over, and was put in Nerily's room with the curtains drawn, although it was still light outside.

My feet and ankles hung over the end of the tiny bed. I could hear Malcolm snoring and chortling in the next room. He had to be up in the morning for his secretarial job, so he'd promised to get me up in time to be in Soho for 9.00. I wanted a cigarette but the roll-ups were downstairs and anyway I couldn't, for Nerily's sake. Even if she did only come here every other week. I lay half propped up on the little pillows and stared at the shape of the laptop computer in the semi-darkness. It emanated a dark-grey gloom at me. It seemed to grow in size and significance. I tried to roll over on to my side but this rammed my face up too close to the balloon wallpaper. I lolloped on to my other side and succumbed to the evil presence of the laptop.

Grace had started without me. She was calling me urgently. She was already falling. Far down – away from me – screaming. I was late for our usual ritual dreamtime sacrifice. I'd been too drunk. She was falling fast and away. A vast swimming pool. A piranha tank. A concrete crocodile pit. Maybe I had pushed her. I threw myself after her and woke with a start on Nerily's floor. I had fallen off the bed. No protective cot bars for me. It was now very bright outside. Birds sang. I got back under the duvet and tried to warm up.

My shirt was not on the chair where I had tossed it the previous night. After a few minutes, Malcolm knocked on the door twice and came in.

'Cup of tea?' And then he produced my shirt on a hanger and put it on the door handle.

'And I ironed this for you. Leave in eleven minutes. The orange one is the spare toothbrush. And don't put your tampon down the toilet, old boy.'

FIVE

'OK, I WANT you all to think for a minute of your most treasured possession. I don't mean in the world. I mean something that you have with you today. Something that you value more than anything else. It might be your watch, or your shoes, or it might be your credit card!'

Various sheepish low chuckles from all of us. That was meant to be a joke.

'Now, I want you to take it out and look at it and think for a minute about what this possession means to you and why it is so important to you?' Unnecessary upward inflections abounded.

I thought of my Psion, my mobile, which obviously was switched off, my mini-Filofax, my watch. Nothing seemed important, not really important, to me, that is. The fat bearded man opposite me had put his expensive camera on his lap and was looking at it tearfully, as if it were a dead kitten. I felt naked, my clothes meant nothing to me, the contents of my pockets meant nothing to me. There was nothing from my button-down shirt to my Church's brogues which wasn't there for business reasons, nothing that was me. Except the picture of Grace in her bucket, I suppose. That was the only non-business thing, although even that has been used on occasions when networking with family-orientated Yank producers. I took it out and looked at it. I must have had as dumb an expression on my face as the fat bearded bloke.

'Now. I want you to stand up and pick someone in the room and give him your most treasured possession and tell him why it means so much to you. Tell him its story.'

I flicked a glance across at Neil, hoping we wouldn't choose each other. I was pulled gently around by a dangerously thin ginger-haired man in a voluminous army T-shirt and rope waistcoat. He had a beard too. Come to think of it, eighty per cent of the men in the room had beards. Luckily, I hadn't shaved. At least I could blend in a bit.

'These were my father's socks' he said to me reverently, in a nasal drone.

I looked down to see his bony white toes twitching on the parquet flooring. 'My father was a very bad man. He walked all over my mother, so now I wear his socks to achieve balance and wholeness.'

I wondered whether washing the socks was also part of the karmic equation.

'This is my daughter,' I said, and we swapped treasures. Christ! What the Andy Pandy was I doing here? Over the other side of the room, Neil was giving someone a stack of badly typed, unbound pages of manuscript and talking at length to him. Shit, that was probably the next draft of his so-called novel. Neil seemed to have a death-wish these days.

'And now I want you all to take what you have just been given and pass it on to someone else and explain to them why it was so important to the other guy.'

I looked around in desperation for someone to give the socks to and picked the only guy who was wearing a suit.

'His dad's socks,' I said. 'Some kind of Oedipal revenge totem.' And was given a little black notebook by the suited man, who spoke to me in a slow Canadian drawl.

'This is a very special book.' He had a large and beneficent smile on his face. At least someone knew how to enjoy this.

'It contains the phone numbers of over two hundred women. Many of whom have had sexual encounters with its owner.' I searched around the room, trying to guess which man was the stud, but noticed instead the thin redhead handing my picture of Grace to a large, earringed, shaven-headed guy, who could have been a paedophile for all I knew, definitely looked like a paedophile. I did not know how to enjoy this.

Apart from anything else, Neil's scant manuscript was probably now in the hands of an unscrupulous bootleg publisher with a photographic memory. We all had to sit back down and close our eyes and think about how we felt about letting go of our possessions. I sneaked a look at Julian, the group facilitator, who was standing on tiptoes waving his arms around, with his thumbs and forefingers pinched together. The conductor of a very strange and bearded orchestra.

'Now, staying with those feelings – perhaps feelings of anger? Of greed? Of insecurity? – and keeping our eyes closed, I want us to say what comes into our heads, however bad it might seem, however unacceptable?' The upward inflections were too studied to be natural. 'Remember this is experiential? There are no value judgements meant to be put on this, and . . . I'll start?'

I peered round through half-closed eyelids at the rest of the group. All eyes seemed closed. Was I really the only one cheating?

There was one professorial-looking bloke who was breathing deeply into his nostrils and exhaling very noisily. He'd been wearing glasses earlier. I was glad I had the book of phone numbers and not this guy's specs. Too much responsibility. I continued my surreptitious glance around the circle and saw the glasses sitting precariously on the lap of a shaggy man with filthy fingernails.

'OK?' said Julian in reassuring tones. 'I am angry that, since she's a successful journalist, my partner has always earned more than what I get as a workshop co-ordinator, and sometimes it makes me unable to offer her the support she needs and I end up shouting at her. Yeah?'

He had an annoyingly chirpy voice, which made everything he said sound as if it was a refrain from a jolly English folk song. There was a pause, a few seconds of quiet – apart from the inhaling professor – while we all tried to think of a contribution.

'How Men Need to Change' was the name of the weekend. What had Neil got me into? I know I said I'm the sort of agent who gets involved with his clients, and I had indeed chanted with Barbara Stenner in Primrose Hill, but this was taking representation too far.

A whole weekend workshop and Neil was missing two days' writing. I should have just cracked the whip and told him to get on with it. But then weekends were becoming occasions to dread now from the ivory tower of Mullin and Ketts in Soho, and I'd long ago given up my social life – friends, I mean – in order to keep financially afloat for Grace and bloody Liz.

In the silence, I thought about weekends and what they used to be. If I'm honest, all of my friends, the only ones in whom I've confided, at any rate, have been women, like Susan Planter. I am, I suppose, somewhat suspect in this respect. I learned at school, and of course from my brother earlier on, that competitiveness is so ingrained that to confess a weakness to another man would be to lay oneself open to attack or theft.

'I realize that I have been abusive, I have been selfish and I closed myself off from intimacy with my wife. I just wasn't strong enough to be gentle.' Must be the man from Kleenex. Who was that goody-goody? Full marks for him. I couldn't see who had spoken but he had obviously been to one of these before.

'I'd like to be able to afford to have a holiday every now and then and to spend more time with my girlfriend.' A squeaky mousy-voiced man to my left.

'It's only when I listen to my woman and learn to feel with her, to really feel what she's feeling, that I can please her, and I want to please her.' A Spanish-sounding guy. Well done that man. Ay thank yoh.

I decided that I was definitely not going to say anything during this bit. Maybe I'm just not a workshop animal.

'Sometimes I just want to kill someone. Push them under the water and drown them.' This was Neil's throaty voice. I hoped he didn't mean his agent.

'I'd like a harem,' said a down-to-earth voice nearby suddenly. 'I'd like to have enough money to hire a different expensive hooker every day, or maybe two, and have them do whatever I told them and never have to work again.'

There was a nasty moment's silence. Someone laughed in it. Julian, our facilitating leader, coughed a little cough.

'That's OK?' he said sagely. 'Remember, we're meant to be saying whatever we feel, whatever comes into our heads? However awful it might seem?'

The earthy voice continued: 'I'd like to whip them with belt straps and make one of them talk dirty in my ear, while another one sucks my knob.'

Unfortunately, I couldn't crane my neck round to see who was speaking without it being obvious. Then came the Canadian guy's voice.

135

'After my divorce, I had to get away. I took an old camper waggon and lived down by the ocean for a few months, with the waves and the sky. It was good.'

I felt certain that, like me, the general democratic majority of the group were waiting to hear more from the harem belt-buckle bloke and were not really that interested in the Canadian guy's commune with nature.

There was another little silence. The professor had stopped wheezing.

'Anything else?' said Julian the facilitator in a nursery-school tone. He was referring to the group as a whole, but his remark seemed to refer in our minds only to the pervy guy on my right. We all waited to hear if this lone voice would have any further exciting revelations for us. He didn't let us down.

'I'd like to invite all my friends round to fuck my ex-wife, one after the other,' he continued. 'I'd watch. Two or three of them at a time. The queue of men would go round the block. She'd be wearing a blindfold.' I wondered if it was his black book that I was holding.

'The whole thing would go on for hours. After the mess she's made of my life, after what she's put me through, it would be a pleasure to see her suffer. They could fuck her up the arse. Some of the men would be allowed to kick her. I'd laugh. Then I'd drag her out across my front drive, scraping her face on the gravel . . .'

He paused because a lump of saliva had come up in his throat. While he swallowed and took breath, Julian facilitated.

'OK, right. And now we can open our eyes?' He stood there still on tiptoe, in his lemon-yellow Marks and Spencer cardigan, smiling.

'So we can see, there's a lot of this aggression in us.' He mimed quote marks around the word aggression, as if he were making some deep intellectual point.

'And it can be even, well, frightening? Yuh?'

I don't think I was the only man there secretly thinking it can also be a bit of a turn-on. Lovey.

Immediately on opening our eyes, we all looked to my right to see if we could identify the monster man, but there were only two very gentle hippy-looking guys and the Canadian in the suit. The large bald paedophile was right over the other side of the room, so it wasn't him.

As you can imagine, lunch was a tawdry affair. Organic everything and small portions of rice. There was a thick chocolate brownie cake but that had run out by the time I had got to the head of the droopy queue. There was plenty of carrot cake, of course. There's always plenty of carrot cake.

I drifted with my paper plate through the alternative bookstall. A thousand pamphlets about men and yet nothing which mentioned football, birds or lager. Tell a lie, there was a small flyer leaflet called 'Men, Violence and Alcohol, a Weekend Intensive', with a photo of the big bald paedophile on the cover, Simon Dukowski, Group Co-ordinator.

'Do you think anyone would notice if we nipped out for a beer?' I turned round to see big Mr Dukowski himself looking at me.

'Only joking,' he said, and laughed all by himself at his own magnanimity. One of his front teeth was missing. 'How're you finding it?' he asked. And while I stumbled for an appropriate and believable expression of appreciation, he continued, 'It's better than last year's, I think. More experiential. Mind you, I couldn't really get into that possessions exercise.'

He reached deep into his tracksuit trousers pocket, which jingled with keys and change – seemingly groping around his balls – and took out what looked like a large carwash token, on which was embossed the words 'Three Years' and the initials NA. Narcotics Anonymous. Uh oh.

'That's my most treasured possession, but when it came to it I copped out, you know? I couldn't bring myself to show anyone?'

He seemed to have caught the upward inflection disease from Julian.

'Three years?' he said proudly. 'I keep it in my pocket at all times so that I can just hold it if I start to feel a bit, you know, wobbly?'

'But you don't mind showing me?' I said. I was catching it now too. My remark did not seem to register with him.

'Three years since I have had any kind of narcotic.'

'Well, that's very . . . impressive.' But my voice trailed off with my attention, which was drawn over his shoulder to a man standing alone on the other side of the room. A man I recognized and whom I hoped would not recognise me. James Rhys-Evans. Until last month Head of Series and Serials at the BBC, and before that Head of Drama at Central. What was he doing here? I leaned my weight behind the large, shaven-headed, toothless ex-drug addict, using him as a shield. Rhys-Evans was standing, miserably eating from his paper plate. He must have only just arrived or been in the other group for the morning session, because he hadn't been in my workshop. I hoped it was the latter, because I didn't want to be caught publicly airing confidences and sharing treasure with an important TV exec, however experiential the experience might be.

'And they're doing more on alcohol and drug-related problems this year, which is good,' the shaven head went on, through mouthfuls of his second banana. It was he who had had the last of the brownie, too. It sat there on his paper plate, waiting for him to finish both bananas. I could see over his shoulder that Rhys-Evans had noticed me and was as studious as I was in avoiding a recognition of this if at all possible.

'Oh, well. Body sculpting this afternoon. That should be good,' said Simon Dukowski cheerfully, starting at last on the brownie.

Body sculpting with Julian turned out to be possibly my worst nightmare on legs. Also, they had reselected us into a larger group in the big hall, to allow more room for physical self-expression – something I tend usually to keep down to a minimum by choice – so I had to face up to Rhys-Evans and he had to face up to me.

I shouldn't have been so worried, I suppose. He was not one of the five really big cheeses in television and he had just been made redundant, so he might be now a spent force, a non-person in a silk suit. An executive with nothing to execute. But those in power change jobs about once every eighteen months, so one can never be sure where they may suddenly re-emerge with added attributes, departments and even share-option schemes to boot.

Obviously, being an agent, I can't name these heavy five grands fromages, let alone say what I really think of them, well, not until they fall from power anyway, and then one has to be pretty sure there is absolutely no chance of a rebirth from the ashes as head of some independent film commissioning body or what-have-you.

As an agent, one is part of that gaggling throng who have a vicious claw at those in power as they plummet from favour, all from the safety of one's own throne of non-commitment, of course. Actually, why should I care any longer? OK, there's Stephen 'Mr Indecision' Ronson, there's Matthew 'The Pudge' Praslin, there's Peter 'The Big Man' Winner – we like him this season – there's Jane 'Give me a Crotch Shot' Poke-Warner – we've all gone off her, too much of a self-publicist, not enough actual television being made – and lastly, there's Sir David Frost, 'Frostie,' or Kellogg, as he's known.

Of course there are far more important people behind this lot, accountants and shareholders and executives who wield the money power. But for the producers, directors, writers, actors, technicians, designers and, of course, agents, these five are the ones that matter, and don't let any head of department or independent production company exec tell you otherwise. Any proposal to end up on British TV will have had to have passed across one of those five desks. So, if you have been turned down by one, you might as well go home. They don't like taking each other's cast-offs and they all read the same papers and they all eat in roughly the same places and they all, funnily enough, live in the same area of London, apart from Peter Winner, of course, who, seeming not to care how naff he looks, lives in a newly built home in Hertfordshire. We all love him for that. 'Up yours' he seems to be saying to the poncy privileged crowd. Mind you, we are fickle, we like him this year because he had such a success with *Pointings*, which gave so many of our clients work and won a clutch of awards.

Last year Stephen Ronson was fave, because he was new and he seemed to be commissioning new dramas like they were Pringles crisps. Now he's faded from grace because of the *Ice-Cream in Barcelona* fiasco, which actually wasn't of his making; he inherited it, so it is totally unfair. We are fickle, it is unfair. Not that our nittering and nattering makes an eence of difference. We are like a colony of mice, whose offices are joined by interconnecting passages beneath the floorboards, with occasional holes in the skirting through which we push young narcissists, blinking in the glare. Every specialized trade serving the industry is like this. Ask a make-up artist what she or he thought of *Les Liaisons Dangereuses* and they will say, 'Terrible film, you could see the wig lace.' Whereas a member of a camera crew will go on about the lens filters used, or mention the name of some new computerized editing technique, like 'Harry' or 'Skid'.

'Now, this afternoon I've stacked all the chairs away, so there can be no hiding in the wings, OK?' said Julian, slipping out of his lemon-yellow cardigan and delicately rolling up his sleeves, ready for some kind of action. We had had to take off our shoes and put them round the edge of the hall. Unavoidably, Rhys-Evans and I acknowledged each other at the row of shoes. Neil was already in the centre of the room, swinging his arms by way of a warm-up. Alright for him, he was a performer, a thesp, a doer. There was no workshop on the schedule called 'Persuading People to Do Things By Talking on the Phone', so I was not to be in my element all weekend. Nor, I suspected by the look of him, was James Rhys-Evans.

'OK, that's good? A few deep breaths and relax and then I'm going to say a word, and what I want you to do is allow yourself to express your feelings about that word . . . through your body.' Inverted commas again. 'Just through your body. You can make noises and move around the room but not too much thinking, OK?' Big joke. 'Just let it come out through your body, like making a sculpture?'

I had that feeling when you climb up to the diving board at the swimming baths and it's obvious the moment you get there that you're not going to have the guts to do it. But you can't just climb back down again in front of the whole school, so you compound the embarrassment by standing pointlessly a foot from the edge for the next twenty minutes.

'And the word is . . .' an elfin smile on his soft-skinned face, 'the British economy.'

That's two words, I thought, well, three if you count the 'the'. But the old professor guy, with his glasses restored, was already squatting down beside me and howling, in rather badly acted agony. Next please, daughter, I thought.

The Canadian started a low hum and his eyelids flickered. Obviously, for him, the British economy had something to do with transcendental meditation. Fair enough.

All around me, bearded men were rising and contorting themselves. Their willingness to join in was disturbing. Lawyers, hippies and estate agents groaned and swore and wriggled in simulated pain on the floor. The collective gibberish rose into the echoey ceiling, like thunder breaking backwards. The individual noises ran into one another, making an ugly and frantic non-stop bark. The British economy yapping in the rafters. So this was how men needed to change, this was what they wanted to change into. A bunch of naff amateur dramatics auditioning for the part of Caliban in an all-canine production of *The Tempest*.

Thinking only of the British economy, I curled into a ball on the floor and tried to blank out the deafening roar above. Neil was doing a sort of t'ai chi mime show; James Rhys-Evans had disappeared into the rugby scrum at the centre of the hall.

'And . . . freeze?' shouted Julian, clapping his hands together.

Simon Dukowski, the fat druggie, was caught on one leg and tried, meaningfully, to stay like that.

'Now, I want you to think of the sculpture you have made of yourself? And, in your own time, slowly return to your normal position?'

The thunder was still roaring in my ears as Julian divided us down the middle for an expression-and-release-of-conflict-and-aggression exercise.

I could just leave now. I could quietly get up, retrieve my shoes and go out of the room. But what would Rhys-Evans think? He showed no sign of wanting to leave. Mind you, I showed no sign of it either. It would have been foolish to show a sign of it, and now we were shouting at each other across a chalk line which Julian had drawn along the centre of the room. He was definitely getting off on this, probably wearing silk underwear underneath his neat, clean jeans.

'You fucking arsehole, you never ever ever made me feel wanted.' The thin redheaded guy seemed to be shouting specifically at me. He gave me full-on son-to-father eye contact. 'You stopped me, every time, you . . . you . . .' He began to tremble and cry. I couldn't think of anything to shout back at him across the chalk line: it seemed a rather horrid thing to do anyway, poor little ginger.

He was sobbing hugely now and I became a little concerned. Various phrases rose above the din.

'I am going to fucking kill you, I'm going to fucking kill somebody,' recognizable to my left from Neil. 'Push them into the water and drown them.' He'd certainly got in touch with his anger this weekend, if that was what we were meant to be doing. I turned my attention away from the redhead and shouted, 'You idiot' to no one in particular. It would have been worse not to join in at all. People were red in the face, saliva spots flecked the chalk. The sound was like having one's own private roadworks piped through headphones.

The Canadian was humming again. A man dressed all in green joined him, and then a few of the hippies. Over the top of the humming and the shouting, Julian screeched, 'Yes, that's good?' More men started humming and then some wandered, like dazed bomb victims, across the chalk and started to hug one another.

Apart from one or two stragglers, it was almost all humming now, except for the redhead, who was beyond hope. He was quaking all over, and still the sobs continued, reverberating back off the rafters. I was seriously concerned for him now. Shouldn't someone call a doctor? I hoped they had some professionals around to cope with this sort of thing. Two or three guys went to hug him. More joined them until he was lost under a scrum of shaggy love. I was jealous. No one hugged me.

James Rhys-Evans caught my eye and went to the other side of the room. There was no way we were going to do any bonding or what-have-you. Imagine his position next time he got his hand on the steering wheel of the entertainment station waggon. You can't cut throats in a cutthroat world if you have been workshopping each other's inner child the night before, now can you? We both knew that and respected it.

The redhead was lifted up on the shoulders of the bearded scrum and carried round the room. His sobbing had transformed itself into manic laughter now. Too manic. This was like a scene from a Peter Brook extravaganza, circa nineteen bloody sixty-eight.

The redhead needed help, I thought, and was not going to get it from Julian, whose smile seemed also to have become Gothic at its twitchy edges. I wondered if he was secretly videoing the whole thing for private perusal at home afterwards.

It's questionable whether it was a changed man who crept down the stairs of Neil's West Hampstead house into the chilly Monday morning. Definitely a man who needed to change his clothes. I'd been in the same corduroys and button-down shirt all weekend. The weekend experience had made me sweat and I hadn't had a bath or shower since Friday morning.

My hair was mussed, and sleeping on Neil's floor with a jacket for a blanket had left me creased, crumpled and stiff. I had woken with the Sunday-afternoon communal drumming still in my ears. It had joined the other sounds in the menagerie in my head: the urgent rustling of poplar leaves in the wind; the dangerous rushing of water; a baby – Grace, probably – crying as if on a tape loop; and now, of course, this mêlée of drumming, so syncopated as to make one homogeneous din, like the oversound in the swimming pool on schools morning: 'Whwwrrrrroooaaahhh.' I must remember to pay a visit to my GP.

I clunked Neil's front door behind me and tottered uneasily on to the street, blinking in the light, although the day was grey. We'd ended up at Neil's with wine and a bottle of vodka, not drifting into sleep until at least 4.00 a.m. The weekend had loosened Neil's tongue and he told me things about himself I'd never known. Things I don't really need to know. But he'd been quite funny, almost like I remember him before, and I had been happy to sit and listen, even when the orange juice had run out and we were drinking the vodka with tap water, or eventually straight from the bottle.

He told me that originally, before he'd met his partner Karen – the trick cyclist, that is – he'd been bisexual. And a funny story about himself in the back end of a pantomime cow in Southend in 1977 which featured a knight of the theatre in it somewhere. It had stopped the buzzing in my ears for an hour or so.

There were about fifteen people at the West End Lane bus stop and I joined them with my jacket collar turned up, hoping that nobody in the business would be heading for Soho this early in the morning and clock me in my current dishevelled state. Hardly a good advertisement for Mullin and Ketts, nor indeed for those in the representational field in general.

I began to get nervous. The time was ticking noisily by, the drumming noise was growing. I needed a distraction. A cab came round Dunlever Road with its yellow 'For Hire' light shining invitingly.

I hailed it, feeling like a heel, leaving them all standing there in the cold. Guiltily, I acted looking at my watch again as I got in, so as to deflect their imagined evil thoughts towards me, and slumped back into the seat.

'Women. Huh. They axe for money, they say it's for the children, but I tell you, how much goes to the children, eh? You see?'

'Well, it's very hard for women these days, you know,' I replied, glad for the internal wash of sounds to stop.

'First she take you, know what I mean? And then it's your wallet. You end up with nothing. I tell all men in my cab now, never get married.'

'But it's fair enough for the man to share in bringing up his children, isn't it?' I shouted back over the traffic noise.

'I tell you. The Child Support Agency, man, it worse than the poll tax, man. The money don't go to the woman, it go to the Government. They take all. All.'

'Yes,' I shouted. 'Yes, you're probably right.'

'I tell you this advice: go to prostitutes. It's cheaper in the long run and it's more convenient.'

The cabbie let out a brassy and wheezy laugh, repeating 'more convenient' several times and flashing his gold teeth in the rear-view mirror. It turned out he had thirteen grandchildren to help support, and a fancy woman he saw once a month.

'I tell you, my wife, she got no complaints, as long as I don't put her money down.' He laughed again.

We parted quite jovially and I had spent the last tenner from my wallet. I'd have to go to a cashpoint later on, but right now I needed a full valet service before the women arrived.

And then, a rather dated comedy sketch happened.

The taxi had dropped me at the junction of Wardour and

Meard. I clonked up the crooked stairs, bursting for a piss and aching for a coffee, or three. I undid the double lock and swung the door . . . and . . . I'd come to the wrong office. It's the oldest gag in the book, isn't it? From Alan Bennett's 'Visiting T.E. Lawrence' monologue, to Noel Edmonds' *House Party*. Even Jeremy Planter has used it on at least two occasions: build up a sketch with jokes and misunderstandings, then tag it with the 'You've come to the wrong house, mate, you want number twenty-seven over the road' routine. Often used in Walter Matthau movies about infidelity in the 1960s, as a matter of fact.

In front of me were three large empty rooms with – apart from one computer – empty tables and desks in them. I checked the keys, stupid, they had opened the door for me, for crying out loud. A fourth desk, through a glass-partition door, still had phones and answerphones and in-trays and out-trays, and framed posters lined the walls in there, but in the main rooms even the corkboards were bare. Silence. Total silence. The lack of noise rang hard in my head. The walls were dirty white without anything on them. The place was bare, like a newly converted flat for sale, but there was no estate agent with me now. The red light on the answerphone on the fourth desk blipped silently with messages. I counted them. Eighteen blips. I let out a short laugh involuntarily and pulled aside the curtain to the kitchen-ette. It was still a cluttered shambles in there. The camp bed roughly folded against the wall where I had left it on Friday evening, the coffee cups unwashed up, the sugar-spill still stuck to the drainer. This was Mullin and Ketts but with the innards ripped out. The main rooms seemed much larger and airier now empty. Had we really had this much space? It had always felt so cramped, so cosy. I walked through the glass-partition door to where the fourth table with the answerphone was. This was my office. Nothing in here had been removed. My room seemed inappropriately cluttered, its reassuring homeliness like a night-watchman's den at a loft art gallery.

What little sunlight there was filled the other three bare rooms and filtered through the glass partition to my desk. On my desk was a bulging envelope with my name on it. My full name. Not just Guy, but Guy Richard Mullin, and the date. It was the only foreign object. I picked it up and went to the kitchenette to put on the kettle. The mini-sofa was still there in the main room but the magazines were gone from the coffee table. Almost all of the box files were gone from the shelves. The up-to-date *Spotlight* casting directories were gone. The piles of hopeful ten-by-eight photographs were gone, the Z-cards from the corkboard, two of the computers and the year planner on Tilda's wall were all gone. In Naomi's room, the grey metal filing cabinets were empty, the sounds I made opening empty drawers reverberated off the walls slightly. My God, the carpet was filthy! We hadn't realized with all our stuff in, but now grey and brown speckles drew the eye embarrassingly to the floor, and around Tania's desk a scuffed and grizzly patch where Cleopatra had spent her days sitting patiently waiting to be walked. I opened the letter.

'All further correspondence to be referred to Ketts Stanton-Walker, 191 Regent Street . . .' fax, phone, e-mail, etc.

Headed note paper already, my dears. Ketts Stanton-Walker and a rather fetching logo, with the K bigger than the S-W.

At the bottom of the page, in small print, the registered office – a firm of accountants I had never heard of – and a list of directors: Naomi Ketts, Tilda Bonelli and Arabella Stanton-Walker. So, Naomi had found someone to buy her out at last, someone with money. Arabella Stanton-Walker. Jeremy Planter's new bedfellow. A past-her-sell-by-date hoofer who had shagged the leading man and bought his agency with money saved, or money from Daddy in Surrey more like.

With my coffee, I sat down on the sofa and smiled. That involuntary nervous mirth common in the face of sudden disaster. Surprise is not an actual feeling, it's more like an absence of feeling. Or had I known all along that this would happen, omitting to acknowledge the signs until now? I could not concentrate on the rest of the large letter. I scanned it, looking for the word 'sorry', a note even, anything personal. But it contained only legal details and contractual bumf. I shrugged and let it fall to the floor. 'Twas ever thus. The hot-water system rumbled into action. Pipes a couple of floors below gurgled. It was quite a pleasant sound. In fact, I felt OK. It would take a few days to sort out the details, the lease, the photocopier, which clients were gone – Jeremy Planter, obviously – but it was OK, honestly it was. My breathing was surprisingly steady. I rang my mother on the cordless. She always took at least ten rings to answer.

Twelve years. Twelve years I've known that Ketts woman. No, fifteen if you count before we started the company. Fifteen years I've seen that woman every day, well, virtually every day. I've been through all her moods with her, her weight loss, her weight gain, her fucking hopeless relationships, on and on about her fucking relationships. I've been drunk with her on countless occasions at do's and even at don'ts. I must have spent more time on the phone to her – any time, day or night, she'd ring – than I've had conversations with everyone else put together, certainly more than I've spent having sex; she always would choose the worst moments to ring. And never, as far as I can remember, a 'How are you?' or an 'Is this a good time to call?' Always straight down to business, always the next thing, always 'Guy, I hear they're casting a new detective series at Yorkshire and there's a part which would be good for Peter or Mary or Solomon or Tunde, and Guy, you know Theresa Undrell, don't you, she's casting, can you get her to see Tunde?' Never an apology, never a break, never a let-up. Always the pink jacket, or the horrible sky-blue suit, or the new shiny shoes, or the 'How do you like my hair, I'm trying to look like Michelle Pfeiffer this week.' I've seen Naomi make mincemeat of lesser folk – several trainees have resigned in tears – and I thought I was OK, I was special, I thought I could handle her. When people complained about her overbearing, insensitive nature, or some slight she had inflicted on them I would defend her: 'That's Naomi, I'm afraid. What you see is what you get,' I'd say, or, 'Yes, she's not exactly easy, is she? But she is good.' Or simply, with a knowing smile, 'That's Ketts for you.' She is good. That's the trouble, she's really good, but that's all she is. She's a machine. She must have realized some time ago that I was turning into a liability. She must have been thinking of this for months. And then seen her opportunity when Jeremy got shacked up with that bimbo. I wonder how long. She must've known about Arabella Stanton-shit-Walker all the time. Two years? Since Grace's ear infections at least. And there's me, like some patsy, some complete jerk-off, some stupid, gullible old crystal-gazing hippy-chick, trying to be nice, trying to make everyone happy, to make everyone feel

147

good. Ruthlessness, that's an attractive quality, isn't it? Bugger it, if I was a client, I'd rather have Naomi Ketts represent me than me. I have to admit it. Damn. You don't want someone kind looking after you, do you now? You want somone ruthless, someone with no conscience, someone who can fight off all the other predators, and fight dirty for you if necessary. Niceness, kindness, what's the point? Naomi Ketts would make a good daddy.

My mother's phone was still ringing. Maybe she wasn't in or wasn't up yet. I hung up, but feverishly tried the number again in case she'd been just about to pick it up, or I'd misdialled. It carried on ringing.

I suppose it's the same with children. It's all very well, isn't it, having cuddlesome, generous, warm-hearted, caring, liberal parents, but what if big monsters come and eat them up? You want to feel safe. You want to know your parents can look after themselves first, don't you? You want to know they can see off the opposition, by whatever means. Then if they give you a bit of attention on top of that, well, it's a bonus, isn't it? I suppose that's why Liz is interested in someone like Bob Henderson, BSCI FTT or whatever fucking letters he's got after his fucking name. He fights to win. Like Naomi. He'll lie, cheat, steal, anything, but he'll win. Naomi should've been in the legal profession, it would have suited her. Skunks. And Liz probably knew exactly what she was doing. She was right to drop me. Little old fat old Guy, faffing about like an auntie trying to get everything right, trying to do all the right things, to have everything in order. That's a servile mentality, that is. Just like my dad. Over-reaching myself, unable to see what's going on right in front of my eyes. Jollying along on my merry jaunt, singing a pretty song, anything to keep me from realizing what a total no-hope, pathetic little turdy little never-has-been wanker I am. Any song will do, any bit of business, any sound in the brain, so long as it keeps the mind from hearing that empty ring of disappointment.

I was looking at my chubby failure of a face in the tiny pink plastic mirror in the kitchenette now with a penetrating loathing. I hung up the phone again. If I felt like this, what chance did Grace have? I'm supposed to set an example, to be the man, the guy, the one she looks to, the one she listens to, the one they all look to, the one they all listen to. The phone rang.

'Guy?' It was my mother. 'What's going on? It's early in the morning, I was asleep.'

'Sorry, Mum. How did you know it was me?'

'I did 1471.'

'Have you looked at the short list of flats I sent you?' She obviously hadn't. I didn't want to drag her around hundreds of unsuitable flats. I wanted her to see one of those photos on the estate agents' details and fall in love with it and then let me make all the arrangements without getting in the way or interfering. Our conversation stalled and she started on at me about Grace.

'You never bring her round to see me, Guy.'

'Well, it's difficult, you know.'

'What about Liz? She never phones me. What does she do all day? She could bring her round and I'd be happy to look after her if Liz wanted to go shopping or something.'

'It's a long way, Mum. It'd take her longer to come to you and then all the way out and back. Why don't you ever come over to us to see her?' I knew she wouldn't, so there was no harm in suggesting it. She had no inkling of my sleeping in the office. I hadn't wanted to upset her, knowing that in the end she would advise and tut-tut her way to controlling everything.

'Oh, you know I can't do that, Guy. I wouldn't want to feel like the proverbial interfering mother-in-law. I don't want to invade another woman's home, and besides, there's nowhere to park.'

It's funny that no matter how much you pay for it, you DIY it, you share in the bin-emptying of it and the fridge-filling, even if you do a fair share of housework, you sleep in it and you eat in it, as far as your mum is concerned, it's still another woman's home. It's still not yours.

'OK, Mum,' I said. 'But you must come round for tea sometime, we'd love to see you, and let me know what you think of the flats I've sent you. The one with the small kitchen has a great view over Bishop's Park and you'd be so much nearer us. You could walk, you could see Grace every day. And you'd be much nearer Tony too, which is a sort of mixed blessing, I'll grant.'

I knew the idea of walking anywhere would put her off, but what the hell. I just wanted her at least to look at the details. Rather pointless persuading her to come and live near Grace when I wasn't even there myself. But I did want to have her sorted out. One less thing to worry about. We said goodbye. She hung up and I sat, listening to the dialling tone. It was better than the unbearable deafening silence, which would hurt my ears if I were to put the receiver back in its cradle. I felt a strong desire to speak to Grace, so I rang home – if you can call it such.

Liz had changed the outgoing message on our answerphone. Instead of my voice there, there was now hers, speaking in a very clipped and measured way. 'You've reached, etc., and for work enquiries for Liz Garnet, please call . . .' She sounded overly formal. I remembered when we'd first got that answerphone, second-hand from Mullin and Ketts, of course, and she'd claimed to be unable to work out how to use it, so I'd had to do it while she giggled in the background.

There were seven short bleeps before the long one, and it was Monday morning so she wasn't picking up her messages. Maybe she had spent the weekend at Bob Henderson's, maybe she had taken Grace with her, maybe Grace called Bob 'Daddy' now. Maybe Bob Henderson had connections with a paedophile ring in Belgium and Grace was even now in a crate in the Channel Tunnel.

'Hello, it's Dad here,' I said on to the machine, with as much of a jovial lilt as I could muster. 'Just ringing up to see how you are and I'll see you in a few days.' And then, lowering my voice to adult tones in order to address Liz, 'I could pick her up from nursery on Wednesday and drop her off, or would you like me to put her to bed at home? Just tell me which suits you better. Please ring me back to confirm.'

Then the silence again, banging around in the vaulting emptiness of Mullin and Ketts, Meard Street, the painful silence again. Or rather, just Mullin now. I would have to arrange new notepaper. The 'Ketts' had flown and was now in Regent Street. I looked at my watch: 8.55. They probably wouldn't be in yet. I could go round there and piss through their letterbox, or post them a turd. I could ring the Ketts Stanton-Walker number and leave obscene messages on the answerphone. I could burst in

150

after ten o'clock and shout at them a lot and get thrown out by the police. I could get my lawyers to threaten them with injunctions. I could hire hit men to go round and fell them all with guns with silencers on: shtip, shtip, sthip.

I thought of the 'How Men Need to Change' weekend. If only all this had happened on Friday. I would have had something to scream about in the large hall. Something to talk about in the circle with our eyes closed. I remembered the confession of the pervy guy and unwillingly put Liz into his violent gang-rape fantasy. When it came to the bit where he dragged her face down across the gravel path, unwillingly again, I got an erection. My phone rang, thank God. I snapped it out of its cradle.

'Hello.'

'Oh, hello, Guy, it's you. I wasn't expecting a person. You're in early.' It was Susan Planter. 'Listen, Guy, I've had a terrible weekend. They're all over me like a rash. I've got three of them outside right now. They clicked away when I took the kids to school and followed us halfway up the road. It's a nightmare. It's like Princess Di, it's ridiculous, I mean, I'm not even wearing a split skirt or anything. I've taken the day off work. I can't face going out of the door again. They keep trying to show me photos of him with that slut to see if they can get a reaction out of me, and the phone hasn't stopped ringing. I don't deserve this, Guy. I don't deserve it.'

I told her how to arrange Call Divert and offered to do it for her.

'And as for that little shit. You said I shouldn't talk to any of them, but he's been blabbing his mouth off to anyone who cares to ask. The little shit, the bastard. How could he?'

Evidently Jeremy had been splashed all over the weekend tabloids attending some awards ceremony with Arabella in a backless, low-cut evening gown. I hadn't read a paper since Thursday, too busy workshopping my masculinity. So Arabella Stanton-Walker had had a busy weekend. A flashy celeb do on the Friday night and then a get-in at her spanking-new Regent Street office on Saturday, although, no doubt, she would have got her people to do anything which required heavy lifting. Like my client files, for example.

151

'I feel like telling the first one to offer me any serious money that Jeremy's got a very small penis, Guy, I really do. I know it's wrong but I've got to do something. I can't handle this. He's a total shit. He's a . . .'

She was lost for words and quite hysterical on the end of the line. It sounded as if she'd dropped the phone, and from further away. I heard a crash and a shout. She picked up the receiver again, out of breath.

'Sorry, Guy. I'm just so angry I can't control myself any more.' She was crying now and I envied her the ability. 'I can't cope,' she sobbed, sounding just like Liz used to when Grace had her ear infection. 'Guy, I can't cope.' This time, though, there was no one in the office with me to cover up for.

'I'm not looking after the kids properly, Guy. I just scream at them. Could you help, Guy? Take them off my hands for a bit before I end up hitting them or something. Dave is driving me mad. He keeps asking questions. It's as if he's blaming me, and, and I can't give him what he needs, Guy, because I look in his eyes and all I can see is that shit Jeremy, and I hate him. I hate my own child, Guy. It's not his fault but I hate him and he can see it. I'm losing him too, Guy.' She subsided into inarticulate snivels.

The post arrived with a patter on the floor. There was a lot of it. The young runner from the film company below very kindly sorts it for the whole building and delivers it. He'll sometimes nip out and get you a sandwich too if he's got nothing else to do. Very keen and probably unpaid. Should go far. I'm always nice to him. May end up running the BFI or something.

I was still cordless, so I walked across and picked up the mail while murmuring sympathetically to the distraught Susan. I advised her again not to talk and not to accept money from the gutter, but my words were hollow. I couldn't really convince myself, let alone her.

I offered to pick up Dave and Polly from school and take them to a McDonald's. I told her that if she really did want to sell a story, then I'd do the negotiating for her, but that she should think about it for a while first. It was the least I could do. She was calming down now and able to apologize and laugh through the sniffing.

'I'm sorry to do this to you, Guy, I'm so sorry. I feel ridiculous.'

'That's OK. Really. It's what I'm here for,' I said, starting on the mail with the phone crooked in my shoulder: three requests for representation, with drama-school CVs and ten-by-eights. An unpaid invoice from the auditors for Tania to deal with, if she was still working for me, of course. And then a strangely shaped envelope, longer than square, with the documents inside folded lengthways instead of across, making them hard to flatten on the desk.

'You've just got to get through to the end of this school term,' I said to Susan down the phone. The summer holiday was nearly on us. 'It's only a week or so and then you could go away with the kids, get away, let the dust settle. Well, let the shit settle. It's worse than dust, I know.'

The oblong letter was a series of papers and documents, paper-clipped and stapled, with an introductory letter loose on the top from the solicitors Henderson Giggs. It was signed not by Bob himself, but by a senior partner, Ralph Tropier-Potts. Down the side of the front page was printed, in luscious purply-blue: 'Henderson Giggs, Copyright Litigation, Contract and Investment Law', and the registered office – another firm of accountants of whom I'd never heard.

I really must think about redesigning the Mullin and Ketts notepaper, sooner rather than later. Apart from just excising the Ketts, I mean. The designs on these two letters today were far more modern and dynamic. It was something I hadn't thought about for years. Now I looked at it, our M and K logo looked, well, too eighties.

I told Susan that I knew of a very nice hotel in Kent which took children and which would be totally discreet and might give her the chance to get a break and get the unwanted eyes of the media off her. She said she wouldn't be able to take the time off work. I told her she had to. I reminded her to ring Dave and Polly's school to warn them that it would be me picking the kids up today.

Ralph Tropier-Potts had obviously had several conversations with Liz, unless he had been briefed by lover-boy Bob. The letter advised me that Liz was now represented by Henderson

Giggs and that I should appoint a solicitor at my earliest possible convenience. The rest of the package contained a Standard Costs agreement for me to sign — that I would pay Henderson Giggs' fees since Liz had no income — and a petition for divorce on the grounds of my unreasonable behaviour.

In the furniture-smashing rows there had been a few slaps and kicks. Difficult now to say who had inflicted more on the other, quantity-wise. Impossible to say, of course, who started it. No blood ever, no bruises other than the emotional kind. I did concuss myself mildly once banging my head against the bedroom wall, and walked around for a few days feeling sorry for myself. She had been frightened by that, I know, but on the whole, the unreasonableness of our behaviour had been mutual, I would say. In fact, unfathomable would be a more accurate description. Reason for separation m'lud: totally incomprehensible behaviour all round.

The bulkiest document was a Child Proceedings Order which had been filled out already and was supposed to relate to Grace, although the details, from what I could ascertain while conducting a phone call, seemed to bear very little relation to reality.

I looked through the partition at the vacant state where once had been many busy women. Nothing seemed to have much to do with reality today. I wanted to ask Susan's advice about solicitors, since she was one, albeit of the local conveyancing kind, but now was obviously not the time. For instance, was it normal for a contract and investment lawyer to be dealing with a matrimonial issue. Was that allowed?

'Thank you, Guy. Thanks so much for all this.' Susan started to wind up our conversation.

'Give my love to Liz and little Grace. I'm sorry to lose it just then. I'm sure I'll be all right in a while and I'll see you at about six or seven then. I'd offer to make you dinner but we don't want Liz thinking I'm taking you away from her.'

The phone would start ringing for real in a while. I wondered how many lines they'd left me. I threw open the window and took some deep breaths. It felt strangely exciting to be alive. The ringing in my ears had stopped. I didn't have the time for it.

Mid-morning the buzzer went.

I checked who it was through the window. I didn't want

anyone important seeing the depletion of my kingdom. I'd had a moderately successful couple of hours trying to find out, by subtle means or foul, who I might still represent, and it looked as if they were going to be a pretty sad and small bunch. Most of my earners had already been approached and sloped across to Naomi and Arabella's side of Soho.

Kemble Stenner was standing in the street carrying a modelling portfolio. She buzzed again, I let her up.

'God! I hate men.' She came in and threw herself on to the mini-sofa, lighting a Marlboro. She was wearing a minuscule wraparound skirt and a tight midriff-revealing top. It was as if, petite as she was, her clothes had all shrunk in the wash. Nothing joined anything else. At the top of her skinny thighs, hold-me-up stockings stopped an inch and a half short of her skirt hem. Her hair was backcomb-frazzled and the amount of make-up she had on made her look like a piece of jailbait.

'You going for a casting?' I asked, putting the kettle on.

'Just been,' she spat. 'For some incredibly interesting new Japanese beer promotion video.'

'Did you get it?'

'Yeeeeeeees. Of course.' She sighed. 'Easy. Bit of lippie, bit of . . .' She acted out a pouting, dumb sex kitten, wiggling her shoulders and fluttering her eyelashes. She did it very well. I put it immediately on my mental shelf of erotic images to be enjoyed later, and made her a coffee without asking if she wanted one.

'Thanks, doll,' she said and slumped back on the mini-sofa. The aggression she had entered with was subsiding now. I took one of her cigarettes without asking.

'Help yourself,' she said, as I lit it, and then, 'Ooo hoo hoo. What's happened here, then? They all done a runner on you?' She looked around the empty room. Our voices had echoes.

'Yup,' I said.

'Fuuuuuuck,' she said, smiling. I was smiling too. I don't know why.

'You got anybody left? I mean, is there any point in my being here or are you an ex-agent now?'

'Oh, I've got a few.'

'What about Doug Handom? He gone with them?'

'Actually, no. I don't think so,' I said. 'He's coming over from

LA this week.' Doug's message had been one of the eighteen on my machine.

'You've *got* to introduce me to him. I want to shag him so much. I think he's gorgeous. I want to have his babies.'

'Yes, he is, isn't he,' I said.

'So do all my friends.'

'Yes, most women feel like that about Doug,' I said.

'Did you know this was going to happen? I mean, was it planned?'

'Nope. Well, they must have planned it but they somehow forgot to tell me. That must have been part of the plan.'

'God. The bitches!' she said, laughing at the sheer exhilaration of the disaster.

'Yup,' I said. 'They're all down at Regent Street now.'

For a moment she looked like a little old lady, heaped there on my sofa, her bony knees sticking up, her shoulders caved in, waving a cigarette in the air. Child actor, you see, always a mixture of the immature and the ancient. Cynical in the voice and eyes, pre-pubescent in the heart. She must have had several years in her early teens of being the sexy one. The one the boys hit on while her non-professional sisters and friends looked on in envy and self-crushing admiration. Learning too early how to control the overactive hormones and hence behaviour of every acne'd male who came within a ten-yard radius of her. This would have been her first taste of power. Her best grade at GCSE. How unfair that she had been too young to do anything with it, other than practise on older and more predatory men now she was in her twenties. Learning enough of grown-up behaviour and dress sense to get herself accepted way out of her depth in the business world, where sexuality is currency.

'So. Do you want a fuck?' she said, stubbing out her cigarette on the coffee table. 'I'm meeting a girlfriend at twelve, so we've got time.'

'Well, I . . .' I began.

'Yeah, I know you've got a lot of work to do, but you must be shattered, you look really rough. It'd do you good, get rid of some of that pent-up anger.'

She got up and came over to where I was sitting, and straddled my lap, making her skirt rise even further up her thighs, if that were possible. I had to clear my coffee cup out of the way and put it on the floor behind me. As my arm became free, she took hold of my wrist and put my hand down between her legs.

'Just because it's a mercy fuck doesn't mean I'm not wet.' She was wet. I didn't know how I felt about being given a mercy fuck at eleven o'clock in the morning by a twenty-two-year old with the scratchy voice of a pensioner. The phone rang. I let the answerphone take it. It was Tania.

'Guy. I've just heard and I wanted to let you know that I didn't know anything about it. I promise.' She sounded distressed. Cleopatra barked in the background. 'If you're there, Guy, pick up the phone, please. They've asked me to go and work there now. I don't know what to do. I don't know if I'll have time to do both. Are you there, Guy?'

She waited a few more seconds and then, asking me to call her back, she rang off.

Kemble was rubbing herself against my hand now, so I left it there. She lifted up her top and started to squeeze her little girl's nipples. 'You don't have to kiss me if you don't want,' she said. 'You can close your eyes and imagine I'm Michelle Pfeiffer if you like.' I didn't feel like closing my eyes and I'm not that mad on Michelle Pfeiffer anyway, as it happens. I tried to think for a moment if there was anyone else, the vision of whom would drive me wild with passion. But, like the woman on my lap, in the end they're all just actresses in one shape or form. In any case, if it came to erotic fantasy, you couldn't do much better than Kemble Stenner sitting on your lap. But somehow the reality of it was not doing the trick. All right, I had a mild erection, yes, but it didn't pulse with any particular need for fulfilment. It was merely reacting to stimuli. Merely obliging, doing the right thing.

I thought of all the times with Liz, when I had wanted sex and she hadn't. I thought about Hendo and whether he was any good at it. Well, he must be, he must know the right things to do. She'd probably never had to bark instructions at him. With shame, I pictured him fucking her hard, doggie-style, up against the filing cabinets I could see over Kemble's shoulder.

'Oh, now, that's more like it,' said Kemble, smiling wickedly at me. 'Yes.' She moved her hands to my trousers and squeezed my cock through the corduroy.

It felt bad, but the idea of Robert Henderson, Copyright and Investment Litigator, roughing up my wife across the filing cabinet was stimulating the manufacture of semen in my scrotum more than the gyrations or the sight of the very real girl on my lap.

We did use a condom. I kept my shirt and jacket on. Afterwards, there was no hug.

'You all right, gorgeous?' she said. 'You look like you're miles away.'

'Sorry,' I said. 'I was.'

From her bag, she took a pair of jeans and some clean knickers. I sat, unmoving, where I was and smoked her last Marlboro Light while she changed.

'Still want to represent me, then? Or have you given up that idea? Are you giving up the business?'

'I'll represent you,' I said. 'I said I would.'

'And introduce me to Doug Handom, remember?'

'Yes, I can do that if you like.'

She gave me a small kiss on the cheek and took the lit cigarette off me.

'I like you,' she said. And left.

Only parents of children under eighteen know what the Danger Zone is, because it only started in 1991 and children over twelve aren't allowed in. It's pretty good value and it has its own burger and chips bar on site. And if you can stand the fluorescent light, bright-green plastic furniture and constant shrieking of children and blowing of whistles, you can sit and read the paper for three-quarters of an hour while your charges disappear into a chaotic maze of rope bridges and climbing tunnels and sporty youths in matching yellow sweatshirts supervise the letting-off of steam. Despite the aggressive titles of the games there – Killer Fox, Ultimate Challenge, Total Destruction – there are virtually no accidents, no broken teeth, bloodied noses or twisted necks, and tears there are also surprisingly rare. Zombified mums and dads sit around holding discarded sweaty zip-tops, unable to converse with each other over the noise. Like sitting in the middle of a congregating throng of soon-to-migrate birds.

I looked at my watch for what must have been the sixth time. We could go as soon as I could get Dave and Polly in the same place for long enough to do up their shoes. Dave, his cheeks red and his hair hot from running around, was in a surly and disobedient mood.

'I think it's really stupid in Killer Fox, because I'll never be able to run faster than a grown-up, right? So if it was real I'd always get caught.'

'Silly,' said Polly. 'You don't have to run faster than a grown-up if it was real. You just have to run faster than me. The fox would just stop and gobble up whichever one he catched first.'

There we have it, the entire theory of natural selection from the mouth of an eight-year-old. Survival of the most competitive within the species so that we can all play our part in the dog-eat-dog world. Like show-biz. Like marriage. Dave refused to put on his jacket.

'You're not my dad,' he said, just to make sure I didn't feel in any way comfortable.

The hordes of tabloid midges which Susan had described to me over the phone were no longer outside the Planter residence in Chiswick. There was, however, one lonely little hack, pacing up and down in a cheap suit. He must have kicked himself, when I arrived with the children, that his photographer wasn't with him. Mind you, I don't exactly look like hunky new toyboy material. As we approached the front gate he scampered along beside us, asking if I would like to comment, or find out if Susan would like to comment, on the crumpled snapshot in his paw which showed Jeremy with a woman – not Arabella – which could have been snatched on a telescopic at any time in the past five years. I steered the children to the front door and rang the bell. I could have given the little junior journo a story by using the key which I still had in my pocket, but I don't think I could have thought of a suitable explanation for Dave of my having the key to his front door.

'I'm sorry about this,' whined the novice gutter rat, 'but I'm only doing my job, and she is blonde.' Poor little kitten. Sent by his big bad editor to cover a non-event in Chiswick because it might afford the opportunity of printing a picture of a woman who happened to have fair hair. I felt sorry for him, all on his lonesome, no back-up. His colleagues had all obviously been called away to bigger coups abounding with boobs and bubbly.

Susan opened the door to us a few inches and we slid indoors. She was in a charred state, quite literally. My assessment of the quality of the wiring at the Planters' had been correct, and a shoddy connection under the upstairs floorboards outside her bedroom had evidently heated up enough to smoulder on to one of the joists, causing a small fire. She'd put it out with some dead flower water about an hour ago, but the place and Susan smelt smoky. She was wearing dark glasses and was over-cranked, slightly shaky.

Upstairs there were a couple of floorboards blackened, still glistening wet, and that was all. What would have come in handy now would have been my inheritance. That 5 ml cable my father left me in his work cupboard. I did what I could to make the place safe for the night, isolating the downstairs so that Susan could stick Dave and Polly in front of a video until a candlelit bedtime. She'd need to have the house looked over properly as soon as possible.

'You're such a good man,' she said as she watched me stack the burnt floorboards neatly behind the door in the bathroom. 'I wish I'd chosen someone sensible like you. Liz is lucky. But I always went for the dodgy ones, always made the foolish choices.'

It's not that much fun being someone sensible like me. Susan was pissed again – Vera Vodka this time – not ugly pissed, but enough to feel like expressing her feelings rather than experiencing them.

'But that's what you get, isn't it, if you go for the dangerous, exciting, sexy ones. God, I'm such an idiot.' She was getting maudlin. Whoever she got in to rewire would have to chase the cables right back to the consumer unit, and re-earth everything under the sinks in the kitchen and bathrooms.

'I could have seen this coming really. What a stupid girl I've been. I knew what he was like, why couldn't I see it? I must have been closing my eyes to the obvious. I must have known all along, somewhere, I just didn't want to admit it to myself.' She was sniffing now. I wrote her a list of points to make to the electrician – better separation between lighting and telephone circuit, plastic deadeners at all junction boxes, that sort of thing — and put my jacket back on.

'I should have just had a few weeks of amazing sex with the toerag and then moved on. I always go and fall for the wrong man.' I was working fast now to leave. I felt invaded by her, and in a strange way it was as if what she was saying was an attack against my father. Not that I'm macho-proud of him or anything like that, far from it — he was, as I have said, on the greyer side of dull — but her words seemed to gnaw at my memory of him. I washed my hands of the underfloor dirt in the kitchen sink.

'That's all Jeremy was good for: sex,' she said, pouring herself another vodka and offering me one this time. I declined — I wanted to go.

'That and earning lots of money, I suppose. He was always good at that, the little shit. I'll fucking sting him there, if he ever wants to see his children again.' She was standing between me and the front door now. 'You can stay the night if you like, Guy,' she said, and stroked my elbow. There was a pleading in her voice and in her eyes. She wanted me to stay with her and make her feel attractive. I'm sure six months previously I would have been flattered, but now I wasn't. Now that the interesting high-earner had flown, she deigned to sex the sensible one, the also-ran. I was hurt. No doubt she'd insist on withdrawal, she wouldn't want my less-than-alpha genes swilling around inside her, and I'm not the kind of guy to have a condom on him at all times. I was glad to reach the insecurity of Soho once again, and ponder on the inadequacy of my own potency.

Whichever way I looked at it, the figures didn't add up. They couldn't. There was the lease on Meard Street. That had another three years to run and cost a serious wodge every quarter. There was the service lease on the photocopier, for crying out loud. Yes, I know those are a rip-off, but we weren't to know at the time.

It looked as if the clients Naomi had left me were going to turn out to be a paltry lot, and there would be weeks of finessing them with meals and drinks to persuade even them, scraggy as they were, not to abandon a sinking ship.

Strictly speaking, the property at Meard Street was not residential, but I probably had a good few months before I got rumbled, so long as I didn't move in a piano and a four-poster bed.

There was the mortgage for Liz, her so-called salary for 'secretarial work'. There were nursery fees and, oh God, big-school fees in September.

I wish I had got Grace into the local state school, but I had been put off by the cheery notices on their announcement board about how to recognize the symptoms of glue-sniffing in the under-tens.

There would be Henderson Giggs bills, plenty of them – God knows how much they would be – and the injustice of paying for the privilege of having some pinstriped villain sue me made my stomach twist with pain. There would be medical bills soon, no doubt: mine.

My mental arithmetic is actually not that brilliant, but the figure £80,000 and the words 'by this November' wafted cheekily into view in my mind's eye, sending shivers of stress through the old nervous system. My heart rate was up and pounding between my ears.

I could go bankrupt. That sounded nice. That sounded like tweety little birds chirruping away in the cherry blossom. Bankruptcy, tra la la la la. No responsibility. I could give up everything – except Grace, of course. I could look after her and Liz'd have to get a job as a check-out girl to support me. I shouldn't have moved out. Why did I move out? I thought it was the right thing to do. The male thing to do. The woman has the baby, after all. She needs a nest for that. By all that's daft, I'm sounding like the inside of a greetings card now.

I sat back from the computer, where I had all the figures laid out on a spreadsheet, and reached for another cigarette, none left. Yes, I was searching the ashtray for a reasonable butt now. That was sensible, darling. When disaster strikes, smoke yourself to death.

Suicide. That was an option. No, not really, not since Grace. Great male role model that would be. When the going gets tough, the tough top themselves. I could run away to Australia – land of Sheilas and soaps – I could go Antipodean, meet some gymnastic surfie girl, work in television and have lots of blond children with perms and pectoral muscles and great teeth. Naaaaaa. Don't fancy that, m'dear.

I had a short session finishing the five or six butts which had any kind of draw on them, and decided that I'd probably have to go downstairs to the all-night cab station where there was a tobacconist's. By that I mean they usually had a few packets of Rothmans for sale. I shut down the computer. There was no point in looking at it all anyway.

Problems come and then they go away again. Doesn't mean they're not coming back. It's like the tide. Who said that? I put my wallet in my jacket pocket and slipped it on, checking my keys. I'll tell you who said that, my bloody dad. My bloody pedantic old boring old git of a father. Sitting in his stupid Pelican 700 series river boat at Windsor, trying to persuade me and Tony to reharness the mooring ropes and learn about buoyancy gradients, instead of running up and down the deck playing Sink the Plastic Bin Bag. 'In comes the tide,' he said, 'and the water can get quite choppy and you can get apprehensive, and then out it goes again and everything's peaceful and you forget about it and think everything's going to be all right for ever, but it won't be. That's why, when things are going well, you have to make your preparations for the storm.' What did he know? The Thames isn't even tidal up at Windsor.

Down in the street, Soho was throbbing. As usual on the pavement outside the Nine Bells, strange-haired people with studs in their leather clothes and studs in their noses were loud-mouthing in the street. We don't go in there. Oh no, honey-child. The Coach and Horses maybe, that's got musoes and chorus folk. Or even the French House, that's poets and trainee intellectuals. But the Nine Bells? I don't think so.

I crossed to the other side of Dean Street and turned into Old Compton. A couple of pale-faced rent boys in nylon zip-tops with greasy hair matted down their acne'd necks passed me, and one of them casually raised his eyebrows at me – a streetwalking sex-shop assistant, 'Do you need any help, sir?' implicit in his subtle acknowledgement. I pressed on. I only came out for a pack of ciggies, dearie.

I bought some matches too so I could have a smoke on the way home. That word is beginning to haunt me. Home. Where the heart is. Or where you left it, at any rate. Suddenly a fight broke out among the crowd in front of the Turnbull. With a real fight, a nasty one, it's always sudden. Not some trade of insults and macho posturing with the protagonists being held back by their mates and a few wild punches. That's a scuffle. With a bit of real upsy-daisy, the nastiness seems to come from nowhere, inflict horrible and permanent damage and fly away again with the unsettling speed of a bat. Then, minutes later, the sirens and the taking of witnesses' stories, if they haven't also flown.

A man was pushed on the ground and two aroused and seriously aggressive soldier types in yellow T-shirts and night-mare boots were kicking him. Not in the stomach. Not in the balls even, but in the head. They got five or six goal-scoring whacks in, whilst his bonce ricocheted on the pavement, and then they ran. This is where the movie-makers have it wrong. The whole thing must have lasted under five seconds. Sam Peckinpah eat your heart out. I was in the Frith Street phone booth dialling 999 for the ambulance, but a dozen others must have been making the same call.

I crossed the road to where the victim was lying in a pool of brain-damage-type blood. He was surrounded now, of course, the danger having subsided.

A couple of women had come out from the pub, Alberto from Leonardo's also. Some others. There was a mild commotion. I hung around, wondering if I could be useful. Passers-by passed by and stared at us. From the shouted remarks, it was apparent that the aggressors were known to several of the folk now involved in the incident. Someone had put their jacket over the white and limp body. Yellow T-shirts, that was all I could remember, not much use in an identity parade. The sirens came. I left.

It's a horrible world. I gave £2 to a homeless and faceless person in a sleeping bag crouched in the doorway of the De Lane Lee dubbing studio – trendy by day, sordid at night – and chucked my ciggie butt in the gutter.

'Looking for trade?' said a sorry-looking old thing as I turned into Meard Street.

'No thank you, madam,' I said. You have to be polite.

Look, I'm not stupid. I know that what my dad told me was probably very good advice, it just wasn't appropriate at the time. If I'd heeded his words, no doubt I could have seen all this coming, I could have known. When we were coasting, I would have checked all the knots that fastened my security. I would have swabbed the decks and peeled potatoes in the galley, but I didn't, OK? And now I was hideously in debt and probably going to have to convince some welfare officer that the office in seedy old Meard Street was a reasonable place to have fortnightly contact with my child.

SIX

THE COUNSELLOR WAS a woman of about fifty-five who lived in Ealing. Her flat where we sat was small and rather carelessly furnished. I remember the smallest details of the hour we spent there, although since then, Liz has disagreed with me on many of them.

'How did it make you feel when your husband left home?' The tone was gentle and coaxing. Liz whisked her head sideways, looked into the middle distance and paused. How did it all make her feel? Well, from the study in anguish on her face, she did not feel relaxed, happy, fulfilled, any of those things. The counsellor waited for Liz's reply with a practised calm which said, 'Take your time to answer this one. We've got forty-five minutes left of this session, but that's OK. And if you only manage to answer this one question, that's also OK. This is the way we do it here.' Funny how in those flaccid pauses where verbal exchange loses its elasticity, the domestic objects in a room take on an inflated significance. There was a clock ticking, obviously. This was a therapy session. It was pale blue and fifties in design. There were photographs of the counsellor's grown-up children in their garden. No doubt not dysfunctional like the rest of us, no doubt each with a clutch of passed exams in their pockets. The chairs and the rug were ragged and old. There was a hole in one arm of the sofa which someone had tried to mend with incorrectly coloured thread. There was a table lamp without a plug, just a wire dangling down past ancient *TV* and *Radio Times* magazines stacked under the side table, one with a photo of Jeremy Planter on the front. All things which you would recognize if you lived here. Things with histories that you would understand. Things which might define 'home' to you. I

166

thought of the objects in Liz and my former home. The unrepaired chair back, the dishevelled sofa, my record collection, now redundant because of CDs, my thermos with the vintage cars on that my mum gave me when I was ten. I can still remember the serial number and date of each car. What makes home? These objects, do they make home? If, as might be happening soon, they were all put in cardboard crates in a storage safe somewhere, would that depot temporarily be my home? Or the shell of the house, the walls, the floor and roof? Does the spirit of the thing reside in the actual location? It was a nice enough house, particularly the back room, and I'd done a lot of work on it myself. Was that investment of time what made it home? Where was home? Wherever I lay my hat, wherever I lay my wife. Wherever she lays whoever.

Liz sniffled a bit. The counsellor leaned forward and gently pushed the box of Kleenex across the low table towards her. 'New, Man-Size Kleenex!' read the label on the top. 'Like a man, just as much strength, but now with added sensitivity!' Not insisting, merely suggesting that it might be OK to cry, that tissues were available, appropriate. Homely reassurance was on hand. A shiver went through me. To reach Liz, the box of tissues and what they symbolized had been pushed further away from me across the table. She was being offered home. In the aching silence, I wanted to ask, 'Where is this home which I have left? Is it something exclusively Liz's? Does she carry it with her wherever she goes like a tortoise and its shell?' And when she's rolled over and helpless with her Bob, is she at home?

I coughed, clearing my throat as if to speak. The counsellor's eyes darted across to mine. 'Don't blow it now', they said to me, 'it's not your turn.' Liz looked deeper into the pattern on the ragged carpet and exhaled in a big sigh. She took a Man-Size Kleenex from the box, and poked at her nose with it. She too was screaming at me in the silence: 'It's not your turn. You agreed to come here, now you must wait.'

I tried not to speak, but rather to extract myself from the moment. I did not leave home. I coughed again. I said it. 'I did not leave home.' Both women looked at me exasperated, as if to say, 'How could you?'

'Please', said the counsellor. 'I was asking Liz. You can speak later.'

'You asked her how it made her feel when I left home,' I said, 'but I didn't leave home, I went to sleep in the office because we were getting on so badly, arguing in front of Grace, you know, and now she's changed the locks.'

'I think you both know what I meant,' said the counsellor. Liz was nodding now, looking at me and biting her trembling lip.

'Hurt . . . lonely . . . abandoned . . . frightened,' she said, as if she'd been practising. You're not on Oprah Winfrey now, love, I wanted to say.

'I'm just trying to help you two to decide what direction you're going in,' said the counsellor. 'I don't want to carry this on until Christmas. I'll give you three, maybe four sessions maximum, but beyond that, there's truthfully not all that much I can do for you.'

Maybe the counsellor wasn't so bad after all. I piped down in order to let her do her stuff. We'd already covered the subject of Bobbie Henderson, and now it seemed to be closed. Liz had said she'd rather not talk about it, that it had nothing to do with her and me and Grace, that it was a separate issue. When I mentioned his Porsche, parked under our elm tree, Liz accused me of spying on her, and the counsellor seemed to consent to this interpretation by her silence.

'And how about Grace?' she said to Liz, emphasizing the word 'about'. 'How are you coping with her? How is she taking all this?'

'She's driving me mad,' said Liz. 'She won't do anything I tell her and I just lie there at night worrying about her. On my own.' The counsellor was buying all this 'on my own' stuff.

'It *is* frightening, just you and a child on your own, isn't it?'

'She's had glue ear again and she's been on antibiotics, and last time they didn't work and the doctor seemed worried that she might end up going deaf.'

'How is she now?'

'Well, she's been better this week but she just seems to want to make noise all the time just to annoy me. She'll turn up the telly full volume and laugh at me or bang on her drum, blow on her mouth organ, anything. She knows it gets on my nerves. It's like she's trying to push me over the edge, to punish me. Yesterday she worked out how to turn on the radio alarm clock, and she thought it was funny.' It did sound quite funny to me.

Liz sniffed and looked up tentatively with the faintest curl of a genuine smile. Almost as if she was asking my permission to smile at me. I smiled back, and for a moment we caught each other's eyes like it was the first time. I was looking deep down into her and she could see right into me, into my fear. The pleading quality was there in her eyes. She snorted a laugh, full of saliva, and I started to wet my cheeks. For a second I could remember what had been there between us originally. It was too much. I turned away. I didn't reach for the Man-Size Kleenex. Man-Size they might be, but not Man-Style. I blinked it all away. Bob Henderson wouldn't blub. The counsellor let us share this moment. She wasn't bad at all, come to think of it, and only £30.

'And how do you feel about leaving Grace with her father? Does that feel safe?' she asked Liz. My pulse quickened and my skin prickled, but I held myself back. Once again, I thought, I was being sentenced without trial. Once again judged by the behaviour of others, the Jeremy Planters and the Doug Handoms. It must be like this for women when they try to get promotion to the board.

'Oh, he's very good with her. She's always loved her daddy.' Well, thank you, Liz. Decent of you to admit it.

'And if it was possible, would it be all right for her to stay with her daddy every now and again to give you a rest?'

Malcolm Viner was right. I had no say here. Only that which was granted me by the authority of the unwritten law of motherhood. No wonder Grace was playing up. Wouldn't you? You are born into an incomprehensible confusion of foreign objects and there are two of them who seem to be in charge, who seem to be more important than the others in terms of whether you get fed, whether you can stick your fingers in plug sockets, whether bedtime means you go to sleep or can get away with another game of pyjama-tigers.

Then, it seems, the second, slightly less useful one has to go away to be shot at in a war, or just pops out for a paper and a pack of ciggies, never to return, or goes and dies of any one of the major six diseases as men tend to, or just runs out of cash or gets bored or . . . What's going on here? you must think. What are the rules? Am I in charge now? Have I killed him? Have I got Mum all to myself now? Aren't I a little young for that? I think I'll get a rash, that'll teach them, or have a nasty ear infection.

'It's not very savoury, where I'm living at the moment,' I said. 'But there is plenty of room. My partners have all buggered off down to Regent Street.'

'How about a trial weekend, and if that works, then every other weekend for the meantime, until you can see more clearly how things will turn out between the two of you?' said the counsellor. In the pause, whilst Liz thought about this, the pale-blue clock ticked lethargically onwards.

'Mmmmm,' Liz agreed, looking down into her lap. 'Maybe an afternoon, but I couldn't let her stay the night.' I still don't understand why, even with an arbiter present, it was still Liz's call. Nevertheless, with two lots of rent, an £80,000 overhang and a business down the toilet, an afternoon with my kid was about all I could afford. I bought into it. The date for an afternoon contact was set.

The large brown woman didn't recognize me, or wasn't going to show it anyway, why should she? I had just been a half-hour punter to her, a trick. She was differently turned out today, the fake lashes and nails were gone. But I recognized her of course, and having a child with us each removed any threat that there might have been in my striking up a conversation with her. Kids are handy like that.

'Thank God it's cooled off a bit, eh?' I said. 'It can get a bit unbearable, can't it?'

'Oh, yes, I prefer the winter. I like it when it's cold.'

'Well, I wouldn't go that far, but it can get so exhausting in the heat with all the pollution, can't it?'

'Yes. Is this your girl?'

'This is Grace.' Grace was hanging on to me shyly. The large woman's daughter was playing among the tangled weeds over by the fallen gravestones.

'How old are you then, Grace?' she asked her. Grace didn't reply. She looked up at me.

'She's four.'

'Four and three-quarters,' Grace murmured under her breath.

'That's my Jasmine.' The woman indicated the chubby girl with a nod of her chin. 'She's nearly nine.'

'I met you before. You probably won't remember. You gave me your number. I've still got it.' I didn't tell her that actually I could recall the number easily even now. She would have got the wrong idea.

'I remember,' she said. 'There was a storm.'

'I'm Guy Mullin, I work round here. Well, live round here, I suppose.'

'Oho – shouldn't tell me your real name, you know, you bad man.'

'No, it's all right, you don't have to tell me yours.'

'I'm Stella, 38–26–38.'

'Yes, I remember. It's a lovely church, isn't it? Have you been inside?'

'Oh, yes. Jasmine goes to school here.'

'Oh, that's good. They're good, aren't they, the church schools?'

'They're the only proper education in the state system. I was lucky to get her in,' said Stella.

'Only trouble is, you have to go to church regularly to qualify for it.'

'Oh, I don't mind that. I've always gone to church.' She was probably unaware of her eyes returning every few seconds to where her child was playing.

'I went along to get Grace in down in Fulham where I used to live, and the church is full of all these middle-class families who never normally go there at all, pushing their under-five-year-olds to join in with the hymns so they won't have to fork out for school fees. No children over five in there at all.' I dawdled a bit. Stella was still sitting quietly on the bench. I stood awkwardly. I put our lunch rubbish in the litter bin. It had been nicer to sit in the churchyard than under the fluoresence of the Shaftesbury Avenue McDonald's.

'Do you want a biscuit, Grace?' said Stella.

'What kind?'

'Funny Face.'

Grace put out her hand.

'Say thank you,' I said automatically, before she had had the chance to say it. She joined Stella on the bench and ate her Funny Face.

I scanned the trees and looked up at the church spire, not sure whether to sit on the bench myself. Under the gable of the roof were knotty gargoyle faces. One of them was disgorging the leafy branches of an oak tree carved out of the stone. Like the locations of the ancient yew trees across England, around which so many of the first churches were built, originally this must have been a pagan site. Christianity merely grafted on over the top like geological rock strata. Tony would like it here. The Green Man, symbol of growth out of death and destruction. The anarchic and spoiling nature of man epitomized. The cheeky jokester. The one who knows that creativity sometimes comes out of breakage. The one who combats apathy but who doesn't put his toys back in the right boxes. The one who stirs the water with a stick to see what's lying on the bottom, just for the hell of it. Curiosity. Devilment. Surprise. An idea occurred to me. A wicked one. Grace bit the eyes off the top of her Funny Face and held it upside down.

'Look. It's a face the other way round too,' she said to the large woman.

'Oh yes, so it is,' Stella replied. I sat down on the bench beside her. Hooters were blaring in Wardour Street beyond the gates of the church, and some kind of argument was raging.

'I don't want to be rude,' I said, somehow spurred on by the grinning gargoyles, 'but I run a sort of agency myself, and, well . . . entertainment business agency, you know, TV, films, all sorts really . . .'

'Huh! And you think I might be just right for a part in a film that might happen if I just pop along to a photographic session and whip my top off. Listen, Buster . . .'

'No, I don't mean that. To tell you the truth, the TV business is not what it was and, well, to tell you the absolute truth, my business is very much not what it was. OK, I'll be straight with you, it's on its last legs, but . . . I do have all the contacts still and . . .' I kept on going. I was grinning now like the Green Man. It was infectious; Stella smiled back at me. A wicked smile. 'Well, some of my clients are very attractive, but unfortunately out of work, actresses and . . .' She wasn't helping me out, she just kept smiling. 'Then there are the visiting film producers, some of them very well known, if you see what I mean?' Looking over the top of Grace's head, I said with exasperation, 'Can't you help me out here?'

'You have a business proposition to make to me, Mr Guy Mullin? I think I know what you're suggesting and I think, well, I *know*, that I might be able to help you here and that we could come to some agreement. Jasmine!' she called across to her daughter. 'You come here a minute, babe!'

Jasmine shuffled halfway across towards us. 'What?' she shouted.

'Jasmine, this is Grace. You play with her for a bit. Your ma's got to have a talk with her dad.'

'Oh, all right,' said Jasmine with unashamed reluctance, her eyes hitting the sky. And then, very politely, she came up and took Grace's hand and led her to where she'd been playing.

'OK, first off, why do you want to do this thing, big boy? And don't you lie to me. I can always tell.'

I thought for a moment. 'Because they can all fuck off as far as I'm concerned.'

'Alrrrrright!' She laughed wheezily.

'Of course, there are practical reasons, necessities. Money, or lack of it . . . her.' I indicated Grace.

'I understand.' She gave a big sigh. 'I do.'

'And I've got the contacts but it would have to be, well . . .'

'Discreet,' she said. 'High-class . . . expensive.' She smiled big now, and her teeth dazzled in the half-sunlight.

'My thoughts entirely.' I was relaxing into it. 'Like escorts or something.' I would wear the shiny suit, I would drive the Mazda. My shades would look £150 but cost £20 from a Carnaby Street booth. Stella put her hand on mine briefly.

'Well, Big Jim, go slowly, my man.' I gave her my line 3 number, my personal one. She popped it in her bag with a suggestive flash of the eyes and got up.

'Jas, time to go, love.' And then, more quietly to me, with a knowing wink, 'Big Jim. Do you like it?'

'What?'

'Your new name.'

'Oh, yes, thank you. Jim was my father's name, actually.'

'Yes, but was he big? Was he Big Jim?'

'You know, I haven't the faintest idea,' I said.

'You mean you never looked?' She laughed again. Jasmine joined us with Grace trailing behind.

'OK, we'll talk then.' Stella took Jasmine's hand and left the churchyard. Grace came up and sat on my lap. It made it worse having her for the afternoon in Soho, away from everything that was familiar to her. Just the two of us stranded together on a strange and hostile planet called Contact, where there was no bathtime, no familiar monsters or chips and ice-cream for tea. Surely abandonment, or at least absence, would be better for her than to have to comprehend this adult complexity. No, I know that's just a cop-out.

After delivering Grace through a gap in the front door no wider than Susan Planter had opened hers for fear of press intrusion, I returned to Soho via Hamleys and bought a duplicate musical dinosaur, pop-up spider book and Rosie and Jim rag dolls to keep at Meard Street. I would have to make the office home. I fell asleep on the cane sofa with the toys on my lap and a fag on the go. That was mature, wasn't it?

It was in my first week as an accredited absent parent – the week after that first shaky Saturday with Grace – that my recurrent dream took a turn for the nasty. The noise wasn't like the roaring of waves or thunder, it didn't have gaps in it, no bits that were louder or softer than others. Nor was it like a digital tone, it was too ragged and raucous for that. It was like an explosion extended beyond the seconds of impact. An eternal car crash. It was dark subterranean night. There was water, dark water. Grace was sinking fast. I was there to save her, but when I reached her at last we were pushed together into the turbulence, and I held her down under the water. I held Grace down, she struggled, I couldn't look in her eyes. I was pushing her under with all my force. Neither of us could believe that I was doing it. I could only just breathe myself, but I made sure that she couldn't. There was black splash over us both, I held her under the rage. There was wind, and in the dream I was weeping with guilt. I held her down until I woke up, fully clothed and shivering in full daylight. The window was open and the phone was ringing.

'Hello, this is Mullin and Ketts. I'm sorry, we're all busy at the moment, but if you would like to leave your name and number and the time you called, we'll get back to you as soon as possible. Please speak after the tone.'

Tilda's voice. I would have to change the outgoing message soon, but in the meantime I had a few days' grace in which to find out who was still in and who had flown. Naomi wouldn't have bothered to have taken everybody with her. She'd have left behind the more boring ones. Simon Eggleston, no doubt. Joy Trainer, Amy Battle, Simon N'quarbo and anyone who hadn't worked for a while. I was trying to blink away the dream, but its dark, treacly taste remained. This wasn't meant to be my dream. Not drowning my own child. The images from it would not disappear back down the horrid hole of my subconscious whence they had come. There was no one to blame for them: no uncensored video, no foul American movie about infanticide which I could claim had influenced me. It was all mine, but I still could not own the dream. I made myself think about the day and work.

I wondered about Barbara Stenner, dear old bat. Hadn't managed to get through to her yet. Would she have fluttered across to Regent Street with the others? Probably. Been in the business too long not to know where bread gets buttered. She was the only one who gave me a tad of the sads. A voice came on the answerphone. It was Neil. I got up to catch him before he rang off. I needed jolting into the day.

'Where are you?'

'I'm not going to say.'

'Oh, come on, that's stupid, Neil.'

'I've taken three bottles of something. I don't know what.'

'What do you mean, taken?' The sound of the dark rushing water was still in my head. The fear in the dream had been let out like a genie from a bottle, and was treading its dirty footprints all over the office.

'You know, pills.'

'Oh, Hinge and Bracket, Neil! Why?'

'I can't do it, Guy. I can't write it. I'm just a cheap light-entertainment turn. I'm not a writer, I'm not anything. I'm not a man. I haven't even got any kids like you. I can't do it.' The murderous aftertaste of my dream settled on the telephone receiver and projected itself down the line at Neil. At that moment, I would have liked to kill him.

'Where are you, Neil? Where are you?'

175

'What's it matter?'

'Well, it matters to me, Neil. You're my client, for God's sake. How do you think this makes me feel?' I was working hard now. I extemporized. 'How dare you go and take some bottles of pills without telling me first? Have you made a will or anything? Well, have you? What if it turns out that what you've written so far becomes a classic and gets made into a big Hollywood film and I can't get my hands on the rights because you didn't sign all the relevant bumf? Neil . . . Neil? . . . Are you still there?'

He gave a sort of resigned half-laugh, half-cough. 'Yeah, I'm still here.'

'Well, where is that?'

'Aha, trying to trick me, eh? In Sussex somewhere, Edinburgh. What does it matter?'

'Whereabouts in Sussex?' With my free hand, I switched line 2 off the answerphone and picked up the receiver. I dialled his home number in West Hampstead with the thumb of my left hand.

'And who's going to play you in the film, you silly old bugger? Or when it goes to series?' I said.

'You know, Guy? I don't give a monkey's,' he said, and chortled quietly. 'Noel bloody Edmonds for all I care.'

I got through to West Hampstead but it was engaged and had that irritating Call Holding voice on: 'The person you are calling knows you are waiting,' etc. I hung up. I held the line 2 receiver away from line 3 into which I was speaking so that Neil wouldn't hear it. I dialled the operator with my left-hand thumb.

'Neil, listen, hang on a second. I've just got to switch off a tap but I'm still here, I want to talk to you. You hold on, OK?'

'Yeah, all right, Guy, but there's no point in ringing Karen, you know.'

'You still there?'

'Yeah. Guy?' He was slurring now.

'Yes?' I replied.

'You know what? You're a bastard, Guy. You're a complete shit.'

'Yes, I know that, Neil, tell me something new. That's what I take my ten per cent for. Someone's got to do it. It's what you pay me for.'

'Listen, you old shit, I'm upstairs at home. That was you trying to call just now, wasn't it? I wish I was in Sussex, or anywhere, that'd be nice, that'd be . . .' He went silent.

'Neil? Neil?' God, I was angry with him. A day at the hospital I did not need. There was clicking down the line, and another voice joined us.

'Hello? Who is this?' It was American, a woman. Karen, I presumed. 'Neil? Are you using this phone, honey?'

'He says he's taken some bottles of pills. He doesn't sound very well. I'm Guy, his agent, by the way. Hello.'

'Oh, not again,' she sighed, and then, shouting to him, 'Neil baby, I've had enough of this already, do you hear? You put down the phone and get downstairs now!'

'Is he alright?' I asked.

'Of course he's alright. The ones who say they're going to do it never do it.' She shouted at him again, this time away from the phone. 'And have you tidied your room yet?'

I couldn't imagine what sort of relationship they had, how on earth it worked, but who am I to comment? I haven't exactly found the key, have I? She spoke to me again.

'Are you still there, Guy? Listen, don't you worry, you go on and have a nice day. I'm sorry about all this. Really.'

I couldn't leave it like that, I had to double-check. Despite wishing him drowned, I said, 'Only if you're sure he's alright.'

'No, he's not alright. He's driving me mad, if you really want to know. But physically speaking, yeah, he's fine. You can relax. Really. I'll take care of this.'

I said goodbye. Ketts Stanton-Walker had not bothered to take Neil with them to Regent Street, as you can imagine. No, I was stuck with him. Muggins.

And so the second week of non-contact went by. Christ! In Neil's TV sitcom the idea of every other weekend had been so amusing, the men so humorously hopeless – particularly Neil, who usually got the dumber laughs. The kids had been cute and knowing, the dads had been quaintly sentimental but completely incompetent, hence lovable. Good telly. They didn't dream nightly of slaughtering their own offspring in a raging torrent of cold black water, and wake shivering with sweat and admonishments. I had put the Rosie and Jim dolls and the wind-up dinosaur into a filing cabinet now; I couldn't bear the sight of them and what they stirred.

By the Wednesday morning I couldn't take it any longer. I had become seriously worried about Grace. Well, I'd become obsessed, to be sure. Liz hadn't returned any of my calls for a week and, frustrated and depressed with the sight of my empty office and with the lonely toys calling me from inside the filing cabinet – 'Let us out! Let us out!' – I packed the day in after lunch and went down to Fulham by bus to see if I couldn't find out what was going on. Man of action, love, that's me. A big boy with a mission: steely gaze, steadfast purpose, square chin. This whole thing needed fixing and I was the soldier boy to sort it. It had taken me ten days to file the horrible, murderous dream under 'stress at work'.

The upstairs of the number 14 was completely overrun by a gang of thirteen-year-old kids in semi school uniform, throwing insults, sweet papers and cigarettes at each other. I was the only adult up there – the conductress having given up on them – and I retreated into my inner thoughts: fantasies of a dramatic scene at my front door in which Liz refused to let me in to see Grace and I kicked the door down and, finding Hendo in my kitchen, stabbed him with one of the chopping knives which had been given to us as a wedding present by her mum. Then the police arrived and I was taken away with Grace screaming and Hendo pumping blood from his neck wound. I couldn't decide whether Ken Loach, Quentin Tarantino or Martin Scorsese would have been the most suitable director for this scenario. Or was I on my way to kill them all?

'Cheer up, mate, might never happen,' said an untidy schoolgirl as half of the kids piled off the bus and jumped out at the lights. It was true I was looking deranged. I looked at my watch. If I got out here I could go round to the day nursery first. It would be pick-up time in about twenty minutes. I followed the schoolkids and hopped off dangerously, even though the bus was now going too fast, arriving on the pavement at a trot. I felt like some SAS guy with weapons in both socks.

It was hot again, and my thin linen jacket wasn't really strong enough to hold my mobile, which was dragging a bulky lump out of the left-hand pocket. I took it out and hooked it on to my belt. Whichever way you wear a mobile you look like a prat, but it was appropriate today to sling mine like a holster. I bet Hendo has one of those wafer-thin ones that fits in the top breast pocket easily and tells the time in Los Angeles and Tokyo.

As I walked along the Fulham Palace Road I rang Malcolm Viner and asked if he wanted to meet later for a drink. His little terraced cottage in Shepherd's Bush was about fifteen minutes from here. I couldn't get him off the phone as I approached the Little Fledglings school in Harcourt Road, and so, since I was early, I hung about outside still talking to him, feeling like a yuppie dad who fits his children into business schedule windows. Well, I suppose that's what I am really, but then what's in a label?

Malcolm's ex-partner Geraldine was evidently intending to move to Dublin, taking his daughter Nerily with her, and Malcolm, unsurprisingly, was vociferous on the implications. She had found a new boyfriend and claimed to want to start a new life in Ireland. Malcolm was considering whether to go and live there too in order to be near his daughter.

'Trouble is, Guy, mate, I think the whole Dublin thing is just a scam. She knows she couldn't move back to America legally speaking, well, not without a helluva stink from me, so she's using Dublin as an interim measure which takes her outside English custodial waters, so to speak. And from there she could go to America, and there'd be nowt I could do about it.'

'What about your work?' I asked.

'Ha! All this Nerily business put an end to anything resembling a career years ago.'

'Look, I've got to go,' I said. 'They're coming out. I'll catch you later.' I said 'catch you later'. You see, I really am a yuppie.

Various parents had accumulated on the street. One or two were sitting in double-parked Volvo estates. Children holding tissue-paper collages and large poster-paint pictures were coming out and being bustled away by mums, nannies, sisters and one or two sheepish dads in summer suits. Liz was not there. The nursery had nearly emptied. A mum from one of the Volvo estates was extricating her two children from the front playroom.

I stood half in, half out of the open front door. A third child of hers sat in the child-seat in the car. The woman was making more noise than all of the children put together. A certain braying upper-middle-class type have naturally grating and resonant voices – from being brought up in baronial dining halls, I presume – and this woman had the kind of volume that would reach beyond the back of the auditorium of the Olivier at the National and right out into the LWT car park beyond.

'It's ainly one week they'll miss, so thet's Ay Kay. You see, *all* the flights back from the Dordogne are full. It's a *nightmare* getting a seat at all. It's *outrageous*.' I would like to be allowed to shoot her now, with a big Clint Eastwood gun. Blow her face across the nursery wall.

'Hello, Mr Mullin. Grace isn't here.' It was Rosie, Grace's aptly named nursery teacher. 'She hasn't been in all week. You can take her art folder if you like.'

I followed Rosie into the playroom, feeling too large. Apart from all the furniture in there being kiddy-sized, the staff and mums all seemed to be smaller even than me. I hung about testily at the doorway to the room. 'Her collages are in the art tray.'

I didn't know where the art tray was, damn it, and hesitated a moment. The nobby mum with the honking voice clocked my lost look, and as she bundled past me with her brood, she stopped and looked up at me with a bitter look in her Anglo-Saxon eyes. 'You're *learning*,' she said at me with a triumphant and hateful lump in her throat. The 'you' in question presumably being all men in general, and I suspect more specifically her nobby husband, wherever he was right now. Probably shagging his secretary. God knows, I would too if I was married to her.

I couldn't ask Rosie for more information without compromising my position. It was bad enough that I obviously didn't know Grace had been off school. What kind of a parent must she think I am? I took Grace's raffia pictures and got out as quickly as I could. When a whole kindergarten do their glueing and sticking and painting and then their efforts are hung on the wall, the results all look pretty much the same, don't they, except for the one that has your own kid's name at the bottom which somehow has a hidden signal in it, a message which only you can read which tells you that actually your kid is a remarkable individual, a genius maybe. Grace had drawn a large acorn growing into a big oak which had stick-on tissue-paper leaves. And beside it was a squirrel. Rosie had helped her write her name underneath.

In the street I left another message on Liz's machine, more querulous this time. Could she please let me know what was going on? My battery was going flat, so I had to leave it at that. Probably just as well. I went round to the house, our house, and stupidly tried my key in the door, even though I knew she'd changed the locks. I tried the bell. I felt less like Clint Eastwood than like Woody Allen now, standing on my own doorstep ringing the bell with a stack of coloured cards under my arm. I wished I was Jim Carrey, then I could have pulled a stunt and abseiled up to Grace's bedroom window. I left a note, a brief one, and sloped away before the neighbours saw.

It was hot as hell and the dog turds on the street were smouldering. I didn't know what to do and I hate that. I felt like an ice-cream, probably just for comfort, but it was hot, so having an ice-cream would be normal. I was allowed an ice-cream. Yes, I could have an ice-cream without looking like too much of a failure sad-act, for Christ's sake. I would have an ice-cream. I set off for Bishop's Park thinking of Mivvis. I needed a space to work out what to do. I should do something. I couldn't go back to Soho, or to Malcolm's, I had to get some result from my afternoon. Maybe I should just go to the park, have my ice-cream and then shoot a lot of people at random. With my battery flat, I couldn't make a barrage of calls, which would have been my normal reaction to crisis or uncertainty. I did, however, nip into the Langthorne Street phone box and call Liz's mum with the last twenty pence on my phone card.

'Hello, Joy, how are you? . . . Good good good. Look, I'm sorry to trouble you but I'm trying to find out where Grace is. She hasn't been into nursery for three days and Liz isn't returning my calls. I don't know how much you know of what's been going on between me and her, but it's not been, well . . . good for the last few months. I don't know what she's told you, but I would like to know where my daughter is.'

'What did you expect, Guy?'

I didn't know how to react, so I gave a recalcitrant snigger. 'Sorry?' I said.

'I'm sure Liz knows what she's doing, Guy. She's perfectly capable of looking after Grace.'

'I'm sure she is, Joy. I'd just like to know where she is, that's all.'

'You should go away for a while, Guy, calm down, take a holiday, take a month off. You should leave Liz alone, for all of your sakes. Stop putting so much pressure on her. Let her sort things out in her own time.'

'I can't afford to go away, Joy, you know that.' The tone of my voice was making me sound more desperate than I was. No, that's a lie. I was trembling in the kiosk.

'There's no point in losing your temper with me, Guy. Something I hear you do rather a lot of these days. I'm very sad for you both at the moment, as a matter of fact. I really thought she'd found the right man for her this time. But . . .'

Oh yes, Joy. You'd really know about finding the right man, having married three wrong ones and road-tested several others for adequacy on the way. I didn't say that. I wish I had. I said, 'I'm touched that you're concerned for us, Joy, but I do want to know where my daughter is, and if you know I think you should tell me.'

'Get real, Guy,' she said, trying to sound modern I suppose. Obviously in her opinion the way to bring up girls correctly is to secrete them from their fathers. I hung up on her. Maybe she was right, I don't know, maybe I should just go walkabout, or on a world cruise, and become in Grace's eyes a distant figment. An enigmatic role model for her to cling to when in a few years' time she was considering whether to sniff that glue, or kick that old lady off the pavement.

The tea shop by the allotments was closed, so no Mivvi. I gulped from the water fountain by the bowling green. The parakeets and rollers in the mini-aviary squeaked and trilled, but their noise did not trouble me. My mind was singular. I had something specific to worry about. The waste-paper bins had not been emptied and sweet wrappers and lolly sticks were spattered on the paving stones. A toddler was being hand-held

182

along the top of the low wall by her bored au pair. Other children on rollerblades had ordinary ice-creams, so the van must be outside the gate on Stevenage Road, the street where BBC producers live before being promoted to heads of department. I couldn't think whether to sit or stand, to move or be still. The lawns and benches were full of reclining men with their shirts off and women lolling over them with their skirts hitched up.

'Aha! It's the wood-man!' Tony was ambling up towards me, dressed only in his oily shorts and brown work-boots. 'I'm just off to the bushes to partake of this,' he said, and flashing his eyes at me he produced a large conical joint from behind his ear. 'And I was wondering if you would care to join me for a blow, compañero?'

'Well, I've got things I'm meant to be doing, so I shouldn't really.'

'Like what?'

'Well, I'm supposed to be meeting a friend of mine for a drink, and . . .'

Under the sweeping branches of an enormous cedar tree by the back of the duck pond, Tony lit up. The smoke billowed upwards from the wider end of the joint and then two thick jets of it came streaming out of his nostrils. Like the foam and twigs and mud on the drowning man's face.

'Seen the Green Man again lately?' he asked.

'No.'

'Too busy pandering and pimping to see what's going on in the real world, eh?'

'You could put it like that. To be honest, at the moment I think I'm what could be called well and truly fucked.' I could tell him. He wasn't in the biz.

He passed me the whopper and I took a couple of puffs before handing it back to him.

'Help yourself,' he said, but I declined any more.

'I'm looking for my daughter.' It sounded rather drama-queeny now said.

'I never told Mum and Dad this, but I've got a kid, I think. In Sweden somewhere. I was seeing this girl when I was in Europe, I mean, it was real love, you know, we both felt it and everything. Amazing sex. She took me back to see her folks and that was it. They were some big fucking rich Swedish family, like nearly royalty, and they told me where to get off. Made me sign papers and everything saying that when she had the kid I would never come back or make a claim on it or anything.'

'That's ridiculous,' I said.

'As far as they were concerned I just wasn't the right kind of man for her, and I wasn't going to make her life difficult, you know, I loved her. So I just fucked off like a puppy.' He inhaled another huge gulp of the smoke. 'But she was the only one really, you know . . . the one. I often wonder what happened to her. The kid'd be, oooh, seventeen now I should think. She wrote to me once, just after she'd had him, Matthias, that's what they called the poor little fucker. What sort of a name's that? Probably a right little banker by now.'

He flicked the glowing end off, and folding over the loose top, put the joint back over his ear.

'Right, that's enough of that for now. Don't want to get completely blotto. Not yet.'

I was feeling a little woozy myself.

'The Bricklayer's Arms opens at six. You coming or what? You can buy me a pint if you behave yourself. Ask your friend to come along. Or is it by any chance a friend of the female persuasion?'

The river was sluggish brown, as if it too was taking the afternoon off to sunbathe. After Tony had popped into his shed to get his top – a T-shirt with a Tibetan mandala on it over the words 'Despair-Proof Vest' – we passed by the spot where the drowning man had disappeared. I stopped for a minute. Tony stood respectfully in silence, looking out in the same direction as I was. I found that my left thumbnail was scratching at my wedding ring. Maybe it had been doing that for some weeks, but only now had I become aware of it. I took the ring off slowly and chucked it hard into the steady plate of water. It was so small that we didn't see its plop. We walked on.

'Yeah,' said Tony presently, 'life becomes much easier to bear once you make the decision that women are crap.'

That thought was not quite the intention of my action. I told him so.

'No, I don't mean crap as in stupid or wicked or inferior,' he

184

said. 'I mean crap as in the answer to it all. They're not very good as drugs. Things go better once you stop looking to a woman to make it all OK in your life. She can't do that for you, Guido. You gotta do that for yourself.' I wished I could wear a T-shirt like his.

Malcolm Viner didn't like the Bricklayer's Arms, I could tell. He looked almost as out of place there as I did, in his sleeveless shirt and slacks with his clean bald head shining. He ordered himself a half of lager and bought me and Tony a second pint each. It's one of those small, dingy back-street jobs which exist in a permanent dark-brown nicotine-sticky state of December. The bar staff and clientele seem to go back a long way, having grown their impressive bellies together over the years in there. As a concession to the free-market thinking of the eighties and the yuppification of pubs across the land, they bunged four half-broken plastic chairs on the pavement outside during the summer months. Tony, Malcolm and I went out and sat on three of them, using the fourth as a table.

'OK,' said Malcolm, 'there are three claims a wife can have over you financially speaking: one, the capital sum, i.e. a big wodge of cash if you've got it; two, the right to accommodation provided by you; and three, maintenance. Then money for child support comes over and above that.'

'So that's four really, ain't it?' said Tony.

'Well, yes, but they try to separate child maintenance from the rest, even though in practice it all ends up going to the mother.'

'Can't I just give her half of everything and leave it at that?' I said.

'Well, no, Guy, you can't. In this country it's worked out according to what's known as the wife's needs and requirements. You'll have to submit a full and frank declaration of how much you're worth and then what you pay her is worked out according to that, set against her needs and requirements.'

'What about Grace?'

'Well, the judge won't award you residency unless you can prove Liz is unfit to be a mother, which is unlikely, and undesirable in any case. It is assumed that you are unfit to be the principal carer of the child because you are a man. But anyway that's academic because she doesn't really work and you do, so the law assumes you can't look after a child.'

185

'What if I don't want to work any more?'

He laughed. 'What you want is not going to come into any of this.' Tony laughed too. Malcolm went on. He was unstoppable: 'I wouldn't advise you to apply for joint residency either; I tried that. Although the 1989 Children Act does give married fathers joint custody, it's a totally meaningless concession, because custody doesn't mean you actually get to see the child – that's residency – and judges still give residency to females in over ninety-five per cent of cases, regardless of their parenting skills. All you get is something called contact, which is completely unenforceable if she decides she doesn't want to let you see the little blighter, or if she doesn't like you any more, or if, like me, you run out of money.'

As before, Malcolm's zealous fire was consuming all it encountered, and exhausting me in the process.

'It all comes down to money in the end,' said Tony, and offered me his baccy.

'I don't think she ever did like me, now I come to look at it.'

'I hate to sound all negative about this, Guy, but there's no point in being unrealistic, is there? You're in a very bad position not having a home for the Princess Grace to go to when she's with you. There are contact centres nowadays. Awful, depressing places. Heart-rending. I went along at the specified time, but Geraldine just didn't bother to show up and there was nothing I could do about it.'

'I wish I'd never married her.'

'Oh, no, that's your main leverage. It'd be much worse if you'd never married, believe me. You'd have no rights over young Gracie at all, only responsibilities to pay for both of them.'

He started to write down some notes for me.

'So if I'm going to be in court with you as your lay adviser, you've got to get me your tax returns for the last five years, all your property details, shareholdings, assets, income and out-goings, gifts received, oh, and a schedule of your own needs and requirements – might as well bung that in although it's not officially relevant – and a full statement of the time you spend with Grace. And of course any insurance details or other policies you might have . . .'

'I feel like I'm just a chequebook,' I said.

'You are, you are. That's all you are, mate, just a way for the Government to avoid paying single-parent allowance. Let's face it, people like us who don't have total financial security shouldn't really go around having children. A couple of rock stars could keep the human race going, sperm-wise. We're just spare pricks, old son.'

Tony concurred. 'Sounds a bit like the Egyptian system really. The pharaoh had a few hundred wives and thousands of children, while everyone else had to settle for a shag once every couple of decades and then back to hauling the stone slabs around to make his pyramid for him.'

I imagined big Hendo, Bob Rameses Henderson III, and the photo of his three young, expensive sons in tartan ties that had been shown to me by his wife Saara. It was true, a man like that can afford to have as many children as he likes. High priest of the temple, investment and contractual litigation, two hundred and fifty pounds an hour. The wallet-photos of his potential offspring unfolded into infinity like a credit-card concertina.

At last I got through to Liz. I was standing in the bar at the Bricklayer's Arms, shovelling coins into their tabletop payphone. A large, sweaty man who was called Bill was nuzzled with his back up against me. They didn't really want customers having private conversations in here and so the phone was annoyingly placed.

'Where are you?' said Liz, hearing the beery laughter behind me.

'In the pub,' I said.

'I see,' she replied in a told-you-so tone of voice. 'What do you want?' It was difficult to crack her hostility.

'Well, to see how you are. Didn't you get my messages? Is Grace OK?'

'Checking up on your property?' she said.

'They told me she hasn't been in Fledglings for three days. What's going on?'

'Don't start shouting at me, Guy. And I don't like you ringing my mother and shouting at her either.'

'I didn't shout,' I shouted.

'There's no point in us talking, Guy. I'll see you at the counsellor's next time. If you can still be bothered to come, that

187

is. But apart from that I don't really think this is very helpful, do you?' She hung up on me.

I looked around the bar. No one was looking at me, but they all wanted me to leave, I could sense it. I rang her back anyway.

'What?' she said, as if I was the stupidest imbecile on earth.

'Where's Grace, Liz? Where is Grace?'

'She's having her bath, and I have to go and supervise actually because she's had another ear infection and mustn't get any water in it.'

'Have you taken her to the doctor?'

'What do you care, Guy? All you care about is Mullin and bloody Ketts and being the shittest-hottest agent in town. Go and sign a few deals, why don't you? Leave me alone.' She hung up again. God, it was hot, I had to get outside again. Tony and Malcolm broke off their conversation and looked up at me together.

'How did it go?' they said jointly.

'Erm. Pretty good,' I said, fidgeting. 'They're alive. But not well. Grace's got another ear infection, and Liz's . . .'

'Has she been to the doctor?' asked Malcolm helpfully.

'Don't know that yet.'

'So that's a bit of a result this afternoon, I think it must be your round, sir.' Tony offered up his empty glass.

'Just a tomato juice for me,' said Malcolm apologetically.

On returning with the drinks, I found Tony smoking the second half of his big joint, with his scarred brown legs outstretched over the kerb, while Malcolm spouted forth on his favourite subject.

'You see, the actual cause of the breakdown bears absolutely no relation to the terms of the settlement and custody arrangements. It doesn't matter who did what to whom; all that does is decide whether a marriage has irretrievably broken down, and once they've decided that, they completely ignore it, and proceed along no-fault divorce lines, which is actually not what's written down in the 1979 Care and Proceedings Order Bill. But they ignore that completely.'

'You ought to write all this down, pal,' said Tony, offering me the joint. I declined. We were in the street.

'Oh, I do,' said Malcolm. 'I've got it all on my Toshiba. So, for instance, it's actually irrelevant whether Guy here petitions Liz or she petitions him. It will make not a jot of difference in the end. He will pay for her and for the court, and she will get custody, although nowadays it's called residency, of course. Fat lot of difference changing the words made.'

Tony gave me a sad and quizzical look.

'Oh, yes,' Malcolm continued, fishing the lemon out of his tomato juice and sucking on it hard, 'you can't win with that lot. Solicitors. You just can't win. No way.'

'Then why fight them at all?' asked Tony.

Malcolm stopped to reflect for a millisecond.

'I can't think like that,' he said.

'I've got this woman I see every now and then at the moment, I mean, I'm not sleeping with her or anything. Yet.' Tony chuckled. 'And she keeps trying to get me to do stuff for her, you know, fix her car, little bit of carpentry, and I think: hang on, what's this all about? She's in love with some big feller in the city and he takes her out to restaurants and that, and I think: why don't you get him to fix your frigging fridge, eh? OK, if a guy's screwing some woman I think he should do stuff for her, fair enough, otherwise forget it.'

'She obviously knows what she's doing,' said Malcolm. 'She's got your number, mate.' We laughed. It was the beer. 'Oh, yes, Darwin was right, it's very much survival of the fittest, I'm afraid, these days.'

'That was Herbert Spencer who said that, not Darwin,' said Tony, with no hint of point-scoring. 'Poor old Charlie Darwin's a very misunderstood geezer.'

Tony started to hold forth about a possible connection between the genetic make-up and the pair-bonded social behaviour of the kittiwake gull, but I was too frazzled to take it in. I didn't know my brother knew about that sort of thing. I didn't think he knew about anything, actually. Middle-class snob I am. Get me.

'So, my thespian compadre,' he said, 'we going up the West End to some sprauntzy club to get rat-arsed and ogle some females, or what?'

'Count me out,' said Malcolm. 'I've got Nerily tomorrow, I think.'

When the Groucho Club first opened up, it was, give or take the Zanzibar and Two Brydges Place, the only club of its kind in the West End. Before that there had been Legends, the Embassy, Maunkberrys, the Pink Palm Tree, but these all owed more to the seventies than the eighties in terms of style. All had dance floors, very loud music and very expensive cocktails. Clothes were shiny, hair was sparkly, conversation was kept to a minimum by virtue of the noise, and lighting was very low, apart from on the dance floor, where it shazammed around in time to music by the Bee Gees and Chic.

In the late eighties, along with mobile phones, the deconstructed suit and the independent production company, a new style of club was needed. The lounge club. Somewhere television execs could have breakfast meetings with freshly squeezed orange juice and cafetière coffee. Where women company directors could lunch on polenta and monkfish and rocket salad. Where theatre designers could meet for afternoon herbal tea and macaroons and where at six o'clock, the entire advertising industry could blow all its new-found pots of eighties loot on bottles of Moët, Chardonnay, Chablis, Sauvignon, Sancerre, more Moët, more Chardonnay, still more Chardonnay, and smoke cigars and meet impressionable young women.

The new thinking on décor was to be strangely paradoxical. In the same way that the seventies clubs had imported most of their ideas from America – the style of John Travolta in *Saturday Night Fever* in particular – the new lounge club was to emulate the cool style of a Los Angeles residential poolside hotel (the Sunset Marquee, say) where old-world comfort and grace is the intention, pastel shades abound, with pale cream and soft turquoise panelling on the walls, above which hang old prints. Upholstered leather sofas and easy chairs are strewn casually over the lush and warm carpets and the occasional painting by someone fashionable will fill any large wall spaces left. The lighting is subliminal and comes from behind peach-coloured wall lamps. The air-conditioning is relentless, and a real live musician tinkles away on a piano unobtrusively. So, it's a style copied from the Americans, copying what they, in their turn, had imagined to be English.

More recently, increasing numbers of these kinds of club have opened up around Soho. Expensive membership clubs with yearbooks, cricket teams, impenetrable menus and waiters with exotic facial hair. There's Black's and the Soho House and Green's and Moscow's and Sally's and on and on. Some have log fires, some have backgammon boards, all have a sign saying, 'No mobile phones', for these are places where the networking is compulsive.

At night, on the whole, they turn into meat markets. Women who dress to enter the Most Provocative Outfit contest mingle with sexy upper-class publishing girls in baggy pullovers and jeans. Guys sprawl around in shirts buttoned to the top with no ties, seeing who can be the most nonchalant, unshaven and secretly, discreetly rolling in dosh.

Models, even supermodels here, dine on scrambled egg with smoked-salmon bits and chain-smoke their way between courses. Table-hoppers hop tables, and at eleven the casts of West End shows, hyped up on their own self-perpetuating adrenalin, arrive with their celebrity guests. Outside, of course, the homeless congregate in sleeping bags with their dogs. The entrances to these clubs must be prime spots for those with blankets and a smack habit.

My favourite in recent years has been the Soho House on Frith Street, but tonight, seeing as Tony was wearing oily denim shorts and his Despair-Proof Vest, I thought we'd try Sally's on Greek. In any case, I didn't fancy bumping into Jeremy Planter or any of my other scummy turncoat ex-clients, and for this Sally's was a safer bet. It's the newest and is possibly, if I can say this without offending Sally herself, a smidgeon more downmarket than the others. Food's good, though, and Sally herself is a constant and amusing presence. She's a large Thai woman who won't think twice about throwing certain people out personally with much loud cursing and insults. This is done, I suspect, mostly for the entertainment of the other clientele and to make them feel that little bit more exclusive. Her choice of expellee is very astute. Usually the arrogant young aristo-type in a yellow waistcoat, who she play-acts taking a dislike to for his attitude. Yes, she knows her business, Sally, and also I felt she wouldn't bat an eyelid at Tony, who might show me up a touch elsewhere. As it happened, she batted both lids and lashes at him.

Sally sat us down at a table near the open front window of her upstairs room, so we could look down into Greek Street below at the queue outside the Blue Ice basement disco.

'I was a bouncer once, for a month or two. You didn't know that, did you, Guy? Didn't last very long, though, on account of my being such a nutcase,' said Tony, picking up the folded beige card menu and squinting at it. Then, out of the pocket of his shorts, he produced an old aluminium spectacle case and took out a pair of half-moon spectacles and put them on.

He was priceless really, sitting there in this foreign place being totally himself with little-old-man specs on. I wished I was like him, or at least had some of his containment. We ordered more beers and agreed to have some red wine with our food. Grain and grape, I know, but I was on the big dipper now, I might as well get up to the top before coming down whooosh for another go.

There was a woman sitting at the table opposite with her back elegantly revealed by a very low-diving black number. Her beautifully kept hair was shiny and clean and swept up to show off her graceful neck. I couldn't see her face and she was sitting up straight with great poise, but a sudden stiffening of her spine and lifting of her ribcage told me that someone significant had just entered the room.

I glanced across to the open arched doorway to where three or four rich-looking folk had entered, and among them was Doug Handom. Sex on legs. The woman with the back was looking down at her food now, trying to conceal her interest from whoever it was she was with, husband, boyfriend, manager, pimp, but he seemed to be jawing on oblivious, through mouthfuls of bang-bang chicken.

After sitting Doug and his crew down, Sally came over to take our order. Doug Handom too had his back to me. I would hop up and say hello later. He had with him two females of the effervescent variety; an older, curly-grey-haired guy in Ivy League clothes with an outrageous tan – producer, I'd wager big dosh – and that Yank actor, damn what's-his-name? Been in loads of stuff – movies – always the bent copper sidekick, never the lead but major supporting, couple of Burt Reynolds's ages ago, oh, Peter something, Ramp? Ryecart? Rumpash? Balding, rugged, butch – damn.

Tony was asking Sally about the ingredients of just about everything on the menu, not critically, and she was enjoying his interest. His questions were informed and she seemed flattered about his knowledge of Thai cuisine.

'No, the sea bass is baked, just with lemon grass and a little bit of ginger,' she said coyly. He flashed a grin at her and made his choice. He was chatting her up, the old devil.

'I'll just have the pasta,' I said, and handed the designer card back to her.

'Used to be a chef in Lai-sin,' said Tony to me when she'd gone. I wondered whether all the stories Tony told might actually be true after all. 'That's when I did me legs in, falling off the Darai temple at Phuket.'

He put his specs away and took a large gulp of red wine from the bulb glass. 'Pity I run out of blow tonight. Ah well, we'll just have to get slaughtered on the old alco-mo-hol. How're you bearing up?'

'Oh, I'm fine.' I had the fleeting thought that he might have come out tonight to keep me company, to make sure I didn't dive into a maudlin thingy. That he might, dare I say it, think I needed looking after. Tony looking after Guy! That's a new one! I dismissed this thought as a projection of my own. I didn't want the evening to turn into some soppy bonding scenario.

The two girls at Doug Handom's table got up, leaving their jackets over the chairs, to go to the Ladies', followed by the actor man, Peter Saravan. That's it! Peter Saravan, of course! Thank Gawd for that! I'd be able to introduce myself soon. Doug looked around and noticed me at last.

'Guy! Bro! How're you doing?' Although still unmistakably north London in accent, Doug had picked up Stateside phraseology. The woman with the back glanced across to see who I was. She was quite pretty, not Emmanuelle Beart but trying to go in that direction.

Excusing myself to Tony, I went across to Doug's table. I shook hands with the old tanned bloke, Irving Tellman – I was right, producer, a couple of cop shows in the eighties and something to do with an early Tom Hanks movie, I think.

'Hi, Guy. Pleased to meet you, Guy. Won't you join us, Guy,' he said with that ludicrously deep resonance only

Americans are allowed by God to have. I looked around at Tony as Sally arrived with our food. Seeing my table-hop, she immediately offered to draw us up a table next to the Americans and change the place settings. Tony came over and sat on the end of the table to eat his fish, without the least trace of discomfort or embarrassment. He was evidently oblivious to who Doug was, or at least didn't register anything when introduced, and this made Doug comfortable enough to ignore him.

The woman with the back was now contorting herself inside with jealousy. Whoever the man was with her, she would not be doing it with her eyes open tonight.

Doug was still holding my shoulder with transatlantic sincerity. 'Guy! Bro! Good to see ya! Did you get my messages?'

'I certainly did. How long are you in town for?' I asked, even though I knew that Doug was here only for a few days. He had to get back to LA to see if there was anything interesting for him in pilot season. Once a year, the American TV stations make hundreds of pilot episodes for their new shows. In this country it's done slightly differently: once, long ago, we used to make the odd pilot.

Irving Tellman answered, 'Oh, just 'til Tuesday, Guy. We're on Park Lane? It's OK there.'

'We've been to some crap charity do tonight. How about you, Guy? Hey, it's good to see you, bro.' Doug pumped my arm now. At the end of the table, Tony ate his dinner slowly, chewing properly and putting down his knife and fork in between each mouthful.

The two girls returned with Peter Saravan and took their places. It was fairly obvious, by the Catherine wheels in their eyes, that they had been taking cocaine in the downstairs toilets. Doug started the introductions: 'This is Peter . . .'

I interrupted him swiftly, shaking the American actor's hand as hard as I could. 'Peter Saravan, yes, I know. I love your work. Guy Mullin, how're ya doin?'

'And this is Vicky and this is . . . oh, I don't fucking know, what's your name, love?' As sex on legs, Doug could do what he liked and it was OK. The two girls, Vicky and whoever she was, simpered and giggled.

194

'For the sake of argument, let's call her Tracey. Right,' said Doug, 'I'm just off to the toilet.' Irving Tellman also seemed, by some extraordinary synchronicity, to need a wee at that very moment. He stood too. Doug turned to me.

'You fancy a line, Guy, or . . .'

I declined the pleasure of a furtive snort of white powder in the cramped toilets of Sally's. I'm the back-up service, not the main act. It doesn't do for an agent to join in. You have to stand by, go along with things. Tony suddenly spoke up for himself.

'I'll have his if it's going,' he said, breaking decorum somewhat.

'Oh, alright.' Doug was a little fazed. He looked at me for reassurance that my companion was OK, cool, one of us. I gave it. The three men left the dining room and went downstairs. I was left with a middleweight American movie actor and two pretty but completely out-of-their-depth girls, all as high as kites.

Peter Saravan leaned over to me and spoke in my ear.

'So, tell me, Guy, you're a Londoner, right? You're Doug's agent over here, right?' I nodded. 'Do you have any idea where we can see some serious action tonight?' I spluttered a typically British sort of Ealing Comedy giggle, indicating Vicky and the other girl, whatever she was called.

'Oh, them,' he said with disgust. 'Haven't the faintest fucking idea who they are. They just kinda latched on to Doug at this fucking charity do.'

We talked a bit, or rather, I smiled and listened and laughed where necessary. Actors are easy. They only need one, maybe two questions every fifteen minutes or so. In the same way that it would be a truism to say that nurses tend to care for other people, actors do like the sound of their own voices and like them enough not to be overly worried about the content of what they're saying.

I have a reciprocal arrangement with Doug Handom's representation in Los Angeles but it is not exclusive. I can enter into agreements with other US managements over other clients if I so wish. By letting him talk, I had found out from Saravan in under five minutes which company he was with over there, the name of the particular person who looked after him, the names of two producers who might be shooting in England next year, which directors were considered hot at the moment and which British actors, currently living over there, were doing OK.

Unfortunately, Saravan's agents were IGA, well established over here already. Big building in Holborn, so nothing there for me but talent leads to talent. Next time I was out there I could look him up and return the favour. It's all about doing favours. After Doug and Irving returned with Tony, I nipped downstairs solo to do a little favour of my own.

I didn't need an address book, I had Kemble's number there among the thousands of others in the instant-access part of my brain.

'Hi, gorgeous.'

'Hello, m'dear. What are you up to?'

'Washing my hair, watching a vid. Nothing.'

'How long would it take you to get up to the West End?'

'Depends.'

'Doug Handom, Peter Saravan, Irving Tellman. Sally's, Greek Street,' I said.

'Under half an hour. Can you hold them?'

'Please, my dearie darling, if we are to get along, don't ever question my professionalism and I'll never question yours.' I was pissed by now.

On the stairs, I passed the woman with the back and her consort. She smiled at me, even though she hadn't a clue who I was. This was living.

'So tell me. What's Los Angeles like then? Worth a visit?' Tony asked Peter Saravan with a simple directness that was several centuries of time travel away from normal biz-chat. Saravan's answer was formulaic.

'Well, I have a large house in the hills, four cars, a pool. You can have a very nice life there.'

'Well, originally I'm from New York,' said Tellman, joining in. 'But all the major deals are in LA and the weather's OK.' Neither of them bothered to address him by his name, since he was quite obviously a layman, non-useful, not in. I intervened.

'Well, if you work in films, then really it's the only place,' I explained. 'It's the Mecca of movie madness, so why not be there?' The usual guff.

'So you're saying it's a crap place in reality, but you've got to go where the work is?' said Tony innocently.

'You have to follow your dream,' said Doug Handom profoundly. I thought of my first trip there, to set Doug up, looking out at 4.00 a.m. from the window of the forbidding Chateau Marmont Hotel where the Brits used to stay and seeing Sunset Strip, a motorway with neon and hookers and fast food and guns in the middle of a desert.

'Sounds like a risky code of practice to me,' said Tony, 'following a dream. I think I'll stick to listening to my dreams and working out what they're trying to tell me.' But Doug's attention was by now elsewhere. Personally I'd rather not know what my new dream was trying to tell me.

We'd been in the crowded downstairs bar drinking tequila for some twenty minutes by the time Kemble arrived. Well, I say that, but she could have been there for quite a while for all I knew. She was sitting, amongst a group of friends, down by the dead-log-fire end of the room, as if she'd been there all night. As if she had happened by, cool as a stick of celery jutting out of a Pimm's. We clocked each other across the room full of mini-skirts, uplift bras and big hair. She was wearing spectacles. Was there a new fashion thing I'd missed out on? Unlike Tony's, hers were big black-rimmed jobs which made her look Joan Bakewell-ey, intellectual, smart, in control. She looked at me over the top of them, smiled and mouthed, 'Hi, gorgeous.' Doug Handom had clocked her too and Kemble's eyes rested on him accusingly for a tenth of a second, before she turned back to her conversation with her friends, which looked from this distance as if it was very deep and fascinating. It was perfect. The only woman in the room not to want to gaze on those angular cheekbones, that famous jawline, the vulnerable mouth which had kissed Emma Thompson and Julia Roberts in the same film, for Pete's sake. The only woman who had better things to do and big grown-up glasses on. She was brilliant. She knew how to handle herself, this one. He was hooked and he didn't even know it. I sat back to admire a master at work. Or mistress, rather.

Various sycophants came and went, claiming Doug's atten-tion: Liz Trainer, the casting director; Anthony Durant, now a successful theatre director, who once employed Doug in some dull, provincial Chekhov or something; Greg Pride, LWT, and more. But all the while, Kemble's poise and the way she was touching the elbows and knees of the men in her group were working on him. I got waylaid by bloody Jonty Forbes, BBC Comedy, who'd somehow heard about Naomi Ketts's moonlight bunk, and I had to spin him some line about having decided last year to start up my own company. How Jeremy Planter had become a liability ages ago, difficult to work with, drunk, out of ideas, that sort of thing. It's easy to do. It's called sticking the knife in wherever possible. I'm sure that in another part of town at that very minute, Naomi was having an identical conversation in reverse with some semi-important possible employer. Denigrating me in any way possible. Denigrating my clients. Fortifying her own position. 'Guy is a lovely man and I love him dearly but he doesn't have that killer instinct.' Or: 'He's very good at the everyday running of things but when it comes to inspiration he's a bit . . .' Sticking in the stiletto with a few slippery words. I wouldn't respect her if she didn't. It's business.

Doug's eyes kept tripping over to where the bespectacled Kemble was sitting, laughing a carefree laugh. Irving Tellman returned from his third visit to the toilet with Vicky and Tracey-whoever. Kemble noticed, or affected to notice, a tall guy over the other side of the room. She shouted across at him. He turned and recognized her. It was as if everyone there was a player in her game. She had control not only of all the pieces but of the board as well. Nay, the incline of the surface on which the board rested.

She got up and left her group to talk to Terry, whoever he was – I'd put my money on photographer – and swishing past us, stood with her back to Doug Handom. She had on tight black trousers and a wafty silk blouse, no bra. From where we sat, her tight little buttocks were on a level with Doug Handom's smouldering eyeline. She'd ignored me in passing and I let her run the show. She was good. It amused me.

Brother Tony, on whom all this was lost, struck up with the distracted Doug Handom again.

'So tell me. This dream you follow. What about your folks, your children? Don't you miss them? Don't they miss you?' he asked him. Bang on the knuckle really, considering Doug's hasty retreat from familial responsibility and abandonment of everything and everybody close to him. Except me of course, his five per cent foothold in the failing British end of the money-making fantasy.

'Oh, man,' said Handom with acted miserableness. 'I wanted to see my kid so much, you know. But my fucking ex-missus, she won't let me. She tries to make me feel guilty, you know. She's such a bitch.'

On further gentle questioning from Tony, it transpired that Doug had turned up unannounced on the doorstep the day before, at the baby's bedtime, laden with gifts, expecting some movie-style prodigal-father reunion after eighteen months of completely non-communicative absence.

'So, you want it to be like, when you stop dreaming for a couple of seconds, everyone'll be there, available, for you to pick up where you dropped them,' said Tony.

Doug's eyes shifted across to mine momentarily, as if he wasn't sure whether he had just been hugely insulted. I looked between him and Tony: the gorgeous but shifty narcissistic fop and the lofty bow-legged oak tree. My job, no, my instinct, my nature was to defend Doug, to bolster his ego up whatever. My business, my life, depended on his dream.

'I hate that,' Peter Saravan interrupted. 'My kids are grown up now but always that guilt, that guilt. Their mother tried to make me feel guilty.'

'Yeah, right,' said Doug. 'She's always trying to make me feel guilty, the bitch.' I'd been gulping tequila for three-quarters of an hour or so, so that's probably what gave me the headache. It came on suddenly, accompanied by the searing sound of a chainsaw. I didn't need these half-humans.

'No, Doug,' I found myself saying. 'You don't feel guilty, you *are* guilty. Her existence just reminds you of quite how guilty you actually are.' In Tony's presence, I seemed to have lost that invaluable tool of agenting: the ability to dissemble. My brother Tony's feet were like roots, twisting below Sally's maroon carpet and into the floorboards below.

'You scooted off after the big prize, remember?' I continued. 'And you got it. I sometimes wish I'd done the same. But you can't come back now expecting sympathy.'

Kemble moved away from Terry the photographer and diagonally back across the room. Like the queen in chess, she could go in any direction she chose, and she chose to stop ever so casually by me – one of her lowly pawns – for surveillance of the enemy king and his bishops.

I did the introductions, and with the ease and grace of a swan landing in the water, she sailed the conversation past Doug Handom and on to Peter Saravan, leaving Doug out of his accustomed spotlight.

'So, you're the bloke who got done for making that video with the underaged girls, then?' she said with charming frankness to Saravan. She knew her stuff, this one.

'We settled out of court,' said Saravan uncomfortably.

'I know,' Kemble replied. Irving Tellman too became a little uneasy.

'So what did you guys have in mind to do tonight?' Kemble said with great dignity. 'I have a friend who works in a lap-dancing club round the corner. Do you fancy that, or do you just want to go back to your hotel for cocoa and an early night?'

Doug Handom swallowed.

In the urinal, I took some breaths and felt somewhat better, although the noise was still getting to me. While I was splashing my face with water, Tony came in and took a piss.

'Ah, smiler. Listen, Guy, do you mind if I kind of branch out on me own from here on? You be alright, will ya?' he asked with a quaint old-fashioned charm, and bunged a tenner at me for the wine, which I of course refused. Then, coming to wash his hands, he said, 'Tell me. Is she married or anything?' 'Who?' I asked without thinking, but knew immediately that he was referring to Sally, our Thai hostess with the mostest.

'Well, I've never heard of a Mr Sally, if that's what you mean.'

'I could do it with her,' he said.

'I'm sure you will,' I replied.

'You come back down the park and tell me how you got on, alright? And look after yourself.'

And he gave me a hug. He smelled of toolsheds and Rioja and roll-ups. I didn't know quite how to respond. We never did hugs in my family.

SEVEN

IN THE BEGINNING was a long, droning, ringing tone. And something came out of the tone and it was consciousness. A possibly frivolous being said, 'Let there be something,' and there was something and that something was me, I think. So far, I was pure thought, spirit even, and was unaware of having a body. Then there was time too. After a few seconds of it spent trying to work out what I was, I recognized that I had a body too. I acknowledged its presence. It was not in any real pain. It was horizontal. I was lying face down on something. But where? Who was I and was I the only one of them? Was I the only thing that had this consciousness, or were there others? Had a big bang – or even a little one – happened and was I in fact a new universe? I lay blinking. It was dark, completely dark. I decided I must in fact be a person but had no handle on who or when. I struggled for some point of reference, something on which to pin my ranging, homeless thoughts. I moved my head a little. It had been resting on a carpet. Close by my face was the leg of a chair. I was on the floor somewhere indoors and probably in the twentieth century. I felt like rolling over, so I did and the movement jogged the memory of a name. My name. Guy. That's who I was. Guy.

Other snippets followed on the tail of this discovery. I was relieved to have limitations. To come out of the void and build up something tangible. I was Guy and I was in a hotel room. That's where I was. I was asleep on the floor, fully clothed. My knee itched and I scratched it. The rolling-over and the scratching were enough movement for the meantime. I closed my eyes again. The noises inside my head had homogenized into one thin and constant ringing tone. To escape further from it I

201

filled in other historical details about myself. It is educational waking up not knowing who you are, or even if you are. And then the memory puts you through a crash course of the last thirty-five years, bringing you with alarming speed to recent crimes and misdemeanours. There had been a night before, there had been brandy, B52s, tequila slammers, many of them, and champagne from my kitchenette fridge. There must also, I presumed, have been some late-night stumble or taxi ride to get me here. But of that I had no recollection. However, now there was recall of much inordinately bad behaviour.

Oh, ghastly memory. Naughty naughty Guy. There had been three- and four-way sexual intercourse on the floor and desks of my office. Not with me as a participant – I hadn't been on the same expensive drugs as the others – but I had witnessed, facilitated even. There had been Kemble, goddess of domination, controlling her slavering subjects with a sweet and enigmatic humour. A brilliant performance. There had been more laughter than I thought was humanly possible. In short, there had been the kind of night before that ends up in the morning editions were it not for the privacy afforded by the little office in Meard. Thank God no one videoed it.

And there had been the complete and somehow delicious degradation of my role. I would not be working as agent for Irving Tellman in the future. Nor Peter Saravan. Nor Doug Handom probably, after the things I said to him. And as more memories clamoured into this consciousness, I thought it unlikely that I would be working as an agent for anybody ever again, because there had been insults to Jonty Forbes – BBC Comedy – in the foyer of Sally's, there had been pouring of drink over Caroline Armitage and then laughing at her, and there had been the sticking of the tongue into the ear of Tom Gutteridge. Howl howl howl, as Old Queen Lear would say. I'd more than blown it, I'd torn it up, I'd thrown it away, I'd pissed on it.

I heaved myself into a sitting position. My head weighed as much as an elephant seal. The hotel room was empty, I had it to myself. The heavy curtains were drawn, but the digital clock read 10.46. I pulled myself on all fours into the swanky marbled bathroom and switched on the bath taps, putting in lots and lots of bubble bath. I hauled myself upright and took a piss. How did I get here? Had Kemble given me some American producer's room key? Whose room was this? I looked in the bathroom mirror. The person standing staring back at me with his flies still undone had some kind of food in his sticky hair, and brown cakey blood all over his right hand.

I took my clothes off slowly to get ready for the bath, checking to see if there might be any more blood elsewhere. Perhaps I had injured myself. There wasn't. My right hand hurt a little. I ran it under the basin tap. There was hardly a graze on it. Whose blood was this trickling down the posh plughole? My alcohol-poisoned memory would not provide this information yet. I got into the bath through a foot and a half of white bubbles. The crunchy noise they made was delicate and sweet, and intercepted the ringing tone momentarily. The heat from the water below them soon made my face and scalp sweat. Apart from in my head, there was peace.

I stretched and luxuriated. I let the memory return at its own speed. I smiled right down to my balls. I closed my eyes. I felt as if I was floating on a river boat in summer . . . We'd bumped into Jeremy Planter sauntering along Old Compton Street with Arabella Stanton-Walker, and I had punched his face. Not once, several times. I think I'd even shouted things like 'And that one's for Dave and Polly, and that one's for Susan, and this one's from me,' or words to that effect. Embarrassing script, but adequately delivered, I feel. What the hell, my dears, what the hell.

Apart from the shower cap, I made sure to open all the little hotel bottles and soaps: the body cream, the shower gel, the shampoo. I slipped the emergency sewing envelope into my jacket pocket and gave my brogues a rub with the shoe buff. Putting my trousers back on – having made sure to dry myself using all of the beautifully stacked white towels – I found a roll of dollar bills in my pocket, as if some good-luck elf had put them there. I had no memory of how they had arrived there. Maybe I had stolen them, maybe this was hush money from Hollywood, I don't know, maybe I had won a bet. Stupidly I double-checked that these were in fact my trousers. There was getting on for six hundred dollars. Had I woken up in someone else's life?

I drew the curtains and was slapped in the face by daylight rushing in from Hyde Park the other side of the four-lane road. I was quite high up, eight floors or so, I'd say. This room must cost a fortune. I opened the door into the corridor, I was in Room 6031. At my feet was a copy of the *Herald Tribune*; apart from that the corridor was empty. I brought the newspaper back in. The knuckles of my punching hand were throbbing now and a bruise was galloping to the surface. Above the mini-bar I found some Nurofen. This was a very swanky hotel. I rang room service to order coffee.

'Yes, Mr Saravan,' said the receptionist. So where in the name of copulation was he? In a police cell? Lying prone on the ratty threadbare carpets at Meard Street? That would have been a ruder awakening than mine. Or still at it with a fresh supply of women? I dialled out to the office but got the answerphone with Tilda's outgoing message on it still. I tried a few hellos, but no one picked up on me.

The coffee came in under four minutes. This was a very special hotel. I hesitated before signing for it, using Saravan's name. The girl in the dark-green waistcoat and pencil skirt hesitated as well. She knew I wasn't him. I took pleasure in peeling off a twenty-dollar bill from my roll and pressing it into her hand. What the hell. She smiled at me – wouldn't you? – and scurried away. I might not be Peter Saravan, but I seemed to have his wedge.

I put my feet up and riffled through the *Herald Tribune*. The coffee was good. Now I needed a smoke. In a hotel this good they didn't question or even pause at my old codger's request for half an ounce of rolling tobacco, some Rizla reds and a box of Swan Vestas. It did take nearly twelve minutes to arrive, though. Tut tut. I must remember to complain to the manager next time I invite him on to my yacht.

The only spoiler was the ringing in my head, which persisted. I supposed I must have tinnitus. That's incurable, isn't it? I could ring down for an acupuncturist, or for Mr Saravan's personal masseuse. I felt like having an enormously unhealthy breakfast as one does after an enormously unhealthy grapple with the demon alcohol. As if the heart were competing with the liver to see which can collapse from abuse first. I also felt like company with whom to share this temporary luxury. Tony wasn't on the phone and in any case was probably at this moment happily cooking up a Thai breakfast with Sally in some Soho kitchen. Kemble Stenner would know how to enjoy this, but heaven knew where she was. I rang reception and asked to be put through to Irving Tellman's room in case she had ended up there, but there was no reply. So I rang Stella, my new business partner. She was in.

'Hotel visits are a hundred and fifty plus cab fare,' she said, 'and anyway I'm too old for all that lark. You need a younger girl with all the right clothes, and it's early in the morning. I can find yer one, Big Jim.' For a moment I toyed with the idea of hiring five hundred dollars' worth of dolly birds to come and cavort, but Stella was right, it was early in the morning and cavorting sounded too much like hard work. I told her that what I had in mind was more of a business meeting over breakfast. She still wasn't interested. I said I'd pay her sixty dollars for the pleasure of her company, and with a laugh, she agreed to come and brunch with me at my Park Lane address.

Twenty-five minutes and several more Nurofen later, there was a call from reception. Stella had been intercepted on her way to the lift and they were calling me for verification of her claim to be visiting a hotel resident. They seemed to think she was some street hooker! Suitably appalled, I went downstairs to fetch her. When I got there I could see what they meant. She was got up like a parody of herself: fake eyelashes, short red leather skirt, bosom plopping out of exceedingly low-cut black bra and a see-through turquoise macramé top.

'Erm . . . sorry, Mr Saravan, but this lady claims to be a business associate of yours,' said a nervy young man in a bottle-green uniform. Stella was standing a couple of yards off with one of the concierge women.

'It's just 'cos I got a brown skin,' she announced in loud Brummy to the lobby in general.

'We'll eat in the Parkside Lounge,' I said, fobbing off the anxious man with a fifty-dollar bill, and, taking Stella by the arm, I swanned through the marbled hall down plush steps to dine.

After I'd eaten scrambled eggs with everything except the black pudding, and Stella had had a croissant which she filled with plum jam, she went to the ladies' loo. Talking in a sort of invented code which included 'overseas gentlemen' for Arabs and Americans, and 'newer girls' for anyone under thirty-five, we seemed to have come to certain agreements over prices and practice: no phone-box advertisers, no fifteen-minute 'tricks', always a call to say when they'd arrived safely, and one when leaving, like a mini-cab driver's passenger-on-board POB call. We would be dealing with independent women who had their own flats and mobile phones. If Stella was to be believed there was an astonishing amount of trade to be tapped. A working girl – new or otherwise – with a room and a maid could provide services to as many as fifteen clients a day or night. But that was an end of the market Stella was keen to leave behind, and I had no need to enter. We would have girls who preferred to work only once a week or so, but to spend several hours or even days on one job for fees which would make an established voice-over artist turn puce. Girls who could talk on a range of subjects, could be topical, could have an opinion. And the sex would be what Stella called a 'further negotiation'. These would be girls who could sit and stand and walk right, and wear elegant clothes to impress and instil envy into a rich man's business associates. Trophy girls. We were going into the escort business.

I would retain certain Mullin and Ketts phone lines and apart from providing both clients and escorts from the exciting and ravenous world of showbiz, would place ads in hotel entertainment guides, the *Herald Tribune*, *Harpers and Queen*, *The Lady*, *Marie Claire* and also, bizarrely, in the *Yellow Pages*. Apart from this, my outlay would be minimal. I was amazed at some of the figures Stella mentioned, and, as I've said, although my mental arithmetic is slow and I didn't have my calculator with me, even I could manage a few ball-park estimates of probable weekly income, and made a swift decision about how much of this business, if it thrived, it would be possible to accept on plastic and how much would have to remain cash. I'd have to do my own book-keeping though, I couldn't imagine someone like Tania being able to square up to all this. I'm not so naive as to suggest that the necessity of providing for Grace, and for Liz and her lawyers, justified the ethics of my new career move, but this is life, not art. All of life is gratuitous; it is only in politics and art that we have to kid ourselves otherwise.

Stella and I had decided to give each other a month's trial period, and agreed a time and place for a second power breakfast in four weeks' time – Marco's in Shepherd Market. Sartorial matters were gone into, and we had both undertaken to change our image. Stella would get some maturer outfits befitting a woman of her age and stature. Clothes in which she could pass in the Soho club milieu: some suits, scarves, maybe a turban. In fact she would look remarkably like a casting director or agent. And I was to flash it up a bit, de-fogey myself. Use hair gel, maybe a blazer, maybe shiny ties. I poured myself some more coffee and rolled a fat one to celebrate the clinching.

I took a *Daily Mail* from the rack where they were stacked in long wooden clasps like in a gentlemen's club, and stretched my legs. On page sixteen there was a small piece with a photo, which was what set me off. Neil was dead. He'd bloody well gone and done it, the little shit. It wasn't clear from the article how deliberate it had been. The photo was a rather silly and dated shot from the first series of *Every Other Weekend*. Obviously all the *Mail* had on their files at such short notice. What had been a look of dopey innocence then, and had been cute and had probably got him the job in the first place, seemed, in the light of his behaviour of the last few months, to be more one of confused desperation: a deranged and deluded ingenue. Evidently he had drowned in his own vomit and as such was joining a hall of notoriety peopled by far raunchier folk than he: Jimi Hendrix, Jim Morrison, Janis Joplin. No light-ent sit-com players on that list. Except possibly Hancock. However, all people who possibly, just possibly, if they had remembered in their stupefied state to go to sleep lying on their sides in the foetal position instead of blanking out lying on their backs, might just have survived. When chucking up, passed out on pills and alcohol, the breathing passages sometimes clear themselves if the up-chuck goes over the pillow rather than in your face. On your back it just falls back down your throat and chokes you. A sad accident unless the savage cocktails taken were deliberate attempts to finish the cycle, end the pain. But we can never be dead-cert sure what the intentions may have been when the whole lot's gone down, can we?

I pictured Neil's beard all tangled and sodden with the

contents of his rebellious stomach, and wondered what colour it all would have been. This image of Neil as an ancient gargoyle with green sprouting out of his gob would, no doubt, play on my guilt for ever after. The back of my throat felt clarty from the eggs. The article was under one hundred words long – about the size of two postage stamps – and after mentioning that he had not managed to revive his career since *EOW*, ended with the sentence: 'Neil James was unmarried and leaves behind no children.' A teeny layer of sweat zipped up to the surface of my skin under my shirt. Stella came back from the loo.

'Y'e alright, me duck?' she asked.

'Yes,' I said. I showed her the newspaper. 'Except one of my clients has just snuffed it. He topped himself. Sort of all my fault.'

I was what you'd call crying a bit now. By which I mean I had watery plates in my eyes and my throat felt restricted and gluey. But then something awful and for an Englishman completely embarrassing happened. It took over and it came from down below my stomach. Bloody Neil James had lobbed a pinless grenade into the recesses of my intestines where half-digested feelings lay fermenting. Its arrival involuntarily detonated the loudest noise I have ever made. A sort of ogre's belch, or the rutting call of an overweight impala.

When a baby is going to really bawl its head off, there is sometimes that ominous two-second silent hiatus of hypertension before the racket begins in earnest. In this tiny pausette, Stella said, 'Oh right. Here we go then.'

And then came a torrent of heavy weeping, right there in the Parkside Lounge. Most un-Hugh-Grant-like, most un-Cary-Grant-like, nothing at all to do with any self-effacing British movie stars called Grant. A blubbering splatter of honking and salivating and gasping. I felt like a foaming racehorse or Juliet Stevenson in *Truly Madly Deeply*. This couldn't all be for Neil. The little dying bastard had hacked into my central system and was making all my programmes crash like the narcissistic virus he was. I was quaking all over now and out of control, as one by one Neil triggered all my nerve centres like a laughing clown with a big plastic master switch: the drowning man, Grace, Liz, Naomi Ketts all slammed into me like oncoming trains. My fear was that this would be never-ending, that once unleashed this state of affairs would reign forever: the real me at last.

Stella did not try to comfort me, touch me or say anything. Just as well, she would have been thrown off in an instant. She knew when to leave well alone. I'd managed to wail, 'I'm sorry about this' a few times before the oleaginous man in the green suit arrived at our table with a concerned but irritated expression on his face. He took Stella's elbow and was trying, with hotel decorum, to usher us away from the dining room and from the disturbance to his other customers.

'Go fuck yourself, buster,' said Stella to him. 'We're leaving anyway.' And then, 'I think it's your milk that's off, mister.'

She half picked me up, still howling, and led me to the street exit. On my way I managed to peel off some dollar bills and shove them in the fist of the bottle-green man, who was now holding the door open for us to leave as soon as possible. I could have given him hundreds of dollars for all I know. Outside, the air and the traffic slowed me up a tad, but there was still a yeasty ball of pent-up dough in me, waiting to rise.

'I'm sorry about this,' I sobbed. 'It's my father. He died last month and I hadn't really come to grips with . . .' but then I was off again.

'Did you love him specially?' Stella asked, leading me to a pedestrian traffic-light crossing.

'No, hardly at all,' I said, 'that's the point. Hardly ever . . .' I was bent double now and tottered with Stella across the road and into Hyde Park, where she took us to a bench. She was not being tender or using any expressions of care, merely getting on with her job. She sat beside me for a minute or two while I retched like a cat vomiting grass. I was thankful she didn't pat my back or touch me in any way.

As a chap there are two things you learn by the age of five. The first is that if there is a war – whether your side's fault or the other's – you can be forced to go and have your skull shot at. And the second is that to blub where other people can see you is suicide. Your conkers will be stolen, your business sequestered, your girlfriend gang-raped. A discarded page from yesterday's *Daily Mirror* flapped at me mockingly from the path: 'Eastenders star shows his soft side' below a picture of a tough guy holding a baby. Alright for him, he's the one who head-butts people for fun, he can afford to do a bit of designer-infant publicity. If you're male, it's OK to cry so long as you do it nobly like Ralph Fiennes or Daniel Day-Lewis.

'Are yer done, mate?' said Stella matter-of-factly.

'Just about, I think so,' I snivelled, and wiped my nose on my sleeve. I apologized again. 'I didn't know there was anything there,' I said. 'I mean, about my dad.'

'Don't worry. Happens every day. I seem to have this effect on men. They can't do it in front of their wives, can they?'

'You mean guys pay you just to sit with them while they have a bucket?'

'Oh, yeah. All the time. Half of those women don't know what they put their fellers through.'

'Do you charge a normal rate for that, or is it extra?' I snorted a laugh.

'Well, how many of those dollars yer got left, me darling? You bin shedding them like they were autumn leaves.'

I took out the wad and gave her half without counting it properly.

'That'll do for starters,' she said, and got up. 'I'll see you around, Big Jim.'

I thanked her profusely, but this seemed to make her cross.

'And don't start going all gooey on me, mate. None of this tart-with-a-heart shit, OK? Because I definitely have not got one of them when it comes to fellers, right?'

'Whatever you say,' I said. She walked off stuffing dollars into her handbag.

There were still fallen trees in the park from July's storm. They'd been moved out of the road and some had been chopped into neat piles, but one or two were still awaiting the tidy-up, their mangled roots dry now in the summer sunlight. I sat, dazed and deflated, thinking back over the events since my father's death. Wondering whether I had ever actually seen a drowning man in Bishop's Park, or whether I was psychic and what I'd seen was in fact a premonition of Neil James drowning in his own vomit. If so, maybe I could start doing tarot readings from Meard Street as well. That should bring in a few bob.

What had Neil been trying to tell me? Like me, he had been out of his depth, lost. We had both been drowning long before these events. Frustrating that he was unreachable now, unknowable. And why was I alive and he was not? Just because I'd fallen asleep on my stomach and not my back? I found myself resenting him for not having finished his bloody novel. Not just because of possible posthumous royalties – which thought did occur to me, I admit, however shamefully – but more because he no longer needed me in any way. We were separate now. I was alive and he was dead, the creep. I breathed in deeply. My sinuses were beginning to clear. I would get in touch with his Karen, of course, and do all the right things. Poor Neil. I had another, minor flurry of tears for him before leaving the bench.

When I got back to Meard Street, Kemble had tidied up the office and put fresh flowers everywhere, making it all homey, the angel. There was a note: 'Bye, gorgeous. See you at BAFTA.' I wrote her a funny card and put it in my out-tray.

And that's it really. Sorry to carry on for so long, but sometimes just being able to talk things through, or even write them down is meant to help, isn't it? Just the act of admitting them. I think I know that now. You can never prepare for every eventuality, you can't spend your life trying to avoid Peter Pain; it hurts too much.

Knowing, as opposed to feeling or believing, is a reflective thing. There is no combustion in it. The moment something is known it loses its motility. As if the process of gaining knowledge were a dampener. In that instant when instinct becomes describable, accountable, it is frozen as knowledge forever. Nobody really knows what they're doing, or why.

We busy ourselves in everyday talk and tasks, tinkering with our histories to assign motives – base or exalted – to our or others' actions. But these are no more than so many household gods, mini-deities on the shelves of our security. Beneath even our collective unconscious, if such a thing exists, is where our real motors charge. We are all just sperm, the forces working on our survival or destruction outside even our subliminal cognizance.

I'd like to be able to say how Liz is enjoying her new life, how she has adapted, but I can't because I don't know. We dared not speak to each other apart from at the counsellor's, which went on for a couple more sessions before petering out with no conclusions other than that Grace should be with me every other weekend, the accepted norm. I was grateful for that at least.

Liz carried on denying that she was seeing Bob Henderson in any kind of serious way, even swore affidavits to that effect. Must have been on the advice of Ralph Tropier-Potts, because Henderson Giggs could sting me for more cash if she was not cohabiting with anyone, particularly one of the partners in their firm. That wouldn't have looked so good in court, would it? If it had ever come to that, which thankfully so far it hasn't. No. In fact the only person I know who's been anywhere near a court this autumn is my brother, Tony, who got a small fine for hacking down the main overhanging branch of the elm tree in my front drive in Fulham at 6.00 a.m. on the morning of 18 September. The eleven-foot branch fell, rather satisfyingly for me, on to Bob's cherished BH 123 Porsche below, denting the roof, smashing the windscreen and – deep joy – cutting a large gash in the plush white-leather driver's seat. Our Bob paid for all the damage himself rather than press charges, which would have meant owning up to staying the night there. And Tony was only done for borrowing council equipment: chainsaw, belaying pins and parrot-beak pruner. He used his own rope. I paid his fine. In cash, of course. Everything seems to be cash nowadays and I like it like that. There's nothing like having a wedge in your pocket at all times.

I smoke little Café Crème cigars now, instead of roll-ups, which I light with a chunky lighter with my initials on it in gold plate. And I have leathery tassels on my slip-on shoes. I don't wear ties at all any more, leaving my shirts undone a few buttons to show off the silver-inlaid shark's tooth dangling there. I suppose I look like a ponce now, but there's nothing like a little shark's tooth to stop people saying to you, 'Cheer up, mate, might never happen.' I had to buy an entirely new wardrobe in any case, because of the weight gain.

I sometimes get a beer and a bag of chips and sit in the Soho churchyard with the Green Man gargoyles. Sometimes I stay there all afternoon just for the hell of it and get drunk. It's nice to do the wrong thing.

I'll be out of Meard Street soon enough. I've found a two-bedroom residential over in Berwick Street above the fruit market, and Darius, the landlord from the betting shop, says I should be able to move in there in the new year. It's all favours. I bought the tickets for Tenerife today. Yeah, tacky I know, but I feel like a bit of the old slip-slop-slap tanning, and it'll make Stella happy. Liz has said she doesn't mind me taking Grace for a whole week at half-term. Malcolm Viner advised me to get that in writing. He's right, I know, but I don't want to inflame the situation, it's nearly almost just about OK. Grace will be grown up anyway by the time the lawyers have finished dipping their fingers into our arrangements.

'Daddy? My noise has stopped.'

'What noise?'

'My big noise. My shouting noise. Hey, I just realized, it's gone.' Grace and I were sitting in what used to be Tania's spot on the old Mullin and Ketts sofa, having finished a supper of Batman spaghetti and fish fingers.

'When did it go?' I asked.

'I don't know. It was very angry.'

'A very angry shouting noise?'

'Yes, like monsters. And drums.'

'Oh, yes. I know what you mean.'

'Did your shouting stop, Daddy?'

'Yes, it did, I think.'

'Where did you put it?'

'I don't know. I think it must have just got bored and went away.'

'Is it coming back?'

'I don't think so. I hope not.'

'Why?'

She was tugging my ear lobe hard now with one hand, and sucking her thumb with the other.

'I'm not going to start all that "why" stuff, Grace. It's way past your bedtime; you should've been asleep ages ago.'

'If it comes back, I'm going to bite it hard on its bum so it cries.'

'Good idea.'

'I'm going to kill it.'

'You do that.'

We sat for a moment in silence. The strip-joint tape loop started up again below.

'Daddy?' She was a little bit sleepy now and ready for bed. But what the hell, we could crash on the sofa.

'Yes?'

'Why are we all alive?'

I suspected Grace's new teacher at big school was a born-again. Grace had been coming back with a lot of 'Baby Jesus' stuff since the end of the summer.

'Erm. How do you mean? Do you mean like Baby Jesus, and because God loves us and that sort of thing?'

'Naaoooo,' she said, as if I was being really stupid – well, I was being really stupid. 'I don't mean songs. I mean why is Mummy alive and you, and Granny Joy, and Jasmine and Jasmine's mummy and Freddie and . . . robbers, and everybody in the whole world.'

'Well, nobody really knows why. Lots of people think up things which might be true, but nobody actually knows.'

'You know lots of things.'

'Yes, but I don't know everything. Even though you're only five, there's still some things you know that I don't know.'

'You mean like *Teletubbies*?'

'Exactly. I've no idea what they are. I don't know everything, you see.'

She paused to consider this deeply, and then suddenly jumped like Archimedes.

'Hey! I just thought! Maybe we all just *fell* alive. And then we couldn't get back.'

'Yes, that could be it. We fell alive, and now we're stuck here.'

Solving the central problem of the universe seemed to satisfy her totally, and we lapsed into thoughtful silence again. In the street below some Hooray Henrys were pranking around slamming car doors, and girls were laughing loudly, but that sound was separate from our peace. Grace trusted me that this was home.

'Daddy?' she said again.

'Mmmm?' I said nonchalantly, so as to induce torpor.

'Do you know what sex is?' But I declined to answer.